WE MEET HANS SCHNIER

on the night he has just given a drunken and disastrous performance. His Catholic mistress has abandoned him for a loveless but sanctified marriage; his wealthy family has long ago disowned him; he has deliberately ruined a promising career.

Armed with a bottle of cognac bought with his last few marks, he retires to his apartment and the telephone. Throughout the long night he summons his past by phoning everyone he knows.

This is the stark outline of a story so etched in acid, so tempered with human compassion, that the characters created here live as spokesmen for our time.

"Despite its seemingly stark setting, Böll's novel is filled with gentleness, high comic spirits, and human sympathy. It would be a great shame for American readers to shrug it off complacently as another compulsive novel of remorse of the kinds which have grown like weeds out of the rubble of postwar Germany. If there is remorse in this book, it is for all to consider."

—*Robert Kiely*, Christian Science Monitor

Other SIGNET Novels about Germany

BILLIARDS AT HALF-PAST NINE *by Heinrich Böll*

One of the most important novels from post-war Germany, a brilliant chronicle of German history from the days before World War I to the present told through the lives of one family. (T2740—75¢)

CAT AND MOUSE *by Günter Grass*

Both hilarious and tragic, bawdy and thoughtful, this is the highly acclaimed story of an eccentric German schoolboy of World War II. Written by the author of the international success, *The Tin Drum*. (P2479—60¢)

THE BIRTHDAY KING *by Gabriel Fielding*

A brilliantly convincing novel about a German business dynasty under Hitler's regime, bent on exploiting and surviving World War II. By the author of *In the Time of Greenbloom*. (T2440—75¢)

THE FOX IN THE ATTIC *by Richard Hughes*

This highly acclaimed novel, set in Germany during the turbulent years following World War I, is the first in a series dealing with the history of our times by the author of *A High Wind in Jamaica*. (T2281—75¢)

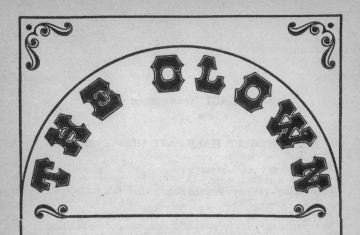

THE CLOWN

HEINRICH BÖLL

Translated from the German by Leila Vennewitz

A SIGNET BOOK

Published by The New American Library

Published as a SIGNET BOOK
by arrangement with McGraw-Hill Book Company,
who have authorized this softcover edition.
A hardcover edition is available from McGraw-Hill Book
Company.

First Printing, February, 1966

Originally published by Kiepenheuer & Witsch,
in Cologne and Berlin, Germany, under the title
Ansichten Eines Clowns; © 1963 by Kiepenheuer & Witsch.

SIGNET TRADEMARK REG. U.S. PAT. OFF. AND FOREIGN COUNTRIES
REGISTERED TRADEMARK—MARCA REGISTRADA
HECHO EN CHICAGO, U.S.A.

SIGNET BOOKS are published by
The New American Library, Inc.
1301 Avenue of the Americas, New York, New York 10019

PRINTED IN THE UNITED STATES OF AMERICA

for Annemarie

Translator's Acknowledgment

I wish to express my deep gratitude for all the help and advice given me in this translation by my husband, William Vennewitz.

Leila Vennewitz

Vancouver, Canada

*To whom he was not spoken of, they shall see:
and they that have not heard shall understand.*

Romans XV, 21

1

It was dark by the time I reached Bonn, and I forced myself not to succumb to the series of mechanical actions which had taken hold of me in five years of traveling back and forth: down the station steps, up the station steps, put down my suitcase, take my ticket out of my coat pocket, pick up my suitcase, hand in my ticket, cross over to the newsstand, buy the evening papers, go outside, and signal for a taxi. Almost every day for five years I had left for somewhere and arrived somwhere; in the morning I had gone up station steps and down again, in the afternoon down the steps and up again, signaled for a taxi, felt in my pockets for money to pay for my ticket, bought evening papers at kiosks, and savored in a corner of my mind the studied casualness of these mechanical actions. Ever since Marie left me to marry Züpfner, that Catholic, these actions have become more mechanical than ever, but without losing any of their casualness. There is a way of calculating the distance from station to hotel, from hotel to station—by the taxi meter. Two marks, three marks, four marks fifty from the station. Since Marie has been gone I have sometimes slipped out of the rhythm and confused the hotel with the station, I would start looking for my ticket as I approached the hotel porter or ask the ticket collector at the station for my room number, something—fate perhaps—must have made me remember my profession and my situation. I am a clown, official description: comedian, no church affiliation, twenty-seven years old, and

9

one of my turns is called: Arrival and Departure, a long (almost too long) pantomime during which the audience confuses arrival and departure all the way through. Since I usually go over this number once more in the train (it consists of over six hundred gestures, and I have to know their sequence by heart, of course), it is not unnatural that now and again I fall victim to my own imagination: rush into a hotel, look round for the departure board, find it, run up or down a flight of steps so as not to miss my train, while all I have to do is go to my room and get ready for the performance. Luckily they know me in most of the hotels. Over a period of five years a rhythm develops with fewer possibilities of variation than one might suppose—besides, my agent, who is familiar with my idiosyncrasies, sees to it that there is a minimum of friction. What he calls "the sensitive soul of the artist" is fully respected, and an "aura of well-being" surrounds me as soon as I get to my room: flowers in an attractive vase, and, almost before I have thrown off my coat and tossed my shoes (I hate shoes) into a corner, a pretty chambermaid comes in with coffee and cognac and runs my bath, and the green bath salts she pours into it make it relaxing and fragrant. While I lie in the bathtub I read the papers, popular ones all of them, sometimes as many as six but at least three, and in a moderately loud voice I sing nothing but sacred songs: chorales, hymns, musical passages I recall from my school days. My parents, devout Protestants, subscribed to the postwar fashion of denominational tolerance and sent me to a Catholic school. I am not religious myself, I don't even go to church, and I make use of the sacred texts and songs for therapeutic purposes: they help me more than anything else to overcome the two afflictions Nature has saddled me with: depression and headaches. Since Marie went over to the Catholics (although Marie is a Catholic herself I feel this phrase is appropriate), the intensity of these two complaints has increased, and even the *Tantum Ergo* or the Litany of Loreto—till now my favorite remedies for pain—are not much use any more. There is one temporarily effective remedy: alcohol; there could be a permanent cure: Marie. Marie has left me. A clown who takes to drink falls faster than a drunk tile-layer topples off a roof.

10

When I am drunk my gestures during a performance become confused—their only justification in the first place is their precision—and I fall into the most embarrassing trap to which a clown is ever exposed—I laugh at my own tricks. A ghastly humiliation. As long as I am sober my stage fright increases till the moment I walk on (I generally had to be pushed), and what some critics have called "that reflective, critical gaiety hiding a beating heart" was nothing but the desperate icy control with which I turned myself into a puppet; it was terrible, incidentally, when the thread broke and I fell back on myself. I imagine monks go through a similar experience when they are in a state of contemplation. Marie always carried around a lot of mystical literature, and I remember the words "empty" and "nothing" occurred very often.

For the past three weeks I had been drunk most of the time and had gone on stage with a deceptive air of confidence, the consequences showed up faster than with a slacker in school who still retains illusions about himself right up until he gets his report; six months is a long time to dream. After three weeks there were already no more flowers in my room, by the middle of the second month I no longer had a room with bath, and by the beginning of the third month the distance from the station was already seven marks, while my fee had shrunk to a third. Instead of cognac, gin, instead of vaudeville theaters, curious clubs which met in gloomy halls where I went on stage with wretched lighting, where my performance no longer even consisted of confused gestures but was reduced to outright clowning for the benefit of the postal and railway employees celebrating twenty-five years of service, or of Catholic housewives and Protestant nurses, and where the beer-drinking army officers whose promotion celebrations I enlivened hardly knew whether they ought to laugh or not when I did what was left of my "Defense Council" act; and yesterday, in Bochum, before an audience of young people, I slipped in the middle of a Chaplin imitation and couldn't get up. There weren't even any catcalls—just a sympathetic murmuring, and when at last the curtain fell I quickly hobbled off, gathered up my belongings and, without removing my make-up, took a cab to my boarding-house where there was a terrible row because my landlady refused to let me have any money for the taxi. The only way I could placate the disgruntled taxi driver was to hand over my electric razor—not as security but as payment. He was decent enough to give me change in the form of a nearly full pack of cigarettes and two marks in cash. I lay down fully dressed on the unmade bed, drank the rest of my bottle, and for the first time in months felt completely rid of depression and headache. I lay on my bed in a state which I sometimes hope will be mine when I end my days: drunk and as if in the gutter. I would have given my shirt for a drink, and only the thought of the complicated negotiations involved in such an exchange discouraged me from undertaking this transaction. I slept marvelously—long and deep, and dreamed that the heavy stage curtain fell over me like a soft thick shroud, yet through sleep and dreams I was aware of my fear of waking up: the make-up still on my face, my right knee swollen, a lousy breakfast on a plastic tray and next to the coffee pot a wire from my agent: "Coblenz and Mainz have canceled stop phoning tonight Bonn. Zohnerer." Then a call from the organizer of last night's show who, I discovered, was head of the Christian Education Society. "Kostert speaking," came his voice over the phone, a mixture of coldness and servility, "we have to clear up the matter of your fee, Mr. Schnier." "By all means," I said, "there's nothing to stop you."

"Oh?" he replied. I said nothing, and when he went on his petty hostility had turned to downright sadism. "We agreed on a fee of a hundred marks for a clown who used to be worth two hundred"—he paused, presumably to give me a chance to be angry, but I was silent and, true to type, he became insulting again and said: "I am the chairman of a welfare organization, and my conscience won't allow me to pay a hundred marks for a clown for whom twenty is a more than adequate—one might even say, a generous fee." I saw no reason to break my silence. I lit a cigarette, poured out some more of the lousy coffee, and listened to his heavy breathing. He said, "Are you listening?" And I said: "I'm listening," and waited. Silence is a good weapon. When I was at school and got called up before the principal or the teachers I always kept silent. I let the Christian Mr.

Kostert sweat it out back there at the other end of the line; he was too small to feel sorry for me, but not too small to feel sorry for himself, and finally he muttered: "Well, what would you suggest, Mr. Schnier?"

"Now listen carefully, Kostert," I said, "I'll make you a deal—take a taxi, drive to the station, get me a first-class ticket to Bonn, buy me a bottle of schnapps, come to the hotel, pay my bill—including tips—and leave an envelope here containing enough money for me to pay for a taxi to the station. Furthermore, undertake on your Christian conscience to pay for sending my luggage to Bonn. O.K.?"

He did some mental arithmetic, cleared his throat, and said: "But my idea was to give you fifty marks."

"All right," I said, "take the streetcar then—that way the whole thing will cost you less than fifty marks. How about that?"

He did some more mental arithmetic and said: "Couldn't you take your luggage with you in the taxi?"

"No I couldn't," I said, "I've hurt my knee and can't be bothered." Evidently his Christian conscience began to make itself felt. "Mr. Schnier," he said in a mild voice, "I'm sorry I—" "Never mind, Kostert," I said, "I am ever so glad I can save the Christian cause between fifty-four and fifty-six marks." I pressed down the hook and put the receiver down by the phone. He was the type who would have called back and spent half an hour relieving his conscience—it was much better to leave him to pick around in it by himself. I felt sick. I forgot to say that not only do I suffer from depression and headaches but I also have another, almost mystical peculiarity: I can detect smells through the telephone, and Kostert gave off a sickly odor of violet cachous. I had to get up and clean my teeth. Then I gargled with some of the cognac that was left, laboriously removed my makeup, got into bed again, and thought of Marie, of Christians, of Catholics, and contemplated the future. I thought of the gutters I would lie in one day. For a clown approaching fifty there are only two alternatives: gutter or palace. I had no faith in the palace, and before reaching fifty I had somehow to get through another twenty-two years. The fact that Coblenz and Mainz had canceled was what Zohnerer would call the "Early Warning

13

Stage," but there was another quality to be taken into account which I forgot to mention: my laziness. There were gutters in Bonn too, and who said I was to wait till I was fifty?

I thought of Marie: of her voice and her breast, her hands and her hair, her movements and everything we had done with each other. Also of Züpfner, whom she wanted to marry. We had known each other quite well as boys—so well that when we met again as grown men we didn't quite know whether to use first names or not—either way we felt embarrassed, and we never got over this embarrassment no matter how often we met. I couldn't understand how Marie could have gone over to him of all people, but perhaps I never "understood" Marie.

I was furious when it was Kostert who aroused me from my thoughts. He scratched at the door like a dog and said: "Mr. Schnier, you must listen to me. Do you need a doctor?" "Leave me alone," I called out, "shove the envelope under the door and go home."

He pushed the envelope under the door, I got out of bed, picked it up, and opened it: it contained a second-class ticket from Bochum to Bonn, and the taxi fare had been calculated exactly: six marks fifty. I had hoped he would make it a round figure of ten marks, and I had already worked out how much I would get out of it if I turned in the first-class ticket and bought a second-class one. It would have been about five marks. "Everything all right?" he called from outside. "Yes," I said, "and now get out, you lousy little Christian worm." "Now wait a minute! You can't—" he said, and I shouted, "Get out!" There was silence for a moment, then I heard him go downstairs. The children of this world are not only smarter, they are also more humane and more generous than the children of light. I took the streetcar to the station so as to save a bit for a drink and some cigarettes. The landlady charged me for a telegram I had sent the evening before to Monika Silvs in Bonn and which Kostert had refused to pay for, so anyway I wouldn't have had enough money for a taxi to the station; I had sent the telegram before discovering that Coblenz had canceled: they had got in ahead of me, and that annoyed me a bit. It would have been better for me if I could have canceled and sent a wire saying "Unable to appear on account of serious knee injury." Well, at least the telegram had gone off to Monika: "Please prepare flat for tomorrow. Regards. Hans."

2

In Bonn the routine was always different from anywhere else; I have never performed there, it is my home, and the taxi I called never took me to a hotel but to my apartment. I should say: us, Marie and me. There was no doorman in the building whom I could mistake for a station official, and yet this apartment, where I spend only three or four weeks a year, is more unfamiliar to me than any hotel. I had to stop myself from hailing a taxi outside the station in Bonn: this gesture was so well rehearsed that it almost led me to make a fool of myself. I had one solitary mark left in my pocket. I stood for a moment on the steps and made sure I had my keys to the building, to my apartment, to my desk; in my desk I would find: my bicycle keys. For some time now I have been considering a pantomime of keys: I have a vision of a whole bunch of keys made of ice which melt away during the performance.

No money for a taxi, and for the first time in my life I could have really used one: my knee was swollen, and I hobbled painfully across the station square to the Poststrasse; it was only two minutes from the station to our apartment, they seemed endless. I leaned against a cigarette vending machine and glanced across to the building in which my grandfather had presented me with an apartment; tasteful units dovetailed nicely into one another, the balconies painted in discreet colors; five floors, five different colors for the balconies; on the fifth floor, where the balconies are all painted terra cotta, is my apartment.

Was I acting out one of my numbers? Inserting the key in the front door, noticing without surprise that it did not melt, opening the elevator door, pressing number five: a gentle hum bore me aloft; looking through the narrow pane of glass in the elevator onto the sections dividing each floor, and, beyond each section, out through the window on each floor: the back of a monument, the square, the church, floodlit; then a black section, a concrete ceiling, and again, in slightly altered perspective: the back of the monument, the square, the church, floodlit: three times, the fourth time only the square and the church. Inserting my key in the lock of my own front door, noticing without surprise that this one opened too.

Everything painted terra cotta in my apartment: doors, woodwork, built-in cupboards, a woman in a terra cotta housecoat on the black sofa would have matched nicely; no doubt it would be possible to get one, the only trouble is: I suffer not only from depression, headaches, laziness, and the mystical ability to detect smells through the telephone, the most terrible affliction of all is my disposition to monogamy; there is only one woman with whom I can do everything that men do with women: Marie, and since she left me I live as a monk is supposed to live; only—I am not a monk. I had wondered whether I ought to drive out to the country and ask one of the priests in my old school for advice, but all these jokers regard human beings as polygamous creatures (that's why they defend monogamy so strenuously), I would be bound to seem like a freak to them, and their advice would be confined to a veiled reference to the domain in which, so they believe, love is for sale. I am still prepared to be surprised by Protestants, as in the case of Kostert, for instance, who actually managed to astound me, but with Catholics nothing surprises me any more. I have always felt a great deal of sympathy and understanding for Catholicism, even when four years ago Marie took me for the first time to this "Group of Progressive Catholics"; she was anxious to produce some intelligent Catholics for my benefit, and of course she secretly hoped I would be converted one day (all Catholics have this ulterior motive). The very first moments in the group were terrible.

17

I was then at a very difficult stage of learning to be a clown, I was not yet twenty-two and I rehearsed the whole day long. I had been looking forward very much to this evening, I was dead tired and was expecting some kind of cheerful get-together, with plenty of good wine, good food, perhaps dancing (we were very badly off and couldn't afford either wine or good food); instead the wine was bad, and the whole evening was rather as I imagine a seminar on sociology under a boring professor. Not only was it exhausting, it was exhausting in an unnecessary and unnatural way. They started off by praying together, and all through this I didn't know what to do with my hands and face; I feel one shouldn't expose an unbeliever to a situation like that. Besides, they didn't merely recite an Our Father or an Ave Marie (that would have been embarrassing enough, with my Protestant upbringing I have had more than enough of all kinds of private prayer), no, it was some text or other composed by Kinkel, very programmatic "and we beseech Thee to give us the power to do as much justice to the traditional as to the progressive," and so on, and only then did they proceed to the "Subject for the Evening," on "Poverty in the Society in which we live." It was one of the most embarrassing evenings of my life. I simply cannot believe that religious discussions have to be that exhausting. I know: it is hard to believe in this religion. Resurrection of the body and eternal life. Marie often used to read me from the Bible. It must be difficult to believe all that. Later on I even read Kierkegaard (useful reading for an aspiring clown), it was difficult, but not exhausting. I don't know whether there are people who use designs by Picasso or Klee for embroidering tablecloths. It seemed to me that evening as if these progressive Catholics were busy crocheting themselves loincloths out of Thomas Aquinas, St. Francis of Assisi, Bonaventure and Pope Leo XIII, loincloths which of course failed to cover their nakedness, for—apart from me—there was no one there who wasn't earning at least fifteen hundred marks a month. They were so embarrassed themselves that later on they became cynical and snobbish, except for Züpfner, who found the whole affair so ghastly that he asked me for a cigarette. It was the first cigarette he had ever smoked, and he puffed away at it unskillfully, I could see he was

18

glad the smoke hid his face. I felt dreadful, for Marie's sake, who sat there, pale and trembling, while Kinkel told the story of the man who earned five hundred marks a month, got along very well on it, then earned a thousand and found it got more difficult, then got into real trouble when he was earning two thousand, and finally, when he reached three thousand, he found that once again he could manage quite well, and from his experience devised the profound formula: "Up to five hundred a month one can manage quite well, but between five hundred and three thousand is utter misery." Kinkel wasn't even aware of the embarrassment he was causing: he rattled on in a kind of Olympian cheerfulness, smoking his fat cigar, raising his glass of wine to his lips, gobbling cheese sticks, until even Prelate Sommerwild, the group's spiritual adviser, began to get fidgety and changed the subject. I believe he introduced the word "reaction" and Kinkel immediately swallowed the bait. He lost his temper and stopped in the middle of his discourse on the subject of a twelve-thousand-mark car being cheaper than one for four thousand five hundred, and even his wife, who embarrasses everyone with her mindless adoration of him, breathed a sigh of relief.

3

For the first time I felt more or less comfortable in this apartment; it was warm and clean, and as I hung up my coat and stood my guitar in the corner, I wondered whether an apartment was perhaps after all something more than a delusion. I have never been one for staying in one place, and never will be—and Marie is even less settled than I am, yet she seems bent on becoming so. She used to get restless when I was booked to appear for longer than a week in one place.

Once again Monika Silvs had been as kind as ever when we sent her a telegram; she had got the keys from the janitor, cleaned the place up, put flowers in the living room, filled up the refrigerator with all sorts of things. On the kitchen table was some freshly ground coffee, and beside it a bottle of cognac. Cigarettes, a lighted candle next to the flowers on the table in the living room. Monika can be terribly sentimental, and sometimes her good taste deserts her; the candle she had put on the table for me was one of those cheap decorated ones and would definitely not have passed the test of a "Catholic Group for Matters of Taste," but most probably she had been in a hurry and unable to find any other kind of candle, or hadn't enough moeny to buy a more expensive, attractive one, and I was aware that it was on account of this awful candle that my affection for Monika Silvs was approaching the borderline set by my confounded inclination toward monogamy. The other Catholics in the group would never risk being sentimental or

20

committing a breach of good taste, they would never expose themselves to criticism, anyway they would sooner do so in a matter of morals than in a matter of taste. I could even still smell Monika's perfume in the apartment—it was much too sophisticated for her, some stuff called, I believe, Cuir de Russie.

I lit one of Monika's cigarettes from Monika's candle, got the cognac from the kitchen, the phone book from the hall, and lifted the receiver. Believe it or not, Monika had fixed that up for me too. The telephone was connected. The high-pitched buzzing seemed to me like the sound of an immense heart, at this moment I loved it more than the sound of the sea, more than the breath of storms or the growl of lions. Somewhere in that high-pitched buzzing were hidden Marie's voice, Leo's voice, Monika's voice. I slowly replaced the receiver. It was the only weapon I had left, and I would soon be making use of it. I pulled up my right trouser leg and examined my grazed knee; the scratches were superficial, the swelling minor, I poured myself a large cognac, drank half of it and poured the rest over my sore knee, hobbled back into the kitchen and put the cognac away in the refrigerator. Only now did it occur to me that Kostert had never brought me the bottle I had insisted on. No doubt he felt that for disciplinary reasons it would be better not to bring me any and had thereby saved the Christian cause seven marks. I made up my mind to call him up and ask him to send me the money. The dirty dog ought not to get off so lightly, besides I needed the money. For five years I had been earning much more than I needed, and yet it was all gone. Of course I could continue to make the rounds of the cheap music halls at the thirty to fifty mark level, as soon as my knee healed up properly; I didn't really mind, in those low-class places the audience is really nicer than in the vaudeville theaters. But thirty to fifty marks a day is simply not enough, the hotel rooms are too small, you keep bumping into tables and chairs while you are practicing, and I don't feel a bathroom is a luxury, or that, when you travel with five suitcases, a taxi is an extravagance.

I took the cognac out of the refrigerator again and had a drink from the bottle. I am not an alcoholic. Alcohol does me good, since Marie has gone. Besides, I wasn't

21

used nowadays to being short of money, and the fact that all I had left was one mark, with no prospect of being able to earn much more in the near future, bothered me. The only thing I could really sell would be the bike, but if I decided to do the cheap music halls the bike would come in very handy and would save me taxi and train fares. There was one condition attached to my possession of the apartment: I was not allowed to sell it or rent it. A typical rich man's gift. There's always a snag. I managed not to drink any more cognac, went into the living room and opened the phone book.

4

I was born in Bonn and know a lot of people here: relatives, friends, former schoolmates. My parents live here, and my brother Leo, who became a Catholic with Züpfner as godfather, is studying at a Catholic seminary here. I would have to see my parents again if only to fix up about the money. But maybe I'll hand that over to a lawyer. I haven't made up my mind about this yet. Since the death of my sister Henrietta my parents no longer exist for me as such. Henrietta has been dead for seventeen years. She was sixteen when the war drew to a close, a lovely girl, with fair hair, the best tennis-player between Bonn and Remagen. In those days the girls were being told they ought to volunteer for anti-aircraft duty, and Henrietta did, in February 1945. Everything happened so fast and went so smoothly that I didn't take it in. I came out of school, crossed the Kölnerstrasse, and saw Henrietta sitting in a streetcar which was just leaving for Bonn. She waved at me and laughed, and I laughed too. She had a small rucksack on her back, and she was wearing a pretty navy-blue hat and her heavy blue winter coat with the fur collar. I had never seen her in a hat before, she had always refused to wear one. The hat altered her very much. She looked like a young woman. I thought she must be going on an outing, though it was a strange time for outings. But in those days the schools were capable of anything. They even tried to teach us algebra in the airraid shelter, although we could already hear the artillery. Brühl, our teacher, sang "Songs

23

of Devotion and Patriotism," as he called them, in which he included "Behold the house of glory" and "Seest thou the dawn in eastern skies?" At night, when for once it was quiet for half an hour, all we could hear was the sound of marching feet: Italian prisoners of war (it had been explained to us in school why the Italians were no longer our allies and were now working for us as prisoners, but to this day I have never really understood why), Russian prisoners of war, women prisoners, German soldiers; marching feet all night long. Nobody knew just what was happening.

Henrietta really looked as if she were off on a school outing. They were capable of anything. Sometimes when we were sitting in our classroom between airraid sirens the sound of real rifle shots came in through the open window, and when we turned in alarm to the window Brühl would ask us if we knew what it meant. By that time we knew: another deserter had been shot up there in the woods. "That's what will happen to all those," said Brühl, "who refuse to defend our sacred German soil from the Jewish Yankees." (Not long ago I ran into him again; he is old now, and white-haired, a professor at a Teachers' Training College, and is said to be a man with a "courageous political past," because he never joined the Party.)

I waved once more in the direction of the streetcar which bore Henrietta away, and walked through the grounds to our house where my parents were already having dinner with Leo. We had thin soup, potatoes and gravy for our main course, and an apple for dessert. Not until we got to the dessert did I ask my mother where Henrietta's school outing was going to. She gave a little laugh and said: "Outing? Nonsense. She has gone to Bonn to volunteer for the Flak. Don't peel your apple so thick. Look, son, watch me," and she actually took the peel from my plate, snipped away at it, and put the results of her frugality, paper-thin slices of apple, into her mouth. I looked at Father. He was staring at his plate and said nothing. Leo was silent too, but when I turned to my mother again she said in her soft voice: "You do see, don't you, that everyone must do his bit to drive the Jewish Yankees from our sacred German soil." She looked across at me, I had a strange feeling, then she

24

looked at Leo in the same way, and it seemed to me she was on the verge of sending us both off to the front to fight the Jewish Yankees. "Our sacred German soil," she said, "and they have already advanced far into the Eifel Mountains." I felt like laughing, but I burst into tears, threw down my fruit knife and ran upstairs to my room. I was afraid, I knew why too, but I couldn't have put it into words, and it enraged me to think of that damned apple peel. I looked at the German soil in our garden covered with dirty snow, I looked toward the Rhine, across the weeping willows to the mountains on the other side of the river, and the whole landscape seemed crazy to me. I had seen a few of those "Jewish Yankees": they were brought down by truck from the Venus Mountain to an assembly point in Bonn: they looked frozen, scared, and young. If the word Jew conveyed anything at all to me, then it was someone more like the Italians, who looked even more frozen than the Americans, much too tired to be scared. I kicked the chair beside my bed, and when it didn't fall over I kicked it again. It finally toppled over and shattered the glass top of my bedside table. Henrietta with her navy-blue hat and rucksack. She never came back, to this day we don't know where she is buried. When the war was over someone came and told us she had "fallen near Leverkusen."

This concern for the sacred German soil is somehow comical when you realize that a good proportion of brown-coal mining shares has been in the hands of our family for two generations. For seventy years the Schniers have been making money out of the scooping and digging the sacred German soil has had to submit to; villages, forests, castles fall in the path of the dredgers like the wall of Jericho.

It was not till some days later that I discovered who it was who might have claimed to be the originator of "Jewish Yankee": Herbert Kalick, then fourteen years old, my Hitler Youth leader. My mother had generously put our grounds at his disposal so we could all be trained in the use of bazookas. My eight-year-old brother Leo was along, I saw him marching past the tennis court with a practice-bazooka on his shoulder, his face as serious as only a child's can be. I stopped him and asked: "What are you doing?" And he answered in deadly earnest: "I'm going to join the Boys' Brigade—aren't you?" "Sure," I said and went along with him, past the tennis court, to the firing range where Herbert Kalick was just telling the story of the boy who at the age of ten had been awarded the Iron Cross, somewhere in Silesia, where he had wiped out three Russian tanks with bazookas. When one of the boys asked the name of this hero, I said: "Superman." Herbert Kalick's face went yellow, and he shouted, "You dirty defeatist!" I bent down and threw a handful of cinders in Herbert's face. They all went for me, only Leo remained neutral, he was crying, but he didn't help me, and in my fear I yelled at Herbert: "You Nazi swine!" I had read these words somewhere, written on the barrier at the railway crossing. I didn't really know what they meant, but I had a feeling they might be appropriate here. Herbert Kalick stopped the fight at once and turned official: he arrested me, and I was shut up in the firing-range shed among targets and wooden pointers, till Herbert had rounded up my parents, Brühl the teacher, and somebody from the Party. I howled with rage, trampled on the targets, and kept on shouting at the boys outside who were standing guard over me: "You Nazi swine!"

After an hour I was taken to our drawing room for a hearing. Brühl was almost beside himself. He kept on repeating: "Ought to be wiped out—wiped out, that's what they ought to be," and I still don't know whether he meant physically or, so to speak, morally. I must write to him care of the Teachers' Training College and ask him to clarify this in the interests of historical accuracy. The chap from the Party, the deputy district leader, whose name was Lövenich, was quite reasonable. He kept saying: "Don't forget, the boy is barely eleven," and because he had an almost soothing effect on me I even answered his question as to where I had come across this dreadful expression: "I read it, on the railway barrier at the Annabergerstrasse." "Didn't someone say it to you?" he asked, "I mean, didn't you actually hear it said?" "No," I said. "The boy doesn't know what he's saying," my father said, putting his hand on my shoulder. Brühl scowled at my father, than glanced nervously toward Herbert Kalick. Obviously he interpreted my father's gesture as being far too strong an expression of sympathy. My mother, who was crying, said in her soft, stupid voice: "You can see he doesn't know what he is doing, he doesn't realize—if he did, I would have to turn my back on him." "Go ahead, turn your back," I said.

All this took place in our enormous drawing room with the heavy dark oak furniture, with Grandfather's hunting trophies up there on the wide oak shelf, the beer mugs and the great bookcases with their leaded-glass doors. I heard the artillery off in the Eifel Mountains, hardly more than ten miles away, sometimes even a machine gun. Herbert Kalick, pale, fair-haired, with his fanatical face, behaving like a kind of prosecutor, kept on beating the sideboard with his knuckles and demanding: "We've got to be ruthless, ruthless." I was sentenced to dig a tank trap in the garden under Herbert's supervision, and that very afternoon, true to the Schnier tradition, I dug up the German soil, although—contrary to the Schnier tradition—with my own hands. I dug the trench clear across Grandfather's favorite rosebed, aiming directly at the copy of the Apollo of Belvedere, and I was looking forward to the moment when the marble statue would fall to my excavatory zeal. I rejoiced too soon: it was demolished by a small freckled boy called Georg. He blew up himself and the Apollo with a bazooka which he let off by mistake. Herbert Kalick's comment on this accident was laconic: "What a good thing Georg was an orphan."

5

In the phone book I looked up the numbers of all the people I would have to call; on the left I made a list of the names of all those I could ask for a loan: Karl Emonds, Heinrich Behlen, both old classmates of mine, one of them had been a theological student and was now a high school teacher, the other a chaplain, then Bella Brosen, my father's mistress—on the right, a list of all the others, whom I would only ask for money as a last resort: my parents, Leo (whom I could ask for money but he never has any, he gives it all away), the group members: Kinkel, Fredebeul, Blothert, Sommerwild; and between these two columns: Monika Silvs, around whose name I drew a nice little loop. I had to send Karl Emonds a wire and ask him to call me. He doesn't have a phone. I would have liked to call Monika first but I would have to call her last. Our relationship was at a stage where it would be both physically and metaphysically discourteous to slight her. Here I was in a terribly difficult position: a monogamist, I had been living a celibate life—against my will yet at the same time in accordance with my nature—ever since Marie had deserted me in "metaphysical horror," as she called it. To be quite honest, I had slipped in Bochum more or less on purpose, and had fallen onto my knee so that I could break off the tour and go to Bonn. I was suffering almost unbearably from what Marie's religious books mistakenly referred to as "desires of the flesh." I was much too fond of Monika to satisfy my desire for another woman with her. If these religious books were

28

to say: Desire for a woman, that would be bad enough, but a good deal better than "desires of the flesh." All I know of flesh is butchers' shops, and even those are not entirely fleshly. When I imagine Marie doing with Züpfner this thing which she ought only to do with me, my depression becomes despair. I hesitated a long time before looking up Züpfner's telephone number as well and writing it in the column of those who I didn't intend to borrow from. Marie would give me money, right away, all she had, and she would come to me and stand by me, especially when she heard of the series of failures that had befallen me, but she wouldn't come alone.

Six years is a long time, and she has no business in Züpfner's house, nor at his breakfast table, nor in his bed. I was even prepared to fight for her, although the word fight has for me almost entirely physical connotations, in other words, a ridiculous idea: a brawl with Züpfner. Marie was not yet dead for me the way my mother is, so to speak, dead for me. I believe that the living are dead, and that the dead live, not the way Protestants and Catholics believe it. For me a boy like Georg, who blew himself up with a bazooka, awkward boy standing there on the grass in front of the Apollo, hear Herbert Kalick shouting: "Not like that, not like that—"; hear the explosion, a few screams, not very many, then Kalick's comment: "What a good thing Georg was an orphan," and half an hour later at supper, at the very table where they had sat to pronounce sentence on me, my mother said to Leo: "You'll do better than that silly boy, won't you!" Leo nodded, my father looked across at me, and found no comfort in the eyes of his ten-year-old son.

Meanwhile for years my mother has been president of the Executive Committee of the Societies for the Reconciliation of Racial Differences; she goes to the Anne Frank House in Amsterdam, sometimes even to America, and lectures to American women's clubs about the remorse of German youth, still in the same gentle, mild voice she probably used when saying goodbye to Henrietta. "Be a good girl, dear." That voice I could hear over the phone any time, but Henrietta's voice never again. She had had a surprisingly dark voice and light laughter. Once in the middle of a game of tennis she dropped her racket, she stood quite still on the tennis court and stared dreamily up at the sky; another time she dropped her spoon in the soup during dinner, my mother shrieked, complained of the stains on her dress and the tablecloth; Henrietta was not even listening, and when she came to she merely picked up the spoon from her soup plate, wiped it on her serviette, and went on eating. On a third occasion, when we were playing cards by the fire and she went off into a trance like this, my mother got really angry. She shouted: "Stop this ridiculous dreaming!" and Henrietta looked up and said quietly: "What's the matter? I simply don't want to play any more," and threw the cards she was still holding into the fire. My mother picked the cards out of the fire, burning her fingers as she did so, and salvaged them all except for the seven of hearts, which was singed, and we could never play cards again without thinking of Henrietta, although my mother tried to behave "as if nothing had happened." She is not spiteful at all, just incredibly stupid, and stingy. She would not allow us to buy a new pack of cards, and I assume the scorched seven of hearts is still in that pack and that my mother is quiet unconcerned when it turns up while she is playing patience. I would have like to phone Henrietta, but the theologians have not yet invented this kind of dialing. I looked up my parents' number, which I always forget, in the phone book: Schnier, Alfons, Dr., Managing Director. The "Dr." was something new—it must be an honorary degree. While I was dialing the number I walked home in my mind's eye, down Koblenzstrasse, turning into the Ebertallee, then to the left toward the Rhine. Barely half an hour's walk. I heard the maid's voice:

"Dr. Schnier's residence."

"May I speak to Mrs. Schnier?" I said.

"Who's calling, please?"

"Hans Schnier," I said, "son of the lady in question." She swallowed, thought for a moment, and I felt along the four miles of telephone wires that she was hesitating. She smelled very nice, incidentally, just of soap, and a little fresh nail polish. Obviously she knew of my existence, but she had been given no positive instructions about me. Probably only dark rumors in her ear: outsider, a radical type.

"Would you please assure me," she finally asked, "that this is not a joke?"

"You may rest assured," I said, "if need be I am willing to give details of my mother's distinguishing marks. A mole on the left side of her face under her mouth, a wart . . ."

She laughed and said: "All right!" and switched me through. Our telephone system is a complicated one. My father alone has three extensions: a red phone for the brown-coal, a black one for the stock exchange, and a private one, white. My mother has only two phones: a black one for the Executive Committee of the Societies for the Reconciliation of Racial Differences, and a white one for private use. Although my mother has a private bank account running into six figures, the telephone bills (and of course her traveling expenses to Amsterdam and elsewhere) are charged to the Executive Committee. The maid had used the wrong switch, my mother answered the black telephone in her business voice: "Executive Committee of the Societies for the Reconciliation of Racial Differences."

I was speechless. If she had said: "Mrs. Schnier speaking," I would probably have answered; "Hans here, how are you, Mother?" Instead I said: "I am a delegate of the Executive Committee of Jewish Yankees, just passing through—may I please speak to your daughter?" I even startled myself. I heard my mother exclaim, then she sighed in a way which told me how old she has become. She said: "I suppose you can never forget that, can you?" I was almost in tears myself and said softly: "Forget? Ought I to, Mother?" She was silent, all I could hear was that old woman's weeping that shocked me so much. I had not seen her for five years and she must be over sixty by now. For a moment I had really believed she could put me through to Henrietta. She is always saying that perhaps she has "a private line to heaven"; she says it archly, the way everyone these days talks about their private lines: a private line to the Party, to the university, to television, to the Ministry of the Interior.

I would have liked to hear Henrietta's voice so much, even if she had only said "nothing" or for that matter "Oh shit." From her lips it had not sounded vulgar at all. That time she said it to Schnitzler, when he spoke of her mystical gift, it had sounded as beautiful as snow (Schnitzler was a writer, one of the parasites who lived with us during the war, and whenever Henrietta went off

31

into one of her trances he always spoke of a mystical gift, and she had simply said "Oh shit" when he began talking about it). She could have said something else: "Today I beat that stupid Peter again," or something in French, "*La condition du Monsieur le Comte est parfaite.*" Sometimes she used to help me with my homework, and it always made us laugh how she was so good at other people's homework and so bad at her own.

Instead all I heard was my mother's old woman's weeping, and I asked: "How's Father?"

"Oh," she said, "he's an old man now—old and wise."

"And Leo?"

"Oh, Le, he works very hard, very hard," she said, "they say he has a future as a theologian."

"My God," I said, "Leo of all people with a future as a theologian."

"Of course it was pretty hard on us when he converted," said my mother, "but the spirit moveth where it listeth."

By now she had her voice completely under control again, and for a moment I was tempted to ask her about Schnitzler, who is still constantly in and out of our house. He was a rather plump, well-groomed fellow, who at that time was always raving about the noble European spirit, about Germanic consciousness. Later on, out of curiosity, I once read one of his novels. "French Love Affair," not as interesting as the title promised. Its highly original feature was the fact that the hero, a French lieutenant, a prisoner of war, was fair, and the heroine, a German girl from the Moselle, was dark. He winced every time Henrietta said—I believe it was twice altogether— "Oh shit," and maintained that a mystical gift could very well go hand in hand with the "compulsion to hurl dirty words" (although in Henrietta's case it was not the least compulsive and she did not "hurl" the word at all, she simply said it), and as proof he dragged out a five-volume work on *Christian Mystics*. Needless to say, there was a lot of grand stuff in his novel, in which "the names of French wines ring out like crystal goblets which lovers raise and touch in mutual adoration." The novel ends with a secret wedding; however, this brought on the displeasure of the National Socialist Writers' Association and he was suspended from writing for some ten months.

The Americans welcomed him with open arms as a resistance fighter and gave him a job in their cultural information service, and today he is running all over Bonn telling all and sundry that he was banned under the Nazis. A hypocrite like that doesn't even have to tell lies to be always on the right side of the fence. And yet he was the one who forced my mother to make us join up, me in the Hitler Youth and Henrietta in the BDM. "In this hour, dear lady, we simply all have to pull together, stand together, suffer together." I can still see him standing in front of the fireplace, holding one of Father's cigars. "Certain injustices of which I have been the victim cannot obscure my clear and objective realization of the fact that the Führer"—his voice actually trembled—"the Führer already holds our salvation in his hands." Spoken about a day and a half before the Americans took Bonn.

"What's Schnitzler doing these days?"

"Oh he's doing splendidly," she said, "they can't get along without him at the Foreign Office." Naturally she has forgotten all that, it is surprising that the Jewish Yankees still arouse any memories at all in her. Now I wasn't sorry any more that I had begun my conversation with her like that.

"And Grandfather, what's he doing?" I asked.

"He is amazing," she said, "indestructible. He will soon be ninety. I simply don't know how he does it."

"That's easy," I said, "these old boys are not bothered by either memories or conscience. Is he at home now?"

"No," she said, "he's gone to Ischia for six weeks."

We were both silent, I was still not quite sure of my voice, whereas she was perfectly in command of hers when she asked me: "But the real reason for your call —I hear you're having money troubles. You've had bad luck in your job, so they tell me."

"Is that so?" I said. "You're probably afraid I'll ask you and Father for money, but you don't have to worry about that, Mother. You wouldn't give me any anyway. I shall take it up with my lawyer; you see, I need the money to go to America. Someone over there has offered me a chance. A Jewish Yankee, as a matter of fact, but I'll do my best to see that racial differences don't arise." She was further from tears than ever. All I heard before

33

I hung up was her saying something about principles. And she had smelled as she always smelled: of nothing. One of her convictions is: "A lady gives off no odor of any kind." This is probably why my father has such a pretty mistress: no doubt she gives off no odor of any kind, but she looks as though she would smell nice.

6

I tucked all the cushions within reach behind my back, put up my sore leg, drew the phone closer, and wondered whether I shouldn't go out to the kitchen, open the refrigerator, and bring in the bottle of cognac.

That "bad luck in your job" coming from my mother had sounded particularly spiteful, and she had made no attempt to conceal her gloating. It was probably naive of me to have supposed that no one here in Bonn knew of my debacles. If Mother knew about them, Father did too, and so did Leo, and through Leo Züpfner, the whole group and Marie. It would be a terrible blow for her, worse than for me. If I gave up drinking entirely again, I would soon be once more on the level which Zohnerer, my agent, called "nicely above average," and that would be enough to carry me through the twenty-two years I still had to go till I reached the gutter. What Zohnerer always speaks so highly of is my "good background as a craftsman"; he has no idea of art anyway, with almost inspired simplicity he judges it entirely by its degree of success. But he does know something about craftsmanship, and he is well aware that I can still play the music halls, keeping above the thirty-mark level, for another twenty years. With Marie it's different. She will be distressed at my "artistic decline" and my poverty, which I myself don't find so terrible at all. For the outsider—and everyone in this world is an outsider in relation to everyone else—something always seems worse or better than it does for the one directly concerned, whether that something is good luck or bad luck, an unhappy love affair or an "artistic decline." I wouldn't at all mind doing some honest slapstick or just plain clowning in stuffy halls to an audience of Catholic housewives or Protestant nurses. The only thing is, these denominational groups have an unfortunate idea of fees. Naturally one of these good ladies, the club president, thinks fifty marks is a nice sum, if he gets that twenty times a month he ought to be able to manage. But when I show her my make-up bill and tell her that in order to practice I need a hotel room somewhat larger than eight by ten, she probably thinks my mistress is as expensive as the Queen of Sheba. But when I then tell her I live almost exclusively on soft-boiled eggs, consommé, meatballs and tomatoes, she crosses herself and thinks I must be undernourished because I don't have a "good hearty meal" every day. Then if I go on to tell her that my private vices consist of evening papers, cigarettes, and parchesi, she probably takes me for a liar. I gave up talking long ago to anyone about money or art. When these two things meet, something is always wrong: art is either under- or overpaid. In an English traveling circus I once saw a clown who was twenty times better than I am as a craftsman and ten times better as an artist, and who got less than ten marks a night: his name was James Ellis, he was in his late forties, and when I invited him for supper—we had ham omelet, salad, and apple pie—he was overcome with nausea: it was ten years since he had eaten so much all at once. Ever since I met James I have given up talking about money and art.

I take it as it comes and expect to end up in the gutter. Marie has quite different ideas; she is always talking about a "message," everything was a message, even what I was doing; she said I was so cheerful, so devout and chaste in my own way, and so on. It is ghastly what goes on in the minds of Catholics. They can't even drink a good wine without somehow twisting and turning, they must at all costs be "aware" of how good the wine is, and why. As far as awareness is concerned, they are as bad as the Marxists. Marie was horrified when I bought a guitar a few months ago and said I would soon be singing songs to the guitar which I had composed myself. She thought this was "beneath" me, and I told her the only thing beneath the gutter was the canal, but she didn't understand what I meant, and I hate explaining a metaphor. Either you understand it or you don't. I am no exegete.

It might have been thought that my puppet strings had broken; on the contrary, I had them firmly in my grasp and saw myself lying there in Bochum on that club stage, drunk, my knee grazed, I heard the sympathetic murmuring in the hall and was ashamed of myself; I had not deserved that much sympathy, and I would rather have had a few catcalls; even the limp was not quite in keeping with the injury, although I actually had hurt myself. I wanted Marie back and had begun to fight, in my own way, simply for the sake of the thing which in her books was described as "desires of the flesh."

7

I was twenty-one, she was nineteen, when one evening I simply went to her room to do the things with her that men and women do with one another. I had seen her that afternoon with Züpfner, they had been coming out of the Youth Club hand in hand, they were both smiling, and it gave me a pang. She did not belong to Züpfner, and this silly holding hands made me sick. Almost everybody in town knew Züpfner, mainly because of his father, who had been kicked out by the Nazis; he had been a schoolteacher and after the war he had refused to return right away to the same school as principal. Someone had even wanted to make him a Minister, but he had got very angry and said: "I am a teacher, and I want to be a teacher again." He was a tall, quiet man who as a teacher I found a bit boring. He substituted once for our German teacher, and read us a poem, the one about the beautiful young Lilofee.

As far as school is concerned, my opinion means nothing. It was simply a mistake to keep me in school for longer than the law required; even that would have been too long. I have never blamed the teachers for the school, only my parents. Actually this idea of "But he has to graduate" is something which should be taken up by the Executive Committee of the Societies for the Reconciliation of Racial Differences. It is really a race matter: graduates and non-graduates, grade school teachers, high school teachers, academic types, non-academic types, all different races, that's all. When

Züpfner's father had finished reading the poem he waited a few minutes and then asked with a smile: "Well, has anyone anything to say?" and I jumped up at once and said: "I think it is a wonderful poem." The whole class burst out laughing at this, but not Züpfner's father. He smiled, but not superciliously. I found him very nice, only a bit on the dry side. I didn't know his son very well, but better than his father. Once I had been walking past the sports ground where he was playing football with his friends, and as I stood there looking on he called out to me: "Don't you want to play?" and I at once said Yes and joined the team playing against Züpfner as left wing. After the game he said: "Won't you come along?" I asked: "Where to?" and he said: "To our club evening," and when I said: "But I'm not a Catholic," he laughed, and the others laughed too; Züpfner said: "We sing—and I bet you like to sing." "Yes," I said, "but I've had enough of youth clubs, I was at boarding school for two years." Although he laughed, he was offended. He said: "Well, if you feel like it, come and play football with us again." I played football a few more times with his group, went with them to eat ice cream, and he never invited me again to come to the club evening. I also knew that Marie and her crowd had their evenings at the same youth club, I knew her well, very well, as I saw a lot of her father, and sometimes in the evening I went to the sports ground when she played volleyball with the other girls, and I watched them. Or to be more precise: her, and sometimes she waved to me in the middle of the game and smiled and I waved back and smiled too; we knew each other very well. At that time I often went to see her father, and sometimes she would sit with us when her father tried to explain Hegel and Marx to me, but at home she never smiled at me. When I saw her that afternoon coming out of the club hand in hand with Züpfner, a pang went through me. I was in an awkward position. I had left schoot at twenty-one in Grade 10. The padres had been very nice, they had even had a goodbye party for me, with beer and sandwiches, cigarettes and chocolate for the non-smokers, and I had put on some of my turns for my classmates: Catholic sermon and Protestant sermon, workman with pay envelope;

also some tricks and Chaplin imitations. I even made a farewell speech "on the Mistaken Assumption that Graduation is Essential to Eternal Bliss." It was a terrific evening, but at home they were bitter and angry. My mother was just horrible to me. She advised my father to send me down into the pit, and my father kept on asking me what I wanted to be, and I said, "a clown." He said: "You mean an actor—very well, perhaps I can send you to drama school." "No," I said, "not an actor but a clown—and schools are no use to me." "But what have you got in mind?" he asked. "Nothing," I said, "nothing. I'll get out of here." Those were two terrible months, because I couldn't pluck up enough courage to really get out, and with every mouthful I ate my mother looked at me as if I were a criminal. And yet for years she had been feeding all kinds of stray hangers-on, but those were "artists and writers"; Schnitzler, that corny fellow, and Gruber, who wasn't bad at all. He was a fat, taciturn, dirty poet who lived with us for six months and never wrote a single line. When he came down to breakfast in the morning, my mother always looked at him as if she were expecting to see signs of his nightly struggle with the demon. It was almost indecent, the way she looked at him. One day he vanished without trace, and we children were amazed and scared when we discovered a whole pile of dog-eared mystery stories in his room, and a few scraps of paper on his desk on which was written the one word, "Nothing," on one piece it was written twice, "Nothing, nothing." For people like that my mother even went down to the basement and brought up an extra chunk of ham. I believe if I had begun to buy some giant easels and had painted some stupid stuff on enormous canvases, she would have been able to reconcile herself to my existence. Then she could have said, "Our Hans is an artist, he will find his own path. He is still struggling." But like this I was nothing but a rather elderly tenth grader, and the only thing she knew about him was that he was "quite good at some kind of tricks." Naturally I refused to pay for that bit of food with "examples of my talent," so I spent hours with old man Derkum, Marie's father, whom I helped a bit in the shop and who gave me cigarettes, although he was not very well off. I only spent two months at home like that, but they seemed an eternity, much longer than the war. I only saw Marie occasionally, she was busy preparing for graduation and was studying with her friends. Sometimes old man Derkum caught me not listening to him at all but staring at the kitchen door, then he would shake his head and say, "She'll be late today," and I would blush.

It was a Friday, and I knew that on Friday evenings Mr. Derkum went to the movies, but I didn't know whether Marie would be at home or cramming with one of her friends. I didn't think about anything, and yet about almost everything, even about whether she would be able to write her exams "afterwards," and I already knew what turned out later to be true, that not only would half Bonn be shocked at the seduction but would add "and just before her graduation, too." I even thought about the girls in her crowd for whom it would be a disappointment, I was terribly afraid of what a boy at boarding school had once called "the physical details," and the question of potency worried me. The surprising thing was that I felt no trace whatever of "carnal desire." I also thought about it being unfair of me to use the key her father had given me to enter the house and go up to her room, but I had no choice, I had to use the key. The only window in Marie's room faced the street, which was so busy till two in the morning that I would have landed in the police station—and I had to do this thing with Marie today. I even went into a drugstore and with the money I had borrowed from my brother Leo bought some kind of stuff which they had said in school would increase male potency. My face was scarlet when I went into the drugstore, luckily a man waited on me, but I spoke so softly that he shouted at me and told me to say what I wanted "loud and clear," and I told him the name of the stuff, was given it, and paid the druggist's wife, who shook her head as she looked at me. Of course she knew me, and when she heard next morning what had happened she probably reproached herself, quite without reason, for two blocks further on I opened the box and let the tablets roll into the gutter.

At seven, when the movies had begun, I walked to Gudenaug Lane, key in hand, but the shop door was still

41

open, and as I went in Marie put her head out on the landing upstairs and called, "Hullo, is there anyone there?" "Yes," I called, "it's me"—I ran up the stairs and she looked at me in astonishment as without touching her I forced her slowly back into her room. We had never talked very much, just looked and smiled at each other, and with her too I didn't quite know what to call her. She had on the gray, threadbare dressing gown she had inherited from her mother, her dark hair was tied back with a piece of green cord; later, when I undid the knot I saw it was a bit of her father's fishing line. She was so startled that there was no need for me to say anything, and she knew exactly what I wanted. "Go," she said, but she said it automatically, I knew she had to say it, and we both knew that it was meant seriously as well as said automatically, but the moment she said "Go" and not "You must go," the matter was settled. There was so much tenderness in that little word, enough, so it seemed to me, to last a lifetime, and I could have wept; she said it in such a way that I was absolutely certain: she had known I would come, at any rate she was not completely taken by surprise. "No, no," I said, "I'm not going—where do you want me to go?" She shook her head. "Shall I borrow twenty marks and go to Cologne—and then marry you later?" "No," she said, "don't go to Cologne." I looked at her and was scarcely afraid any more. I was no longer a child, and she was a woman, I looked at the place where she held her dressing gown together, I looked over to her table by the window and was glad none of her school books were lying around there: just sewing things and a dress pattern. I ran down into the shop, locked the door and put the key in the place where it has been put for the last fifty years: between the gumdrops and the writing pads. When I got upstairs again she was sitting on her bed, crying. I sat down on the bed too, on the other corner, lit a cigarette, gave it to her, and she smoked her first cigarette, unskillfully; we had to laugh, she blew the smoke so funnily out of her pursed mouth that it looked almost flirtatious and when once it happened to come out of her nose I laughed: it looked so depraved. Finally we started to talk, and we talked a good deal. She said she was thinking of the women in Cologne who did "this

42

thing" for money and evidently believed it could be paid for with money, but it was not to be paid for with money, and so all the women whose husbands went there were in their debt, and she didn't want to be in the debt of these women. I talked a lot too, I said I thought everything I had read about so-called physical love and about the other kind of love was nonsense. I couldn't separate one from the other, and she asked me if I thought she was pretty and loved her, and I said she was the only girl I wanted to do "this thing" with, and I had always thought only of her when I thought of this thing, even at school; only of her. Finally Marie stood up and went into the bathroom while I stayed sitting on her bed, went on smoking and thought of the awful tablets I had let roll into the gutter. I began to get scared again, went over to the bathroom, knocked, Marie hesitated a moment before she said Yes, then I went in and as soon as I saw her my fear left me again. The tears were running down her face as she rubbed hair lotion into her hair, then powdered her face, and I said, "Whatever are you doing?" and she said: "I'm making myself beautiful." The tears had made little furrows in the powder, which she had put on much too thick, and she said: "Won't you really go away?" And I said "No." She dabbed on some Eau de Cologne while I sat on the edge of the bath and wondered if two hours would be long enough; we had already wasted more than half an hour talking. At school there had been specialists in these things: how difficult it was, for instance, to make a woman of a girl, and I kept thinking of Gunther who had to send Siegfried on ahead, and I thought of the frightful Nibelung carnage which resulted from this thing, and how at school, when we were doing the Nibelung saga, I had stood up and said to Father Wunibald, "Surely Brunhild was really Siegfried's wife," and he had smiled and said: "But he was actually married to Krimhild, my boy," and I had got mad and maintained that was a typical priest's interpretation. Father Wunibald was furious, struck the desk with his finger, invoked his authority, and said he would not put up with being "insulted."

I stood up and said to Marie: "Please don't cry," and she stopped crying and smoothed out the tear furrows with the powderpuff. Before we went to her room we stood for a moment at the landing window and looked down onto the street: it was January, the street was wet, the lights over the asphalt were yellow, the sign over the grocery opposite green: Emil Schmitz. I knew Schmitz, but I didn't know his first name was Emil, and it seemed to me that Emil did not go well as a first name with Schmitz as a second name. Before we went into Marie's room I opened the door a little and switched off the light inside.

When her father came home we were not yet asleep; it was nearly eleven, we heard him go into the shop downstairs and get some cigarettes before coming upstairs. We both thought he would be bound to notice something: after all, what had happened was so tremendous. But he noticed nothing, listened a moment at the door, and went on upstairs. We heard him taking off his shoes and throwing them on the floor, later on we heard him coughing in his sleep. I wondered how he would react to this thing. He was no longer a Catholic, he had left the church long ago, and he had spoken contemptuously to me of the "hypocritical sexual morals of bourgeois society" and was furious "with the swindle the priests carry on with marriage." But I was not sure whether he would accept what I had done with Marie without raising hell. I liked him very much, and he liked me, and I was tempted to get up in the middle of the night, go to his room, and tell him the whole thing, but then it occurred to me I was old enough, twenty-one, and Marie was old enough too, nineteen, and that certain kinds of manly frankness are more embarrassing than keeping quiet, and I also felt: it really didn't concern him as much as I thought. After all, I could hardly have gone to him in the afternoon and said: "Mr. Derkum, I want to sleep with your daughter tonight"—and what had happened he would find out in good time.

A little later on Marie got up, kissed me in the dark and pulled the sheets off the bed. It was quite dark in the room, no light came from outside, we had drawn the heavy curtains, and I wondered how she knew what had to be done now: pull the sheets off and open the window. She whispered to me: I'm going to the

44

bathroom, you wash here, and she drew me by the hand out of bed, led me in the dark to the corner where her washstand was, guided my hand to the jug, the soap dish, the basin, and went out carrying the sheets. I washed, got back into bed, and wondered why Marie was taking so long bringing the clean sheets. I was dead tired, glad I was able to think of that wretched Gunther without getting into a panic, and then began to feel scared something might have happened to Marie. At school they used to tell terrible stories. It was not pleasant lying there on the mattress without sheets, it was old and lumpy, I had nothing on but my undershirt and I felt cold. I thought once more of Marie's father. Everyone assumed he was a communist, but when after the war he was supposed to become mayor the communists saw to it that he didn't, and every time I started to compare the Nazis with the communists he got mad and said: "There's a difference, my boy, whether someone gets killed in a war which is carried on by a soft soap company—or whether he dies for a cause in which one can believe." What he really was I still don't know, and when Kinkel once called him a "brilliant sectarian" in my presence, it was all I could do not to spit at Kinkel. Old man Derkum was one of the few men I respected. He was thin and bitter, much younger than he looked, and being a heavy smoker he had trouble with his breathing. All the time I was waiting for Marie I heard him up there in his bedroom coughing, I felt like a skunk, and yet I knew I wasn't. He had said to me once: "Do you know why in the houses of the rich, like your parents', the maids' rooms are always next to those of the young sons? I'll tell you: it is an age-old speculation on human nature and compassion." I wished he would come down and find me in Marie's bed, but to go upstairs and report to him, so to speak, that was something I didn't want to do. It was getting light outside. I felt cold, and the shabbiness of Marie's room depressed me. The Derkums had long been considered to have come down in the world, and the decline was attributed to the "political fanaticism" of Marie's father. They had had a small printing plant, a small publishing business, a bookstore, but now all they had was this little stationery shop where they also sold candy to school kids. My father once said to me: "Now you see how far fanaticism can drive a man—yet after the war Derkum had an excellent chance of having his own newspaper since he was a victim of political persecution." Strangely enough I had never found Derkum fanatical, but perhaps my father had confused fanaticism and principles. Marie's father did not even sell prayer books, although that would have brought him in a little extra money, especially before White Sundays.

When it got light in Marie's room I saw how poorly off they really were: she had three dresses hanging in the closet: the dark green one, which I felt I had been seeing on her for a hundred years, a kind of yellow one that was almost threadbare, and the curious dark blue suit she always wore in processions, her old bottle-green winter coat, and only three pairs of shoes. For a moment I felt tempted to get up, open the drawers, and have a look at her underwear but I didn't. I don't think even if I were properly married to a woman I would ever look at her underwear. Her father had stopped coughing long since. It was after six when Marie finally came out of the bathroom. I was glad I had done with her what I had always wanted to do with her, I kissed her and felt happy to see her smiling. I felt her hands on my neck: ice cold, and I whispered: "What have you been doing?" She said: "What do you think I've been doing? I've been washing the sheets. I would have liked to bring you some clean ones, but we only have four pairs, there are always two on the beds and two in the laundry." I drew her down beside me, covered her up and put her ice-cold hands in my armpits, and Marie said they felt wonderful there, warm as birds in a nest. "After all, I couldn't give the sheets to Mrs. Huber," she said, "she does our washing for us, and like that the whole town would have heard about what we've done, and I didn't want to throw them away either. I did think for a moment of throwing them away, but then I felt it would be a pity." "Didn't you have any hot water?" I asked, and she said: "No, the boiler has been broken for ages." Then quite suddenly she started to cry, and I asked her what she was crying for now, and she whispered: "For Heaven's sake, I'm a Catholic, you know I am—" and I said that any girl, Protestant or atheist,

46

would probably cry too, and I knew why; she looked at me questioningly, and I said: "Because such a thing as innocence really does exist." She kept on crying and I didn't ask her why she was crying. I knew: she had belonged to this group of girls for quite a few years and had always taken part in the procession, and she must have constantly talked about the Virgin Mary with the other girls—and now she felt like a cheat or a traitor. I could imagine how terrible it was for her. It really was terrible, but I couldn't have waited any longer. I told her I would talk to the girls, and she sat up in alarm and said: "What—who with?" "With the girls in your group," I said, "it really is a terrible thing for you, and if the worst comes to the worst I don't mind your saying I raped you." She laughed and said: "No, that's nonsense, what are you going to tell the girls?" I said: "I shall say nothing, I shall simply appear before them, do a few of my turns and imitations, and they will think: Oh, so that's that Schnier who did this thing with Marie—that will be much better than just having rumors going around." She thought for a moment, laughed again, and said softly: "You aren't so stupid." Then she suddenly began crying again and said: "I can't show my face here any more." I asked: "Why?" but she only wept and shook her head.

Her hands warmed up under my arms, and the warmer her hands got the sleepier I became. Soon it was her hands that were warming me, and when she asked me again whether I loved her and thought she was pretty, I said of course I did, but she said she wanted to hear me say it and I mumbled sleepily, yes, yes, she was pretty and I loved her.

I woke up when Marie got out of bed, washed and dressed. She was not shy, and I found it quite natural to watch her. It was even more obvious than before: how poor her clothes were. While she was doing up all the hooks and buttons I thought of all the nice things I would buy her if I had money. I had often stood in front of shopwindows and looked at skirts and sweaters, shoes and handbags, and pictured how they would all suit her, but her father had such strict ideas about money that I would never have dared to buy her anything. He had said to me once: "It is terrible to be poor, but it's not very pleasant either just to get by, which is the way most people are." "And to be rich?" I had asked, "what's that like?" I had flushed. He had looked at me keenly and flushed too, and had said: "You'll regret it, my boy, if you don't give up thinking. If I had the courage and faith to believe one could accomplish something in this world, do you know what I would do?" "No," I said. His color mounting again he said, "I would found some kind of society to look after the children of the rich. The idiots always apply the term antisocial only to the poor."

A lot of things went through my mind as I watched Marie dress. It made me glad and at the same time unhappy to see how she took her body for granted. Later on, when we moved together from hotel to hotel, I always stayed in bed in the morning so I could watch her wash and dress, and when the bathroom was so placed that I couldn't watch her from the bed, I lay in the bathtub. On this particular morning in her room I would have liked to go on lying in bed indefinitely and could have wished she would never finish getting dressed. She washed her neck, arms and breasts thoroughly and brushed her teeth vigorously. Personally I have always tried to get out of washing in the morning, and I still loathe cleaning my teeth. I prefer having a bath, but I always enjoyed watching Marie, she was so clean and everything was so natural, even the little gesture with which she screwed the top on the toothpaste tube. I also thought about my brother Leo, who was very devout, conscientious, and precise, and who was always assuring me he "had faith" in me. He was just about to graduate too, and somehow he was ashamed that he had managed to do it at nineteen, while at twenty-one I was still getting annoyed at the phony interpretation of the Song of the Nibelungs. Leo even knew Marie from some study groups or other where young Catholics and Protestants discussed democracy and religious tolerance. By this time Leo and I both regarded our parents just as a kind of couple running a foster home. It had been a terrible shock for Leo when he found out Father had had a mistress for nearly ten years. It was a shock for me too, but not a moral one, I could well imagine how awful it must be to be married to my mother, whose

48

deceptive meekness was a meekness of i and e. She hardly ever said a sentence containing a, o or u, and it was typical of her to have abbreviated Leo's name to Le. Her favorite expression was: "We simply see things differently"—her next favorite was: "In principle I am right, I'm ready to listen to reason." For me the shock of finding out Father had a mistress was more of an esthetic one: it wasn't like him. He is neither passionate nor vigorous, and if I was not to assume that she was some kind of nurse or spiritual therapist for him (in which case the dramatic expression mistress is not appropriate), then the thing that bothered me was that it didn't suit Father. In actual fact she was a nice, pretty, not terribly intelligent singer, for whom he didn't even arrange extra engagements or concerts. He was too upright for that. To me the whole thing seemed pretty confused, for Leo it was bitter. He was wounded in his ideals, and the only way my mother could describe Leo's condition was to say "Le is in a state of crisis," and when he then got a D in an exam she wanted to haul him off to a psychologist. I managed to prevent this by first of all telling him all I knew about this thing men and women do together and then by giving him so much help with his homework that the next time he got a C and then a B—and then my mother didn't think the psychologist was necessary any more.

Marie put on the dark green dress, and although she had trouble with the zipper I didn't get up to help her: it was so wonderful to watch the way she reached behind her with her hands, her white skin, her dark hair, and the dark green dress; I was glad too to see that she didn't get irritated; she finally came over to the bed, and I raised myself up and closed the zipper. I asked her why she got up so terribly early, and she said her father did not go to sleep properly till nearly dawn and would stay in bed till nine, and she had to take in the newspapers and open up the shop, as sometimes children came before mass to buy notebooks, pencils, or candy, and "besides," she said, "you had better be out of the house by half-past seven. I'm going to make coffee now, and in five minutes you can come down quietly into the kitchen." I felt almost married when I went down to the kitchen and Marie poured me out some coffee and buttered me a roll. She shook her head and said: "Face not washed, hair not combed, do you always come to breakfast like that?" and I said, yes, not even at school had they managed to get me to wash regularly in the early morning.

"Then what do you do?" she asked, "you must freshen up somehow?"

"I always rub myself down with Eau de Cologne," I said.

"That's pretty expensive," she said, and immediately blushed.

"Yes," I said, "but I always get it as a gift, a big bottle, from an uncle who has an agency for the stuff." In my embarrassment I looked round the kitchen I knew so well: it was small and dark, just a sort of back room to the shop; in the corner stood the little coal stove where Marie had kept the briquettes glowing the way all housewives do: in the evening she wraps them in wet newspaper, in the morning she stokes up the embers and gets the fire going with kindling and new briquettes. I hate the smell of briquette ash which hangs about the streets in the mornings and on this particular morning hung about the stuffy little kitchen. It was so cramped that whenever Marie took the coffee pot off the stove she had to get up and push the chair out of the way, and probably her grandmother and her mother had had to do exactly the same thing. This morning the kitchen I knew so well seemed for the first time worka- day. Perhaps I was realizing for the first time what this workaday world meant: having to do things which are no longer determined by the desire to do them. I had no desire to leave this cramped house ever again and assume any obligations outside; the obligation to confess what I had done with Marie to her friends, to Leo, even my parents would hear of it somewhere. I would have liked to stay here and sell candy and writing pads to the end of my days, get into bed with Marie at night and sleep with her, really sleep with her, as we had the last few hours before we got up, with her hands in my armpits. I found it terrible and magnificent, this workaday world, with coffee pot and rolls and Marie's washed-out blue and white apron over her green dress, and it seemed to me that it was only women who took the workaday world as much for granted as their bodies. I was proud that Marie was my woman and I did not feel quite as grown-up as I would have to behave from now on. I stood up, went round the table, took Marie in my arms and said: "Do you remember how you got up during the night and washed the sheets?" She nodded. "And I won't forget," she said, "how you warmed my hands in your armpits—now you must go, it is nearly half-past seven, and the first children will soon be coming."

I helped her bring in the bundles of newspapers from outside and unpack them. Across the street Schmitz was just coming back from market with his vegetable truck, and I jumped back into the shop so he wouldn't see me—but he had already seen me. Even the devil's eyes can't be as sharp as the neighbors'. I stood there in the shop and looked at the early morning papers which most men are so crazy about. I am only interested in newspapers in the evening or in the bath, and in the bath the most solemn morning papers seem to me as ridiculous as the evening papers. The headline this morning was: "Strauss: With unshakeable determination!" It might after all be better to leave the composing of an editorial or the headlines to a computing machine. There are limits beyond which idiocy should be prohibited. The shop bell went, a little girl, eight or nine years old, with black hair and red cheeks and freshly washed, her prayer book under her arm, entered the shop. "Gumdrops," she said, "a nickel's worth." I didn't know how many gumdrops could be bought for a nickel, I opened the glass jar and counted twenty into a paper bag and for the first time was ashamed of my not quite clean fingers which were magnified through the thick candy jar. The little girl looked at me in amazement as twenty candies fell into the bag, but I said: "It's all right, run along," and I took her nickel from the counter and threw it into the till.

Marie laughed when she came back and I proudly showed her the nickel. "Now you must go," she said.

"But why?" I asked, "can't I wait till your father comes down?"

"When he comes down, at nine, you have to be back here again. Now go," she said, "you must tell your

51

brother Leo before he hears about it from someone else."

"Yes," I said, "you're right—and how about you," I was blushing again, "don't you have to go to school?"

"I'm not going today," she said, "I'm never going again. Hurry back."

I found it hard to leave her, she came with me as far as the shop door, and I kissed her in the open doorway so Schmitz and his wife across the street could see. They goggled like fish who suddenly discover to their surprise that they have swallowed the hook.

I went off without looking back. I felt cold, turned up my collar, lit a cigarette, made a little detour across the market place, walked along the Franziskanerstrasse and at the corner of Koblenzstrasse jumped on the moving bus, the conductress opened the door for me, wagged a finger at me when I stood beside her to pay, shook her head and pointed to my cigarette. I stubbed it out, put it in my pocket, and went through to the middle. I just stood there, looking out into Koblenzstrasse, and thought about Marie. Something in my face seemed to annoy the man next to me. He even lowered his paper, stopped reading his "Strauss: With unshakeable determination," pushed his glasses down onto his nose, looked at me, shook his head, and murmured "Incredible." The woman sitting behind him—I had almost fallen over a big bag of carrots which was standing next to her—nodded at his comment, shook her head too, and moved her lips soundlessly.

For once I had combed my hair with Marie's comb in front of her mirror, the jacket I was wearing was gray, clean, and quite ordinary, and my beard was never so heavy that one day without shaving would have made me look "incredible." I am neither too tall nor too short, and my nose is not so long that it is noted in my passport under Distinguishing Marks. It says there: None. I was neither dirty nor drunk, and yet the woman with the bag of carrots was quite upset, more so than the man with the glasses, who finally after a last despairing shake of his head pushed up his glasses again and turned his attention to Strauss' determination. The woman swore silently under her breath, making restless movements with her head so as to inform the other passengers of what her lips would not reveal. I still don't know what Jews look like, otherwise I could tell whether she took me for one, I am more inclined to believe it had nothing to do with my appearance but with the expression in my eyes when I looked out of the bus onto the street and thought of Marie. This silent hostility got on my nerves, I got out one stop too soon, and walked the last bit of the Kölnerstrasse before turning off toward the Rhine.

The trunks of the trees in our grounds were black, still damp, the tennis court freshly rolled, red, from the Rhine I could hear the hooting of the barges, and as I entered the hall I heard Anna muttering softly to herself in the kitchen. All I could make out was ". . . a bad end—a bad end." I called through the open kitchen door: "No breakfast for me, Anna," quickly went on and came to a halt in the living room. The oak paneling, the wooden shelf with its tankards and hunting trophies, had never seemed so dark to me. Next door in the music room Leo was playing a Chopin mazurka. In those days he was planning to study music, he got up every morning at half-past five to practice before school. What he was playing transported me to a later time of the day, and I forgot that Leo was playing. Leo and Chopin do not go well together, but he played so well that I forgot him. Of all the older composers, Chopin and Schubert are my favorites. I know our music teacher was right when he called Mozart divine, Beethoven magnificent, Gluck unique, and Bach mighty; I know. Bach always seems to me like a three-volume work on dogma which fills me with awe. But Schubert and Chopin are as earthly as I myself probably am. I would rather listen to them than anyone else. In the garden, down toward the Rhine, I saw the targets in Grandfather's rifle range moving in front of the weeping willows. Fuhrmann had evidently been told to oil them. Sometimes my grandfather drums up a few "old boys," and there are fifteen enormous cars drawn up in the circular driveway in front of the house, and fifteen chauffeurs stand shivering among the hedges and trees or play cribbage in groups on the stone benches, and when one of the "old boys" has scored a bull's eye you can very soon hear a champagne cork popping. Sometimes Grandfather used to send for me, and I would do a few tricks for the old boys, imitations of Adenauer, or Erhard—a depressingly easy thing to do, or I acted out little scenes for them: executive in a restaurant car. And no matter how malicious I tried to make it, they laughed themselves sick, said it was "capital fun," and when I went round at the end with an empty shell carton or a tray they usually put in some folding money. I got along quite well with these cynical old codgers, I had nothing in common with them, I would have got along just as well with Chinese mandarins. A few of them went so far as to say my performances were "tremendous"—"magnificent." Some even announced: "The boy has talent" or "That boy's got something."

While I was listening to Chopin I considered for the first time going after bookings so I could earn some money. I could ask Grandfather to recommend me as solo entertainer at capitalist gatherings or for the enlivenment of board meetings. I had even rehearsed a number called "Board of Directors."

The moment Leo entered the room, Chopin vanished; Leo is very tall, fair, and with his rimless glasses he looks the way a deacon should look, or a Swedish Jesuit. The sharp creases in his dark trousers removed the last traces of Chopin, the white pullover above the sharply creased trousers didn't seem right, nor did the collar of his red shirt, above the white pullover. A sight like that—when I see how someone has tried so hard to look relaxed—always depresses me deeply, like pretentious names such as Ethelbert or Gerentrud. I also saw once again how Leo resembled Henrietta without really looking like her: the snub nose, the blue eyes, the hair line—but not her mouth, and everything about Henrietta which seemed pretty and lively is in Leo touching and awkward. He doesn't look as if he were the best athlete in the class; he looks like a boy who is excused from sports, but over his bed hang half a dozen athletic awards.

He came quickly toward me, suddenly stopped a few steps away, his awkward hands spread slightly sideways, and said: "Hans, what's the matter?" He looked into my eyes, a little below them, like someone who wants to draw your attention to a spot, and I realized I had been crying. When I listen to Chopin or Schubert I always cry. I wiped away the two tears with my right forefinger and said: "I didn't know you could play Chopin so well. Please play the mazurka again."

"I can't," he said, "I have to go to school, they're giving us the German subjects for our exams first thing this morning."

"I'll drive you there in Mother's car," I said.

"I don't like driving in that ridiculous car," he said, "you know I hate it." Mother had at that time got a sports car from a friend "fantastically cheap," and Leo was very sensitive about anything that might be interpreted as showing off. There was only one way to make him lose his temper: if anyone teased him or spoiled him because of our rich parents he would get red in the face and hit out with his fists.

"Just this once," I said, "sit down at the piano and play. Don't you want to know where I was?"

He blushed, looked down at the floor and said: "No, I don't want to know."

"I was with a girl," I said, "with a woman—my wife."

"Were you?" he said, without looking up. "When was the wedding?" He still didn't know what to do with his awkward hands, and he suddenly tried to walk past me with lowered head. I caught him by the sleeve.

"It's Marie Derkum," I said quietly. He drew his elbow away, stepped back and said: "Oh my God, no."

He looked at me angrily and muttered something under his breath.

"What?" I asked, "what was that?"

"That I have to take the car after all—will you drive me?"

I said yes, put my hand on his shoulder, and went with him across the living room. I wanted to spare him having to look at me. "Go and get the keys," I said, "Mother won't mind giving them to you—and don't forget the papers—and Leo, I need some money—have you any left?"

"In the bank," he said, "can you get it yourself?"

"I don't know," I said, "you'd better send it to me."

"Send?" he asked. "Are you going away?"

"Yes," I said. He nodded and went upstairs.

It was only when he asked me that I knew I wanted to leave. I went into the kitchen, where Anna received me grumbling.

55

"I thought you didn't want any breakfast," she said crossly.

"I don't," I said, "just some coffee." I sat down at the scrubbed table and watched Anna at the stove as she removed the filter from the coffee pot and stood it on a cup to drip. We had breakfast every morning with the maids in the kitchen as we found it too tiresome to be waited on formally in the dining room. At this hour Anna was alone in the kitchen. Noretta, the second maid, was with Mother in the bedroom, serving her breakfast and discussing her clothes and cosmetics. Probably Mother was at this moment grinding some wheat germ between her excellent teeth, while her face was covered with some stuff made of placenta and Noretta was reading the paper to her. Perhaps they had only got as far as morning prayers, consisting of quotations from Goethe and Luther and usually with an extra dash of moral rearmament, or possibly Noretta was reading to my mother from her collection of brochures on laxatives. My mother has whole files full of medical prospectuses, divided into "Digestion," "Heart," "Nerves," and whenever she can lay hands on a doctor she pumps him for information on "new treatments," so she doesn't have to pay for a consultation. When one of the doctors sends her a physician's sample she is blissfully happy.

I could tell from Anna's back that she was putting off the moment when she would have to turn round and look me in the face and talk to me. We are fond of each other, although she can never suppress the embarrassing tendency to teach me manners. She has been with us for fifteen years, Mother took her over from a cousin, a Protestant clergyman. Anna is from Potsdam, and the mere fact that, although we are Protestants, we speak the local dialect of the Rhine country, seems somehow weird, almost unnatural, to her. I believe she would think a Protestant who spoke with a Bavarian accent was the devil incarnate. She is tall, slim, and proud of the fact that she "moves like a lady." Her father had been paymaster in something of which all I know is that it was called I.R. 9. It is useless to tell Anna that we are not in this I.R. 9; as far as bringing up children is concerned she refuses to budge from the phrase: "You couldn't have done that in I.R. 9." I have never quite

56

understood what this I.R. 9 is, but have since discovered that in this mysterious educational establishment I could probably never have had a chance as a latrine cleaner even. It was chiefly my washing habits that called forth Anna's references to I.R. 9, and "this horrible habit of staying in bed as long as possible" disgusts her as if I had leprosy. When at last she turned round and came over to the table with the coffee pot, she kept her eyes lowered like a nun serving a slightly disreputable bishop. I was sorry for her, like the girls in Marie's group. With her nun's instinct Anna had undoubtedly realized where I had been, while my mother, even if I were secretly married to a woman for three years, would probably never notice a thing. I took the pot from Anna's hand, poured myself some coffee, held Anna firmly by the arm, and forced her to look at me: she did so with her pale blue eyes and fluttering eyelids, and I saw that she was actually crying. "Damn it, Anna," I said, "look at me. Surely even in your I.R. 9 people look each other manfully in the eye."

"I'm not a man," she whimpered, I let her go; she stood facing the stove, mumbling something about sin and shame, Sodom and Gomorrah, and I said: "My God, Anna, just think for a moment what they really did in Sodom and Gomorrah." She shook my hand off her shoulder, I left the kitchen without telling her I was planning to leave home. She was the only person I sometimes talked to about Henrietta.

Leo was already standing outside the garage, and looked anxiously at his watch. "Did Mother notice I was out?" I asked. He said, "No," gave me the keys, and held open the garage door. I got into Mother's car, drove out and let Leo get in. He looked strenuously at his fingernails. "I have the savings book," he said, "I'll get the money during break. Where shall I send it?" "Send it to old man Derkum," I said. "Please," he said, "let's go, it's getting late." I speeded up, along our driveway, through the gates and had to wait outside at the streetcar stop where Henrietta had got on the streetcar to go and join the Flak. A few girls of Henrietta's age got on the streetcar. As we overtook the streetcar I saw more girls of Henrietta's age, laughing the way she had laughed, wearing blue berets and coats with fur collars. If a war

57

came, their parents would send them off just like my parents had sent off Henrietta, they would give them some pocket money, a few sandwiches, pat them on the back and say, "Be a good girl." I would have liked to wave to the girls, but I didn't. Things are always taken the wrong way. When you drive a ridiculous car like that you can't even wave at a girl. I had once given a boy in the park half a bar of chocolate and pushed his fair hair back from his dirty forehead; he was crying and had smeared the tears on his face onto his forehead, I only wanted to comfort him. There was a terrible scene with two women who nearly sent for the police, and after all their abuse I really felt like a fiend, because one of the women kept saying to me: "You filthy swine, you filthy swine."

It was horrible, I found the scene as perverse as I do a real sex maniac.

As I drove along the Koblenzstrasse, much too fast, I kept my eye open for a ministerial car to scrape, Mother's car had projecting hubs with which I could have scratched up another car, but at that early hour no cabinet minister was about. I said to Leo: "How about it? Are you really going into the army?" He colored and nodded. "We discussed it," he said, "in the study group and came to the conclusion that it's in the interests of democracy." "Go ahead then," I said, "by all means go and take a hand in this nonsense, I'm sorry I'm not liable to be called up." Leo looked at me questioningly, but turned away his head when I tried to look at him. "Why?" he asked. "Oh," I said, "I would like to see the major again who was billeted with us and wanted to have Mrs. Wieneken shot. I'm sure he's a colonel by now, or a general." I stopped at the Beethoven School to drop him off, he shook his head and said: "No, park over there to the right behind the hostel," I drove on, stopped, shook hands with Leo, but he smiled miserably and went on holding out his hand to me. My thoughts were already far away, I didn't understand, and it irritated me the way Leo kept looking anxiously at his watch. It was only five to, and he had plenty of time. "You don't really want to go into the army, do you?" I said. "Why not," he said angrily, "give me the car key." I gave him the car key, nodded to him, and walked off. I was thinking all the time of Henrietta and thought it was madness that Leo wanted to be a soldier. I crossed the park, past the university and on toward the market square. I felt cold, and I wanted to see Marie.

The shop was full of kids when I arrived. The children took candies, pencils, erasers from the shelves and put down the money for Derkum on the counter. When I pushed my way through the shop to the back room he did not look up. I went over to the stove, warmed my hands on the coffee pot and thought, Marie will be coming any minute now. I was out of cigarettes, and I wondered whether I should just take some or pay for them when I asked Marie for them. I poured myself out some coffee and noticed there were three cups on the table. When it got quiet in the shop I put down my cup. I wished Marie were there. I washed my face and hands in the sink next to the stove, combed my hair with the nailbrush lying in the soap dish, smoothed down my shirt collar, pulled up my tie, and had another look at my nails: they were clean. I suddenly knew I must do all these things I never did otherwise.

When her father came in I had just sat down, I stood up at once. He was as embarrassed as I was, and just as shy, he did not look angry, only very serious, and when he stretched out his hand toward the coffee pot I started, not much but enough to notice. He shook his head, poured himself some coffee, offered me the pot, I said no thank you, he still didn't look at me. During the night, upstairs in Marie's bed, in thinking it all over I had felt very confident. I would have liked a cigarette but I didn't dare take one out of his packet lying on the table. Any other time I would have. Standing there, bent over the table, with his large bald head and the gray untidy ring of hair, I thought he looked very old. I started to say in a low voice, "Mr. Derkum, you have every right," but he banged his hand on the table, looked at me at last, over the top of his glasses, and said: "Damn it, did you have to do that—and so that the whole neighborhood had to know about it?" I was glad he was not disappointed and didn't start talking about honor. "Was that really necessary—you know how we've skimped and saved for this damned exam, and now," he closed his hand, opened it, as if he were setting a bird free, "nothing." "Where's Marie?" I asked. "Gone," he said, "gone to Cologne." "Where is she?" I shouted, "where?" "Keep calm," he said, "you'll find out. I suppose you are now going to talk about love, marriage, and so on—don't bother—go on, go. I shall be interested to see what becomes of you. Now go." I was afraid to go past him. I said: "And her address?" "Here," he said and pushed a piece of paper across the table. I put it in my pocket. "Anything else?" he shouted, "anything else? What are you waiting for?" "I need some money," I said, and was relieved when he suddenly laughed, it was a curious laugh, hard and angry, like the only time I had heard him laugh before, when we talked about my father. "Money," he said, "that's a joke, but come along," he said, "come on," and he pulled me by the sleeve into the shop, went behind the counter, jerked open the cash register, and tossed out small change with both hands: dimes, nickels, and pennies, he scattered the coins over the notebooks and newspapers, I hesitated, then slowly began to pick up the coins, I was tempted to scoop them up in the palm of my hand, but then I picked them up one by one, counted them, and put them in my pocket. He watched me, nodded, took out his purse, and handed me a five-mark piece. We both blushed. "I'm sorry," he said quietly, "I'm sorry, Oh God, I'm sorry." He thought I was offended, but I understood him very well. I said: "May I have a pack of cigarettes too?" and he at once reached toward the shelf behind him and gave me two. He was crying. I leaned over the counter and kissed him on the cheek. He is the only man I have ever kissed.

8

The thought that Züpfner might be able to watch Marie getting dressed, or be allowed to see how she puts back the cap on the toothpaste, made me feel quite ill. My leg was hurting, and I began to doubt whether anyone would still have booked me even at the thirty to fifty-mark level. Besides, it was torture to think it might mean nothing to Züpfner to watch Marie put back the cap on the toothpaste: in my modest experience, Catholics have no feeling whatever for detail. I had Züpfner's phone number on my sheet of paper, but I was not yet sufficiently fortified to dial the number. One never knows what someone will do under ideological pressure, and perhaps she had really married Züpfner, and to hear Marie's voice on the phone saying: "Mrs. Züpfner speaking"—it would have been unbearable. In order to phone Leo I had looked in the phone book under Catholic seminaires, found nothing, and yet knew that these two places existed: Leoninum and Albertinum. At last I felt strong enough to lift the receiver and dial Information, for once it wasn't engaged, and the girl at the other end even spoke with a Rhineland intonation. There are times when I long to hear the Rhine dialect so much that I call up a Bonn telephone service number from some hotel or other, just to hear this utterly nonmartial way of talking which barely pronounces the R's, the very sound military discipline is based on.

I heard the "One moment, please" only five times, then a girl answered, and I asked her about these "places where they train Catholic priests"; I told her I had looked under Catholic seminaries, found nothing, she laughed and said these "places"—she said the quotations marks very nicely—were called colleges, and she gave me the numbers of both. The girl's voice on the phone had made one feel a bit better. It had sounded so natural, not prim, not coy, and typically Rhineland. I even managed to get through to the telegraph office and send off a wire to Karl Emonds.

I have never been able to understand why everyone who would like to be thought intelligent tries so hard to express this compulsory hatred for Bonn. Bonn has always had certain charms, drowsy charms, just as there are women of whom I can imagine that their drowsiness has charms. Of course Bonn cannot stand up to exaggeration, and people have exaggerated this town. A town which cannot stand up to exaggeration cannot be described: a rare quality, after all. Besides, everyone knows the climate of Bonn is a climate for retired people, there is some connection between atmospheric pressure and blood pressure. The thing that doesn't suit Bonn at all is this defensive irritability: I had plenty of opportunity at home to talk to government officials, deputies, generals—my mother is a great one for parties —and they are all in a state of irritated, sometimes almost tearful defensiveness. They all smile at Bonn with such martyred irony. I don't understand what all the fuss is about. If a woman whose charm lay in her drowsiness suddenly began to dance a wild can-can, you would assume she had been doped—but to dope a whole town, this is beyond them. A dear old aunt can teach you how to knit sweaters, crochet little doilies, and serve sherry—but I wouldn't expect her to make a witty and knowledgeable two-hour speech on homosexuality or to suddenly start talking like a floozy. False hopes, false modesty, false speculation on the unnatural. It wouldn't surprise me if even the papal nuncio began complaining about the shortage of floozies. At one of our parties at home I met a politician who was on a committee for the suppression of prostitution and complained to me in a whisper about the shortage of floozies in Bonn. Bonn used really not to be so bad with all its narrow streets, book-stores, fraternities, little bakeries with a back room where you could have a cup of coffee.

Before trying to call Leo I hobbled out onto the balcony to look out over my native town. It is really a pretty town: the cathedral, the roofs of what used to be the Elector's Palace, the Beethoven Monument, the Little Market and the park. It is Bonn's destiny that nobody believes in its destiny. Up there on my balcony I drew in great breaths of the Bonn air, which strangely enough made me feel better: as a change of air, Bonn can work wonders, for a few hours.

I left the balcony, went back into the room and without hesitation dialed the number of the place where Leo was a student. I was nervous. Since Leo has become a Catholic I have not seen him. He informed me of his conversion in his childishly correct manner: "My dear brother," he wrote, "This is to inform you that after mature consideration I have reached the decision to join the Catholic church and to prepare myself for the priesthood. Doubtless we will soon have an opportunity to discuss this decisive change in my life personally. Your affectionate brother Leo." Even the old-fashioned way he tries desperately to avoid beginning the letter with "I," instead of I am writing to inform you, saying This is to inform you—that was typically Leo. None of the polish he brings to his piano-playing. This way of doing everything in a businesslike manner increases my depression. If he goes on like this one day he will be a noble, white-haired prelate. On this point—style of letter-writing—Father and Leo are equally at sea: they write about everything as if they were dealing in coal.

It was a long time before someone at this place deigned to come to the phone, and I was just in the mood to start berating this ecclesiastical sloppiness with harsh words, said "Oh shit," then someone lifted the receiver at the other end and a surprisingly hoarse voice said: "Yes?" I was disappointed. I had been expecting a gentle nun's voice, smelling of weak coffee and dry cake, instead: a croaking old man, and it smelled of pipe tobacco and cabbage, so penetratingly that I began to cough.

"Excuse me," I said at last, "may I speak to Leo Schnier, a theology student?"

"Who is speaking, please?"

"Schnier," I said. This was evidently beyond his powers

of comprehension. He was silent for a long time, I began to cough again, pulled myself together and said: "I will spell it: School, Charles, Henry, Norman, Ida, Emil, Richard."

"What are you talking about?" he said finally, and he sounded as if he felt as desperate as I did. Maybe they had put a nice old pipe-smoking professor in charge of the phone, and I hastily scraped together a few Latin words and said humbly; *"Sum frater leonis."* I felt I was taking an unfair advantage, I thought of all the people who perhaps felt the urge now and again to speak to someone there and who had never learned a word of Latin.

Strangely enough he tittered and said: *Frater tuus est in refectorio*—at dinner," he said, raising his voice slightly, "the students are having dinner and they must not be disturbed at mealtimes."

"The matter is very urgent," I said.

"A death in the family?" he asked.

"No," I said, "but almost."

"A serious accident then?"

"No," I said, "an internal accident."

"Oh," he said, and his voice sounded somewhat milder, "internal hemorrhage."

"No," I said, "spiritual. A purely spiritual matter." Obviously this was a foreign word for him, he maintained an icy silence.

"My God," I said, "after all a man consists of body and soul."

His rumblings seemed to express doubts as to this statement, between two puffs of his pipe he muttered: "St. Augustine—Bonaventura—Cusanus—you are quite wrong."

"Soul," I said obstinately, "please tell Mr. Schnier that his brother's soul is in danger and ask him to phone me as soon as he's finished dinner."

"Soul," he said coldly, "brother, danger." He might just as well have said: Muck, manure, milkman. To me the whole thing seemed quite funny: after all, the students were being trained there as future spiritual advisers, and he must have come across the word soul somewhere. "The matter is of the utmost urgency," I said.

He merely went "Hm, hm," he seemed quite unable to understand that something connected with soul could be urgent.

"I'll give him the message," he said, "what was that about school?"

"Nothing," I said, "nothing at all. The matter has nothing to do with school. I merely used the word to spell my name."

"I suppose you think they still teach children spelling in school. Do you seriously believe that?" He became so animated that I assumed he had finally hit on his favorite topic. "The methods are much too mild these days," he shouted, "much too mild."

"Indeed they are," I said, "they ought to use the strap much more in school."

"Yes, oughtn't they?" he exclaimed eagerly.

"Yes," I said, "especially the teachers, they ought to be strapped much more often. You won't forget, will you, to give my brother the message?"

"I've made a note of it," he said, "urgent spiritual matter. To do with school. Listen, my young friend, may I as doubtless the older of us give you some well-meant advice?"

"By all means," I said.

"Stay away from St. Augustine: skillfully formulated subjectivity is not theology, not by a long shot, and it's harmful to young souls. Nothing but journalism with a few dialectical features. You won't take offense at this advice?"

"No," I said, "I shall immediately go and throw my St. Augustine into the fire."

"That's right," he said almost jubilantly, "into the fire with him. God bless you." I was on the point of saying Thank you, but it didn't seem appropriate, so I merely hung up and wiped the sweat off my face. I am very sensitive to smells, and the intensely strong smell of cabbage had mobilized my vegetative nervous system. I also thought about the methods of ecclesiastical authorities: of course it was nice to make an old man feel he was still useful, but I couldn't see why they would give such a crotchety deaf old fellow the job of answering the phone. The cabbage smell was something I remembered from boarding school. A padre there had once explained to us that cabbage was supposed to suppress sensuality. I find the idea of suppressing mine or anyone else's sensuality disgusting. Evidently they think day and night of nothing but "desires of the flesh," and somewhere in the kitchen a nun sits drawing up the menu, then she talks it over with the principal, and they sit opposite each other and don't talk about it but think with each item on the menu: this one inhibits, that one encourages sensuality. To me a scene like that seems a clear case of obscenity, just like those confounded football games that went on for hours at school; we knew it was supposed to make us tired so we wouldn't start thinking about girls, that made football disgusting to my mind, and when I think that my brother Leo has to eat cabbage so as to suppress his sensuality, I want to go to that place and sprinkle hydrochloric acid over all the cabbage. What those boys have in store for them is hard enough without cabbage: it must be terribly hard to proclaim these extraordinary things every day: resurrection of the body and eternal life. To dig away in the vineyard of the Lord and see precious little visible result. Heinrich Behlen, who was so kind to us when Marie had the miscarriage, explained it all to me once. He always spoke of himself to me "as an unskilled laborer in the vineyard of the Lord, with regard to outlook as well as wages."

When we left the hospital at five I walked home with him since we had no money for the streetcar, and as he stood there at the front door and pulled his keyring out of his pocket there seemed to be no difference between him and a workman coming home from night shift, tired, unshaven, and I knew it must be terrible for him: to read mass now, with all the secrets Marie always used to tell me about. When Heinrich unlocked the door, his housekeeper was standing there in the hall, a grumpy old woman in loose slippers, the skin of her bare legs quite yellow, and not even a nun, or his mother or sister; she hissed at him: "What's the meaning of this? What's the meaning of this?" This shabby, musty bachelor atmosphere; damn it all, I'm not surprised some Catholic parents are afraid to send their daughters to a priest at his home, and I'm not surprised these poor devils sometimes lose their heads.

I almost phoned the deaf old pipe-smoker at Leo's college again: I would have liked to talk to him about carnal desire. I was afraid to call up someone I knew: this stranger would probably be more understanding. I would have liked to ask him whether my conception of Catholicism was correct. For me there were only four Catholics in the world: Pope John, Alec Guinness, Marie, and Gregory, an old negro boxer who had once nearly become world champion and who was now eking out a meagre living as a strong man in vaudeville. Now and again I would run into him during a tour of engagements. He was very devout, a real churchgoer, was a member of the Third Order and always wore his scapular on his huge boxer's chest. Most people thought he was mentally deficient because he hardly ever uttered a word and apart from pickles and bread hardly ate a thing; and yet he was so strong that he could carry me and Marie on his hands across the room like dolls. There were a few more Catholics with a fairly high degree of probability: Karl Emonds and Heinrich Behlen, and Züpfner too. As for Marie, I was already beginning to have my doubts: her "metaphysical horror" was something I didn't understand, and now if she went and did all those things with Züpfner which I had done with her, then she was doing those things which in her books are described unmistakably as adultery and fornication. Her metaphysical horror was concerned simply and solely with my refusal to be married at a registry office, to have our children brought up as Catholics. We didn't have any children yet, but we talked all the time about how we would dress them, how we would talk to them, how we would bring them up, and we agreed on all points except the Catholic upbringing. I was willing to have them baptized. Marie said I must put it in writing, otherwise we could not be married in church. When I consented to the church wedding, it turned out we also had to go through a civil ceremony—and then I lost patience and said we ought to wait a while after all, a year didn't make much difference now, and she cried and said I just didn't understand what it meant to her to live in this state and with no prospect of having our children brought up as Christians. It was terrible, because it turned out that on this point we had been talking at cross purposes for five years. I really hadn't known one has to have a civil wedding before one can be married in church. Of course I ought to have known, as an adult citizen and a "fully responsible male person," but I simply did not, just as I didn't know till recently that white wine is served cold and red wine warmed. I knew, of course, that such things as marriage license offices existed and that certain marriage ceremonies took place and documents were issued there, but I thought that was something for people who didn't go to church and for those who as it were wanted to give the state a little treat. I got really angry when I found out you have to go there before you can get married in church, and when Marie then started in about my giving a written guarantee that our children would be brought up as Catholics, we began quarreling. That seemed like blackmail to me, and I didn't like it at all that Marie was so completely in agreement with this demand for a written guarantee. After all, she could have the children baptized and bring them up as she saw fit.

She wasn't feeling well that evening, she was pale and tired, spoke rather loudly to me, and when I finally said, Yes, all right, I would do everything, even sign those things, she got mad and said: "You're just agreeing now out of laziness and not because you are convinced of the justness of abstract principles of order," and I said, Yes, it was true I was doing it out of laziness and because I wanted to have her by me my whole life long, and I would even go over properly to the Catholic church if that was necessary in order to keep her. I even got quite dramatic and said an expression like "abstract principles of order" reminded me of a torture chamber. She took it as an insult that, in order to keep her, I even wanted to become a Catholic. And I had thought I was paying her an almost exaggerated compliment. She said it was no longer a question of her and me, but of "order."

It was evening, in a hotel room in Hanover, in one of those expensive hotels where, when you order a cup of coffee, you only get three quarters of a cup of coffee. They are so sophisticated in those hotels that a full cup of coffee is considered vulgar, and the waiters know much better what is sophisticated than the sophisticated

68

people who play the part of guests there. I always feel in these hotels as if I am in an ultra-expensive and ultra-boring boarding school, and this evening I was dead tired: three performances one after the other. In the early afternoon to some kind of steel shareholders, later in the afternoon to some graduate teachers, and in the evening in a vaudeville theater where the applause was so weak that I could already sense my approaching downfall. When I ordered some beer sent up to my room in this stupid hotel, the head waiter said in an icy voice on the phone: "Certainly, sir," as if I had asked for liquid manure, and they brought me the beer in a silver tankard. I was tired, all I wanted to do was drink some beer, play a little parchesi, have a bath, read the evening papers and fall asleep beside Marie: my right hand on her breast and my face so close to her head that the smell of her hair would become part of my sleep. The feeble applause still sounded in my ears. It would have been almost more humane if they had all turned their thumbs down. This tired, blasé contempt for my performance was as flat as the beer in the stupid silver tankard. I was simply incapable of carrying on an ideological discussion.

"It's the principle of the thing, Hans," she said, not quite as loud, and she didn't even notice that "thing" has a special meaning for us; she had apparently forgotten. She walked up and down by the foot of the bed and every time she gesticulated she jabbed the air so precisely with her cigarette that the little smoke clouds looked like full stops. She had meanwhile learned how to smoke, in her pale green pullover she looked beautiful: her white skin, her hair darker than it used to be, I saw for the first time tendons in her neck. I said: "Have a heart, let me have a good night's sleep first, tomorrow at breakfast we'll talk over everything again, especially the thing you're worried about," but she noticed nothing, turned round, stood in front of the bed, and I could see from her mouth that her behavior was caused by motives she did not admit to herself. When she drew on her cigarette, I saw a few little lines round her mouth I had never seen before. She shook her head as she looked at me, sighed, turned round again and walked up and down.

"I don't quite understand," I said wearily, "first we quarrel about my signature to this blackmail form—then about the civil wedding—now I have agreed to both, and you are angrier than ever."

"Yes," she said, "it is too quick for me, and I feel you are avoiding the issue. What do you really want?" "You," I said, and I don't know of anything nicer you can say to a woman.

"Come here," I said, "lie down beside me and bring the ashtray, we can talk much better like that." I could no longer say the word "thing" in her presence. She shook her head, put the ashtray beside me on the bed, went over to the window and looked out. I was afraid.

"There's something about this conversation I don't like —it doesn't sound like you!"

"What does it sound like then?" she asked quietly, and I was deceived by her voice which had suddenly become so gentle again.

"It reminds me of Bonn," I said, "of the group, of Sommerwild and Züpfner—and all that crowd."

"Perhaps," she said, without turning round, "your ears imagine they have heard what your eyes have seen."

"I don't understand," I said wearily, "what do you mean."

"Oh," she said, "as if you didn't know that there's a Catholic Congress going on here now."

"I saw the posters," I said.

"And that Heribert and Prelate Sommerwild might be here, didn't that occur to you?"

I hadn't known Züpfner's first name was Heribert. When she said the name I realized she could only mean him. I thought once again of them holding hands. I had already noticed that in Hanover there were more Catholic priests and nuns about than the town seemed to call for, but it had not occurred to me that Marie might be meeting someone here, and even if she were—after all, when I had a few free days we had sometimes gone to Bonn, and she had been able to enjoy the whole "group" to her heart's content.

"Here in the hotel?" I asked wearily.

"Yes," she said.

"Why didn't you let me meet them?"

"You were hardly here," she said, "on the road for a whole week—Brunswick, Hildesheim, Celle . . ."

"But now I'm free," I said, "phone them, and we'll have a drink downstairs in the bar."

"They've gone," she said, "they left this afternoon."

"I'm glad," I said, "you were able to breathe 'Catholic air' so long and so plentifully, even if it was imported." That was her expression, not mine. Sometimes she had said she had to breathe Catholic air again.

"Why are you angry?" she asked; she was still standing facing the street, had lighted another cigarette, and this was another strange thing about her: this feverish smoking, it was as strange to me as the way she spoke to me. At this moment she could have been anybody, any pretty girl, not very intelligent, who was looking for any excuse to leave.

"I'm not angry," I said, "you know I'm not. Tell me you know."

She didn't say anything, but she nodded, and I could see enough of her face to know she was holding back the tears. Why? She ought to have cried, loud and long. Then I could have got up, put my arm around her and kissed her. I didn't. I had no desire to, and to do it out of mere routine or duty didn't appeal to me. I stayed lying on the bed. I thought of Züpfner and Sommerwild, and that for three days she had been chatting with them without telling me a thing about it. For certain they had talked about me. Züpfner was a member of the Executive Committee. I hesitated too long, a minute, half a minute or two, I don't know. When I got up and went over to her she shook her head, pushed my hands away from her shoulder and began talking again, about her metaphysical horror and about principles of order, and I felt I had been married to her for twenty years. Her voice took on a disciplinary note, I was too tired to follow her arguments, they flew past my ears. I interrupted her and told her about my failure at the vaudeville theater, the first in three years. We stood side by side at the window, looking down onto the street below where taxis kept driving by taking the Catholic committee members to the station: nuns, priests and solemn-looking laymen. In one group I recognized Schnitzler, he was holding the taxi door open for a very distinguished-looking elderly nun. When he was living with us he had been a Protestant. Either he must have converted or be here as a Protestant observer. He was capable of anything. Down below suitcases were being carried and tips pressed into the hands of hotel staff. I was so tired and confused that everything swam before my eyes: taxis and nuns, lights and suitcases, and all the time that horrible feeble applause was ringing in my ears. Marie had long since broken off her monologue about principles of order, she had stopped smoking too, and when I moved away from the window she followed me, grasped me by the shoulder and kissed both my eyes. "You are so sweet," she said, "so sweet and so tired," but when I wanted to put my arms round her she said softly: "Please, please, don't," and I made the mistake of really letting her go. I threw myself fully dressed on the bed, fell asleep at once, and when I woke in the morning I was not surprised to find Marie had gone. I found the note on the table "I must take the path that I must take." She was nearly twenty-five, and she ought to have been able to think of something better than that. I was not offended, it just seemed a little inadequate. I sat down at once and wrote her a long letter, after breakfast I wrote her another one, I wrote her every day and sent all the letters to Fredebeul's address in Bonn, but I never got an answer.

9

It was a long time before anyone at the Fredebeuls came
to the phone; the constant ringing got on my nerves, I
imagined Mrs. Fredebeul asleep, then being woken up
by the ringing, then falling asleep again, then being woken
up again, and I suffered all the agony that this call was
causing her ears. I was just about to hang up but told
myself this was an emergency and let it go on ringing.
The idea of waking Fredebeul himself out of a deep
sleep would not have bothered me in the least: the
fellow doesn't deserve undisturbed sleep; he is pathologi-
cally ambitious, probably always has his hand poised on
the telephone ready to call someone up or take calls
from government department heads, editors, executive
committees and the party. I like his wife very much. She
was still a schoolgirl when he took her for the first time
to a group meeting, and the way she sat there, following
the theological-sociological discussions with her beautiful eyes, quite upset me. I could see she would much
rather have gone dancing or to a movie. Sommerwild,
in whose home this meeting was taking place, kept
asking me: Is it too warm for you, Schnier, and I said:
No, sir, although the sweat was pouring off my forehead
and cheeks. Finally I went out onto Sommerwild's balcony because I couldn't stand all that talking any more.
She was the one who had started off this whole palaver by
saying—à propos of nothing, by the way, as actually
they were discussing the size and extent of provincial-
ism—she thought some things Gottfried Benn had written

were "quite nice really." Whereupon Fredebeul, who was supposed to be her fiancé, went scarlet, for Kinkel gave him one of his famous speaking looks: "How come? Haven't you straightened her out about this yet?" So he straightened her out himself and chipped away at the poor girl, using the whole Western world as a chisel. There was practically nothing left of the nice girl, the chips flew, and I was annoyed at Fredebeul for being such a coward and not intervening because with Kinkel he was "committed" to a certain ideological line, I have no idea whether left or right, at any rate they have their line, and Kinkel felt morally obliged to straighten out Fredebeul's fiancée. Sommerwild didn't lift a finger either, though he represented the opposite line from Kinkel's and Fredebeul's, I can't remember which: if Kinkel and Fredebeul are left, Sommerwild is right, or vice versa. Marie had gone a bit pale too, but she is impressed by erudition——I have never been able to talk her out of it—and Kinkel's erudition impressed the future Mrs. Fredebeul too: with almost lascivious sighs she submitted to the torrent of information: from the Church Fathers to Brecht, it poured down like a tropical storm, and when I came back refreshed from the balcony they were all sitting there totally exhausted, drinking punch—and all because the poor child had said she thought some of Benn's writings were "quite nice really."

Now she already has two children by Fredebeul, is barely twenty-two, and while the phone was still ringing in their apartment I imagined her somewhere busy with baby bottles, talcum powder, diapers and cold cream, utterly helpless and confused, and I thought of the mountains of dirty diapers and the unwashed, greasy dishes in her kitchen. Once when the conversation became too exhausting for me I had helped her make some toast, cut sandwiches and put on the coffee, chores of which I can only say that they are less repellent to me than certain forms of conversation.

A very hesitant voice said: "Yes?" and I could tell from the voice that the kitchen, bathroom and bedroom looked more hopeless than ever. I could hardly smell anything this time: only that she must be holding a cigarette.

"Schnier speaking," I said, and I expected an exclamation of pleasure, such as she always gives when I call her up. Oh, you're in Bonn—how nice—or something like that, but there was an embarrassed silence, then she said feebly: "Oh, that's nice." I didn't know what to say. Formerly she always used to say: "When are you coming to give us a show again?" Not a word. I was embarrassed, not for my sake, more for hers, for me it was only depressing, for her it was embarrassing. "The letters," I finally said with an effort, "the letters I sent to Marie care of your address?"

"They're lying here," she said, "returned unopened."

"Where did you forward them to?"

"I don't know," she said, "my husband took care of that."

"But you must have seen on the letters that came back what address he wrote on them?"

"Are you cross-examining me?"

"Oh no," I said mildly, "no, no, I simply thought in all modesty that perhaps I had a right to know what happened to my letters."

"Which you, without asking us, sent here."

"Dear Mrs. Fredebeul," I said, "please, do be human now."

She laughed, faintly but audibly, but said nothing.

"What I mean is," I said, "there is a point at which human beings, even if for ideological reasons—become human."

"Does that mean that up to now I have behaved inhumanly?"

"Yes," I said. She laughed again, very faintly, but still audibly.

"I am very unhappy about this whole thing," she said finally, "but more than that I can't say. You have disappointed us all terribly."

"As a clown?" I asked.

"That too," she said, "but not only that."

"I suppose your husband isn't home?"

"No," she said, "he won't be back for a few days. He is on an election campaign in the Eifel Mountains."

"What?" I exclaimed; that was news indeed, "surely not for the CDU?"

"Why not," she said in a voice that made it clear she would like to hang up.

"Oh all right," I said, "is it asking too much if I ask you to send me my letters."

"Where to?"

"To Bonn—to my address here in Bonn."

"You're in Bonn?" she asked, and it sounded as if she was suppressing a "For Heaven's sake."

"Goodbye," I said, "and thank you for so much humanity." I was sorry to be so angry with her, I was fed up. I went into the kitchen, took the cognac out of the icebox and had a long drink from it. It didn't help. I had another, that didn't help either. Mrs. Fredebeul was the last person from whom I would have expected a brush-off like that. I had been prepared for a long sermon about marriage, with reproaches about my behavior toward Marie; she could be dogmatic in a nice, consistent way, but usually when I was in Bonn and phoned her she would ask me laughingly to help her again in the kitchen and with the children. I must have been mistaken about her, or perhaps she was pregnant again and in a bad mood. I didn't have the nerve to phone again and maybe find out what was the matter with her. She had always been so nice to me. The only way I could account for it was that Fredebeul had given her "strict instructions" how to treat me. I have often noticed how wives are loyal to their husbands to the point of absolute madness. Mrs. Fredebeul was no doubt too young to know how deeply her unnatural coldness would hurt me, and I really couldn't expect her to realize that Fredebeul is little more than an opportunist, full of hot air, intent on becoming a success at all costs and prepared to "drop" his own grandmother if she got in his way. No doubt he had said, "Write Schnier off," and so she simply wrote me off. She was under his thumb, and as long as he had believed I was useful in some way, she had been allowed to follow her natural instincts and be nice to me, now contrary to her instincts she had to be unkind to me. But maybe I was doing them an injustice, and they were both merely following the dictates of their conscience. If Marie was married to Züpfner, it was no doubt sinful to arrange a contact between us—that Züpfner was *the* man in the

76

Executive Committee and could be useful to Fredebeul didn't interfere with their conscience. Doubtless they must do what was right and proper even when it was to their advantage. I was less shocked at Fredebeul than at his wife. I had never had any illusions about him, and not even the fact that he was now on an election tour on behalf of the Christian Democratic Union could surprise me.

I put the cognac bottle away in the refrigerator for good.

I decided I might as well ring them all, one after the other, so I could get the Catholics out of the way. Somehow I was wide awake now and wasn't even limping any more when I came back to the living room from the kitchen.

Even the clothes closet and the door to the broom closet in the hall were terra cotta.

I didn't expect to get anywhere by phoning Kinkel—but I dialed his number just the same. He had always declared himself to be an enthusiastic admirer of my art—and anyone familiar with our profession knows that even the tiniest scrap of praise from a stagehand makes us nearly burst with pride. I had the urge to disturb the peace of Kinkel's Christian evening—and the idea at the back of my mind that he might tell me where Marie was. He was the brain of the group, had studied theology, then broken off his studies on account of a pretty woman, went in for law, had seven children and was said to be "one of our most capable social legislators." Perhaps he really was, I couldn't judge. Before I met him Marie had given me one of his pamphlets to read, *Ways to a New Order,* and after reading it, and liking it very much, I had imagined him as a tall, slight man with fair hair, and then when I saw him for the first time: a heavy-set, short chap with thick black hair, "bursting with vitality," I couldn't believe it was him. Maybe it was because he didn't look the way I had imagined that I was so unjust toward him. Whenever Marie began to enthuse about Kinkel, old man Derkum had always talked about the Kinkel cocktails: mixtures of various ingredients: Marx plus Guardini, or Bloy plus Tolstoy. The first time we were invited there, things went wrong right from the start. We arrived much too early, and somewhere in the

77

rear of the apartment Kinkel's children were quarreling noisily, with much hissing, subdued by still further hissing, as to whose job it was to clear the supper table. Kinkel came in, smiling, still chewing, and tried desperately to hide his irritation at our premature appearance. Sommerwild came in too, not chewing, but grinning and rubbing his hands. Kinkel's children shrieked atrociously in the background, an embarrassing contrast to Kinkel's smile and Sommerwild's grin, we could hear faces being slapped, a brutal sound, and behind closed doors, I knew, the shrieking went on worse than ever. I sat there beside Marie and out of sheer nervousness, thrown completely off balance by the row going on in the background, I smoked one cigarette after another, while Sommerwild chatted with Marie, that "forgiving, generous smile" never leaving his face. It was our first time back in Bonn since our flight. Marie was pale with emotion, also with awe and pride, and I understood very well what she was feeling. It was important to her to "become reconciled with the Church," and Sommerwild was so kind to her, and Kinkel and Sommerwild were people she looked up to in awe. She introduced me to Sommerwild, and when we sat down again Sommerwild said: "Are you related to the brown-coal Schniers?" I was annoyed. He knew quite well who I was related to. Almost everyone in Bonn knew Marie Derkum had run away with one of the brown-coal Schniers, "just before her graduation, too, and she was such a religious girl." I ignored Sommerwild's question, he laughed and said: "Sometimes I go hunting with your grandfather, and occasionally I play skat with your father at the Union Club in Bonn." This annoyed me too. Surely he couldn't be so stupid as to suppose I would be impressed by this nonsense about hunting and the Union Club, and he didn't look to me the type of man who would say something just for the sake of talking. I finally opened my mouth and said: "Hunting? I always thought the Catholic clergy were forbidden to hunt." An awkward silence followed, Marie blushed, Kinkel hunted irritably around the room for the corkscrew, his wife, who had just come into the room, shook some salted almonds onto a glass dish which already contained olives. Even Sommerwild blushed, and it didn't suit him at all, his face was red enough in the first place. He said in a low yet slightly

offended voice: "For a Protestant you are well informed."
And I said: "I am not a Protestant, but I am interested
in certain things because Marie is interested in them."
And while Kinkel poured us all some wine, Sommerwild
said: "There are certain rules, Schnier, but there are
also exceptions. I come from a family in which the profession of head game warden was hereditary." If he had
said profession of game warden I would have understood, but his saying profession of head game warden annoyed me again, though I said nothing, just looked sour.
Then they began again with their eye-language. Mrs. Kinkel said with her eyes to Sommerwild: Leave him alone,
he's so terribly young. And Sommerwild said with his
eyes to her: Yes, young and pretty badly behaved, and
Kinkel as he filled my glass, the last one, said with his
eyes to me: God, how young you are. Aloud he said to
Marie: "How's your father? Still the same?" Poor Marie
was so pale and upset that she could only nod dumbly.
Sommerwild said: "What would our nice devout old city
be like without Mr. Derkum." That annoyed me still further, for old man Derkum had told me that Sommerwild
had tried to warn the Catholic schools kids, who still
bought candy and pencils at his shop, against him. I said:
"Without Mr. Derkum our nice devout old city would be
even dirtier, at least he is not a hypocrite." Kinkel looked
at me in surprise, raised his glass and said: "Thank you,
Mr. Schnier, you have given me my cue for a good
toast: let's drink to Martin Derkum's health." I said:
"Yes, to *his* health with pleasure." And Mrs. Kinkel spoke
again with her eyes to her husband: He is not only
young and badly behaved—he is also insolent. I have
never understood how later on Kinkel could always refer
to that "first evening with you" as the nicest. Shortly
afterwards Fredebeul arrived, with his fiancée, Monika
Silvs and a certain Von Severn of whom, before he came,
it was said that "although he had just converted he was
very close to the Socialist Party," which was evidently regarded as a terrific sensation. I also met Fredebeul for
the first time that evening, and there again the same thing
happened as with almost all the others: in spite of everything they liked me, and in spite of everything I didn't
like any of them, except Fredebeul's fiancée and Monika
Silvs; I felt neither one way nor the other about Von

Severn. He was a bore and seemed firmly determined to rest on the laurels he had acquired from the sensational fact that he was a convert *and* a member of the Socialist Party; he smiled, was friendly, and yet his rather prominent eyes always seemed to be saying: Look at me, it's me! I didn't find him bad at all. Fredebeul was very jovial with me, he talked for almost three quarters of an hour about Beckett and Ionesco, rattling off a lot of stuff which I could tell he had pieced together from his reading, and his smooth handsome face with the surprisingly wide mouth radiated goodwill when I was stupid enough to acknowledge having read Beckett; everything he says seems so familiar to me, as if I had read it somewhere before. Kinkel beamed at him admiringly, and Sommerwild looked around, his eyes saying: We Catholics aren't behind the times, are we, eh? All this was before prayers. It was Mrs. Kinkel who said: "I think, Odilo, we can say prayers. It looks as if Heribert is not coming today"— they all looked at Marie, then away again, much too quickly, but I didn't understand why there was again such an awkward silence—it was only in Hanover in the hotel room that I suddenly realized Heribert is Züpfner's Christian name. He did come later after all, after prayers, when they were in the midst of the topic for the evening, and I found it very sweet the way Marie went up to him as soon as he came in the room, looked at him, and gave a helpless little shrug before Züpfner greeted the others and sat down next to me with a smile. Sommerwild then told the story of the Catholic writer who lived for a long time with a divorced woman, and when he finally married her an eminent church dignitary said to him: "But my dear Besewitz, couldn't you have just kept her on as a concubine?" They all laughed rather boisterously at this story, and Mrs. Kinkel almost obscenely. The only one who didn't laugh was Züpfner, and I liked him for it. Marie didn't laugh either. No doubt Sommerwild told his story to show me how generous and warm, how witty and colorful, the Catholic church is; that I was also living with Marie as my concubine, as it were, that they didn't think of. I told them the tale of the workman who had lived quite near us; he was called Frehlingen, and in his little suburban house he had also lived with a divorced woman, and even supported her three children. One day the priest came to see Frehlingen and with a grave face and the use of certain threats he called upon him to "put an end to these immoral goings on," and Frehlingen, who was a good Catholic, had actually sent the pretty woman and her three children away. I also told them how the woman later went on the streets to support her children, and how Frehlingen took to drink because he had really loved her. Again there was the same awkward silence which occurred whenever I said anything, but Sommerwild laughed and said: "But Mr. Schnier, you can't really compare the two cases, can you?" "Why not?" I said. "You can only say that because you know nothing about Besewitz," he said angrily, "he is the most sensitive author worthy of being called a Christian." And I got angry too and said: "Do you know how sensitive Frehlingen was—and what a Christian workman he was." He merely looked at me and shook his head and raised his hands in despair. There was a pause, during which all one could hear was Monika Silvs clearing her throat, but as soon as Fredebeul is in the room no host need be afraid of a pause in the conversation. He immediately broke into the short silence, led the conversation back to the topic for the evening, and talked about the relative nature of poverty, for about an hour and a half, till he at last gave Kinkel a chance to tell the story about the man who between five hundred and three thousand marks a month had gone through sheer hell, and Züpfner asked me for a cigarette to hide his embarrassment behind the smoke.

I felt as bad as Marie did when we took the last train back to Cologne. We had scraped the money together for the trip because it had meant so much to Marie to accept the invitation. We felt physically sick too, we had not had enough to eat and had drunk more than we were used to. The journey seemed endless, and when we got out at Cologne West we had to walk home. We had no more money for fares.

At Kinkel's someone answered the phone right away. "Alfred Kinkel speaking," said a self-confident boy's voice.

"This is Schnier," I said, "might I speak to your father?"

"Schnier the theologian or Schnier the clown?"

"The clown," I said.

"Oh dear," he said, "I hope you're not taking it too hard?"

"Hard?" I said wearily, "what am I not to take too hard?"

"What?" he said, "haven't you read the paper?"

"Which one?" I asked.

"The Voice of Bonn," he said.

"A panning?" I asked.

"Oh," he said, "I think it's more of an obituary. Shall I get it for you and read it out?"

"No, thank you," I said. This boy had a nice sadistic undertone to his voice.

"But you ought to have a look at it," he said, "so as to learn from it." My God, he had tutorial ambitions too.

"Who wrote it?" I said.

"Someone called Kostert, described as our correspondent in the Ruhr. Extremely well written, but pretty nasty."

"Oh well," I said, "he's a Christian, after all."

"Aren't you?"

"No," I said, "I suppose I can't talk to your father?"

"He doesn't want to be disturbed, but for you I'll be glad to disturb him." It was the first time sadism had ever been useful to me. "Thanks," I said.

I heard him lay the receiver down on the table, go across the room, and again I heard that awful hissing in the background. It sounded as if a whole family of snakes had got into a quarrel: two male snakes and one female. I always find it embarrassing when my eyes or ears witness something not meant for my eyes or ears, and the mystical gift of being able to detect smells through the telephone is far from being a pleasure, it is a burden. In the Kinkels' apartment it smelled of beef broth, as if they had cooked a whole ox. The hissing in the background sounded ominous, as if the son was about to kill the father or the mother the son. I thought of Laocöon, and the fact that this hissing and abuse—I could even hear sounds of blows and scuffling, Ows and Ohs, cries of "you disgusting beast," "you big bully"—was going on

82

in the home of the man who had been called the "gray eminence of German Catholicism," did nothing to cheer me up. I also thought of that bastard Kostert in Bochum, who must have gone to the phone yesterday evening and phoned through his text, and yet this morning he had scratched at my door like a humble dog and pretended to be full of Christian brotherhood.

Evidently Kinkel was struggling literally hand and foot against having to come to the phone, and his wife—I was gradually able to decipher the sounds and movements in the background—was even more determined that he shouldn't, while the son refused to tell me he had made a mistake, his father was out. Suddenly there was absolute silence, the silence of someone bleeding to death, really: it was a deathly silence. Then I heard dragging footsteps, heard someone lift the receiver from the table and was expecting the receiver to be replaced. I remember exactly where the phone is in Kinkel's apartment. Precisely under the one of the three baroque madonnas which Kinkel always says is the least valuable. I would almost have preferred him to put back the receiver. I felt sorry for him, it must be terrible for him to speak to me now, and for myself I expected nothing from this conversation, neither money nor good advice. If he had sounded out of breath, my sympathy would have got the upper hand, but his voice was as booming and vigorous as ever. Someone once compared his voice to a whole body of trumpeters.

"Hullo, Schnier," came booming out at me, "how delightful of you to call."

"Hullo, Doctor," I said, "I'm in a fix."

The only malicious thing in what I said was the Doctor, for his title, like Father's, is a brand-new honorary one.

"Schnier," he said, "are we on such a footing that you feel you have to address me as Doctor?"

"I have no idea what footing we're on," I said.

He let out a particularly booming laugh: vigorous, Catholic, frank, filled with "baroque merriment." "My feelings for you are unchanged." I found that hard to believe. Probably I had fallen so low in his eyes that it was no longer worth while to let me fall any lower.

"You have reached a crisis," he said, "that's all, you are still young, pull yourself together and everything will

83

be all right." Pull yourself together, that sounded like Anna's I.R. 9.

"What are you talking about?" I asked mildly.

"What do you think I'm talking about," he said, "about your art, your career."

"But I don't mean that at all," I said, "on principle I never talk about art, you know I don't, and least of all about my career. I mean—I am looking for Marie," I said.

He produced a scarcely definable sound, something between a grunt and a belch. I heard the last of the hissing at the other end of the room, heard Kinkel putting down the receiver on the table, picking it up again, his voice was smaller and darker, he had stuck a cigar between his lips.

"Schnier," he said, "forget about the past. Your present is your art."

"The past?" I asked, "just try and imagine that your wife had suddenly left you for another man."

He was silent in a way that seemed to say: If only she would, then he said, chewing around on his cigar: "She wasn't your wife, and you haven't had seven children together."

"Oh," I said, "so she wasn't my wife?"

"Oh for God's sake," he said, "this romantic anarchy. Be a man."

"Damn it," I said, "it's just because I am a member of that sex that the whole thing is so terrible for me— and the seven children might still come. Marie is only twenty-five."

"By a man," he said, "I mean someone who resigns himself to a situation."

"That sounds very Christian," I said.

"God, you of all people are trying to tell me, I suppose, what is Christian."

"Yes," I said, "as far as I am aware, according to Catholic belief married people offer each other the sacrament?"

"Of course," he said.

"And if they are married ten times over, in church and not in church, and don't offer each other the sacrament, then the marriage is non-existent."

"Hm," he went.

"Listen, Doctor," I said, "would you mind very much taking the cigar out of your mouth? It all sounds as if we were talking about the stock market. Somehow it embarrasses me to have to listen to your chewing."

"Now wait a minute," he said, but he took the cigar out of his mouth, "and you'd better realize that the way you think about it is your affair. Miss Derkum evidently thinks otherwise and is acting according to the dictates of her conscience. Quite right too—is all I can say."

"Then why doesn't one of you lousy Catholics tell me where she is? You're hiding her from me."

"Don't be ridiculous, Schnier," he said, "we're not living in the Middle Ages."

"I wish we were living in the Middle Ages," I said, "then she would be allowed to be my concubine and wouldn't be at the mercy of her conscience all the time. Oh well, she'll come back."

"I wouldn't be so sure if I were you, Schnier," said Kinkel. "It's too bad you obviously have no sense of metaphysics."

"Everything was fine with Marie as long as she was worried about my soul, but you people taught her to worry about her own soul, and now it's got to the point where I, who have no sense of metaphysics, am worrying about Marie's soul. When she marries Züpfner, then she will really be sinning. That much I have grasped of your metaphysics: what she is doing is fornication and adultery, and Prelate Sommerwild is acting the pimp."

He actually managed a laugh, although not a very booming one. "That all sounds very funny when you stop to think that Heribert is so to speak the temporal eminence and Prelate Sommerwild the spiritual eminence of German Catholicism."

"And you are its conscience," I said, furious, "and you know perfectly well I'm right."

For a while I heard his heavy breathing up there on the Venus Mountain under the least valuable of his three baroque madonnas. "I'm just aghast at how young you are—and yet I envy you for it."

"Never mind that, Doctor," I said, "never mind about being aghast and envying me, if I don't get Marie back I shall kill your most eminent dignitary, I shall kill him," I said, "I have nothing more to lose."

He was silent and stuck the cigar back in his mouth.

"I know," I said, "at this moment your conscience is working overtime. If I killed Züpfner, you'd have no objection: he doesn't like you and is too far to the Right for you, while Sommerwild is a big help to you in Rome where—quite unjustly by the way, in my modest opinion—you are suspected of being pretty much of a Leftist."

"Stop this nonsense, Schnier. What on earth's the matter with you?"

"I don't trust Catholics," I said, "because they take advantage of you."

"And Protestants?" he asked with a laugh.

"I loathe the way they fumble around with their consciences."

"And atheists?" He was still laughing.

"They bore me because all they ever talk about is God."

"Then what are you?"

"I am a clown," I said, "at the moment better than my reputation. And there is one Catholic creature I need very badly: Marie—but she's the very one you have taken away."

"Nonsense, Schnier," he said, "do get these notions of abduction out of your head. We are living in the twentieth century."

"That's just it," I said, "in the thirteenth century I would have been a nice court jester, and even the cardinals wouldn't have cared whether I was married to her or not. Now every Catholic layman is jumping around on her wretched conscience and driving her to a life of fornication and adultery all because of a stupid scrap of paper. In the thirteenth century, Doctor, your madonnas would have meant your excommunication and interdict. You know perfectly well they were lifted from churches in Bavaria and the Tyrol—I don't need to tell you that even today robbing churches is still considered a pretty serious crime."

"Just a minute, Schnier," he said, "are you trying to get personal? I'm surprised at you."

"For years you have been interfering in my most personal affairs, and when I pass a trivial remark and confront you with a truth that might be personally inconvenient, you get mad. When I have some money again I shall hire a private detective to find out where your madonnas originally came from."

He wasn't laughing now, he merely cleared his throat, and I realized he still hadn't grasped the fact that I meant it. "Hang up, Kinkel," I said, "put down the phone, otherwise I shall start talking about the subsistence level. I wish you and your conscience good evening." But he still didn't understand, so I was the one who hung up first.

10

I was well aware that Kinkel had been surprisingly nice to me. I think he would have even let me have some money if I had asked him for it. But this talk of metaphysics with his cigar in his mouth and the way he suddenly took offense when I mentioned his madonnas was too disgusting. I didn't want anything more to do with him. Nor with Mrs. Fredebeul either. To hell with her, and as for Fredebeul, one of these days I would give him a punch in the nose. It's no use fighting him with "spiritual weapons." Sometimes I regret that dueling is a thing of the past. The business between Züpfner and me over Marie could only have been settled by a duel. It was horrible for it to have been carried on by abstract principles of order, demands for written guarantees, and secret discussions going on for days in a Hanover hotel. After her second miscarriage Marie was so depressed and jittery, she was forever running to church, and was cross when I didn't take her to the theater, to a concert or a lecture, on my free evenings. When I suggested we play parchesi the way we used to, drinking tea and lying on our stomachs on the bed, she got crosser than ever. Actually it all began with her playing parchesi with me simply out of kindness, to help me relax or to be nice to me. And she had also stopped going with me to the movies I enjoy seeing so much: the ones small kids are allowed to go to.

I don't believe there is anyone in the world who understands a clown, even one clown doesn't understand another, envy and jealousy always enter into it. Marie came close to understanding me, but she never quite understood me. She always felt that as a "creative person" I must be "deeply interested" in absorbing as much culture as possible. She was wrong. Of course I would get into a taxi at once if I had a free evening and heard Beckett was being played somewhere, and I enjoy going to the movies once in a while, come to think of it I like going often, and always to those films which small kids are allowed to see. Marie could never understand that, a large part of her Catholic up-bringing consisted after all simply of psychological information and of a rationalism decked out with mysticism, of the order of "make them play football so they won't think about girls." And I was so fond of thinking about girls, later only about Marie. At times I felt like a monster myself. I like going to movies for children, because there is none of that grown-up nonsense in them about adultery and divorce. In movies about adultery and divorce, somebody's happiness always plays such a big part. "Make me happy, darling" or "Do you want to stand in the way of my happiness?" Happiness that lasts more than a second, perhaps two or three seconds, is something I can't imagine. Real whore films, now, those I quite like, but there are so few of them. Most of them are so pretentious that you can't tell they really are whore films. There is another category of women who are not whores and not wives, women of compassion, but they are neglected in films. Most films which children are allowed to see are full of whores. I have never understood what the boards who grade the films have in mind when they pass this type of film for children. The women in these films are either whores by nature, or they are whores in a sociological sense; they are almost never compassionate. In some Wild West saloon there are these blondes dancing the cancan, while rough cowboys, goldminers, or trappers, who have spent two years in the wilderness chasing skunks, watch these pretty young blondes dancing the cancan, but when these cowboys, goldminers, or trappers then go after the girls and try to go up to their rooms with them, they usually have the door slammed in their face, or some brutal swine cruelly knocks them down. I take it this is meant to express something like virtuousness. Cruelty where compassion would be the only humane thing. No wonder the poor devils start beating each other up and shooting—it's like football at school, only it is even crueller, since they are grown men. I don't understand American morals. I suppose over there a compassionate woman would be burned as a witch, a woman who does it not for money and not out of passionate love for the man, but simply out of pity for masculine nature.

What I find particularly embarrassing are films about artists. Most films about artists must be made by people who would have paid Von Gogh not even an ounce of tobacco for a picture but only half an ounce, and later would have regretted even that because they realized he would have sold it even for a pipeful of tobacco. In films about artists the suffering of the artistic soul, the poverty and the wrestling with the demon, are always put in the past. A living artist who has run out of cigarettes, can't buy shoes for his wife, is of no interest to film people because three generations of nincompoops haven't yet confirmed that he is a genius. One generation of nincompoops would not be enough for them. "The turbulent searching of the artistic soul." Even Marie believes in it. It is embarrassing, such a thing does exist, but it ought to go by a different name. What a clown needs is quiet, the simulating of what other people call leisure. But the point is that these other people don't understand that for a clown the simulating of leisure consists of forgetting his work, they don't understand because they—as is absolutely natural—can devote themselves to so-called art during *their* leisure time. A different problem is the one of artistic people who think of nothing but art but don't need any time off because they don't work. So when someone starts calling an artistic person an artist it leads to the worst kind of misunderstanding. Artistic people always start talking about art at the very moment when the artist happens to feel he is enjoying something like time off. Usually they hit the nerve exactly, in these two or three, up to five minutes when the artist forgets art an artistic person starts talking about Van Gogh, Kafka, Chaplin, or Beckett. At such moments I would like to commit suicide—when I begin thinking *only* about the thing I do with Marie, or

90

about beer, or falling leaves in autumn, about parchesi or some corny, perhaps sentimental thing, some Fredebeul or Sommerwild brings up the subject of art. At the very instant when I have the incredibly exciting feeling of being quite normal, as normal and low-brow as Karl Emonds, Fredebeul or Sommerwild start talking about Claudel or Ionesco. Marie is a bit like that too, she used to be less so, recently more. I realized this when I told her I was going to begin singing songs to the guitar. According to her, this offended her esthetic instincts. The non-artist's leisure hours are the working hours of a clown. Everyone knows what leisure is, from the highly paid executive to the humblest laborer, whether they drink beer or shoot bears in Alaska, whether they collect stamps, Impressionists or Expressionists (one thing is certain, anyone who *collects* art is not an artist). Even the way they light up their knocking-off-work cigarettes, putting on a special expression, can absolutely infuriate me for I know this feeling just well enough to envy them because they can enjoy it so much longer. There are leisure moments for a clown—then he may stretch his legs and know for as long as it takes to smoke half a cigarette what leisure means. What is really hell is a so-called vacation: apparently the others go through this for three, four, six weeks! Marie tried a few times to give me this feeling, we went to the sea, we went inland, to resorts, to the mountains, by the second day I was ill, I was covered from head to foot with hives and my soul was full of murderous thoughts. I think I was ill with envy. Then Marie had the appalling idea of going away with me to a place where artists spend their vacations. Needless to say they were all artistic people, and on the very first evening I had a fight with an idiot who is a big noise in the film business and who got me involved in a conversation about Grock and Chaplin and the clowns in Shakespeare's plays. Not only did I get quite nicely beaten up (these artistic people who manage to make a good living in quasi-artistic jobs never do any work and are bursting with health), I also got a nasty attack of jaundice. As soon as we got out of that terrible place I felt fine right away.

What worries me so much is my inability to limit myself, or, as my agent Zohnerer would say, to concentrate my talents. My acts are too much of a mixture of pantomime, artistry, clowning—I would be a good Pierrot, but I could also be a good clown, and I vary my acts too often. I could probably have lived for years on my turns called a Catholic and a Protestant sermon, a Board of Directors meeting, traffic, and a few others, but when I have done an act ten or twenty times I find it so boring that I can hardly keep from yawning right in the middle, literally, I have the worst time controlling my mouth muscles. I am bored with myself. When I stop to think that there are clowns who perform the same acts for thirty years, my heart sinks as if I were condemned to eat a whole sack of flour with a spoon. I must enjoy doing a thing, otherwise I get sick. It suddenly occurs to me that I might possibly be able to juggle or sing: just excuses to get out of practicing every day. At least four hours' practice, six is better, even longer if possible. I had neglected that too during the past six weeks and just done a few headstands, handstands, and somersaults every day and some exercises on the rubber mat I always carry around with me. Now my injured knee was a good excuse for lying on the sofa, smoking cigarettes, and inhaling self-pity. My latest new pantomime, the Minister's Speech, had been quite good, but I was fed up with caricatures and anyway never got beyond a certain point. All my lyrical attempts had failed. I had never managed to portray human nature without being horribly corny. My acts Dancing Couple and Going to School and Returning from School were at least artistically passable. But then when I tried a man's career, I always dropped back into doing a caricature. Marie was right when she said my attempts to sing to the guitar were an attempt at escape. What I do best are the absurdities of daily life: I observe, add up these observations, increase them to the nth degree and draw the square root from them, but with a different factor from the one I increased them by. Every morning at all the big railway stations thousands of people arrive to work in the city—and thousands leave by train to work outside the city. Why don't these people simply exchange their places of work? Or take the long lines of cars crawling past each other during rush hour. Exchange the places where people work or live, and all the stink and fumes, the dramatic arm-waving of the policemen, could be avoided: it would be so quiet at the intersections they could play parchesi there. From this observation I composed a pantomime where I use only my hands and feet, my face remains immobile and snow-white in the middle, and with my four extremities I manage to give an impression of a tremendous amount of rushing movement. My aim is: as few props as possible or, even better, none at all. For the act Going to School and Returning from School I don't even need schoolbooks; the hands holding them are enough, at the last moment I run across the street in front of clanging streetcars, jump on buses, off them again, shopwindows divert my attention, I write misspelled words with chalk on housewalls, I stand—late—in front of the scolding teacher, put down my books and slide into my seat. The lyrical quality of childhood is something I manage to portray quite well: in a child's life there is a greatness in the banal, it is strange, random, always tragic. A child, too, never takes time off as a child; time off does not begin until the "principles of order" have been accepted. I observe all the various ways of knocking off work with fanatical zeal: the way a workman puts his pay envelope in his pocket and gets on his motorbike, the way a broker finally lays down the telephone, puts his notebook away in a drawer and locks it, or the way the girl in the grocery store takes off her apron, washes her hands and fixes her hair and lips in the mirror, picks up her handbag—and away she goes, it is all so human that I sometimes feel inhuman because I can only portray time off as one of my acts. I have discussed the question with Marie of whether an animal can take time off, a cow chewing the cud, a donkey dozing beside the fence. She said she thought animals that worked and so could take time off would be blasphemous. Sleep might be something like time off, a wonderful thing that humans and animals have in common, but the leisurely quality of leisure consists after all in the conscious experiences of it. Even doctors have time off, and recently even priests. That annoys me, they have no business to and they should be able to understand that about the artist. They need to know nothing about art, about mission, calling, and all that nonsense, but about the nature of the artist. I have always argued with Marie as to whether the God in whom she believes takes time off or not, she always insists he does, gets out the Old Testament and reads me the story of the Creation: And He rested on the seventh day. I countered with the New Testament and said it was possible the God of the Old Testament had taken time off, but the idea of a Christ taking time off was quite inconceivable to me. Marie went pale when I said that, she admitted she found the idea of a Christ taking time off blasphemous, that he might have enjoyed himself but had hardly enjoyed leisure.

I can sleep like an animal, dreamlessly as a rule, often only for a few minutes and yet with the feeling I have been gone for an eternity, as if I had stuck my head through a wall beyond which lies endless darkness, oblivion and leisure, and what Henrietta was thinking of when she suddenly dropped her tennis racquet on the ground or her spoon in the soup or tossed the playing cards into the fire: nothing. I asked her once what she thought about when it came over her, and she said: "You really don't know?" "No," I said, and she said softly: "Of nothing, I think of nothing." I said, but it's not possible to think of nothing, and she said: "Yes, it is, I am suddenly quite empty and yet kind of drunk, and I long to throw off my shoes and my clothes—to get rid of all ballast." She also said it was such a wonderful feeling that she was always waiting for it, but it never came when she waited for it, always unexpectedly, and it seemed to last forever. It had happened to her a few times in school too, I remember my mother's vehement phone conversations with the teacher and the expression: "Yes, yes, hysterical, that's the word—and please punish her severely."

Sometimes I get a feeling of wonderful emptiness like when I play parchesi when it has gone on for more than three or four hours; just the sounds, the rattle of the dice, the taptap of the little men, the click when one is taken. I even managed to get Marie, who prefers chess, addicted to this game. It was like a drug for us. Sometimes we played it for five or six hours on end, and the waiters and chambermaids who brought us tea or coffee showed the same mixture of uneasiness and annoyance in their faces as my mother did when it came over Henrietta, and sometimes they said what the people in the bus had said when I went home from Marie's: "Incredible." Marie invented a very complicated system of keeping score with points: according to whether you got thrown out or threw the person out, you got points, she worked out an interesting chart, and I bought her a four-color pencil so that she could mark down the passive values and the active values, as she called them. Sometimes we played it on long train journeys, to the amazement of respectable passengers—until I suddenly realized Marie was only going on playing with me because she wanted to please me, to soothe me, to relax my "artist's soul." Her thoughts were far away, it began a few months ago when I refused to go to Bonn, although for five days in a row I had no performance. I didn't want to go to Bonn. I was scared of the group, was scared of meeting Leo, but Marie kept on saying she had to breathe "Catholic air" again. I reminded her of how we had gone back to Cologne from Bonn after the first evening with the group, tired, miserable and depressed, and how she had kept saying to me in the train: "You are so sweet, so sweet," and had fallen asleep against my shoulder, waking up only a few times when the conductor called out the names of the stations: Sechtem, Walberberg, Brühl, Kalscheuren—each time she jumped, started up, and I pressed her head down again onto my shoulder, and when we got out at Cologne West she said: "We should have gone to a movie." I reminded her of all that when she began talking about having to breathe "Catholic air," and I suggested we go to a movie, or go dancing, or play parchesi, but she shook her head and went off to Bonn by herself. I have no idea what she means by "Catholic air." After all, we were in Osnabrück, and the air there couldn't be all that un-Catholic.

11

I went into the bathroom, poured some of the stuff
Monika Silvs had put out for me into the tub and turned
on the hot water. Having a bath is almost as good as
sleeping, just as sleeping is almost as good as doing "the
thing." That's what Marie called it, and I always think of
it in her words. I simply could not imagine that she
would do "the thing" with Züpfner, my imagination just
hasn't room for such ideas, just as I was never seriously
tempted to poke around in Marie's underwear. I could
only imagine that she would play parchesi with Züpfner,
and that infuriated me. There was nothing I had done
with her that she could do with him without seeming like
a traitor or a whore. She couldn't even spread butter on
his toast. When I imagined her picking up his cigarette
from the ashtray and smoking it I nearly went out of my
mind, and the knowledge that he didn't smoke and
probably played chess with her was no consolation. After
all, she had to do something with him, go out dancing
or play cards, he had to read aloud to her or she to him,
and she had to talk to him too, about the weather or
about money. Actually the only thing she could do for
him without having to think of me all the time was cook,
for she did this so rarely for me that it would not necessarily be treason or whoring. I felt like phoning Sommerwild right away, but it was still too early, I had made
up my mind to wake him up at two thirty in the morning
and have a long talk with him about art. Eight o'clock in
the evening, that was too respectable an hour to call him

up and ask him how many principles of order he had fed Marie with already and what commission he would get from Züpfner: a thirteenth-century crucifix, or a fourteenth-century madonna from the Rhineland. I also considered the method I would use to kill him. Probably the best way to kill esthetes is with valuable objets d'art so that in death they can still get mad over an act of vandalism. A madonna would not be valuable enough, and it would be too solid, he could die happy in the knowledge that the madonna had been saved, and a painting is not heavy enough, although the frame might be, only then again he would find consolation in the thought that the painting itself might be spared. Perhaps I could scrape the paint off a valuable painting and suffocate or strangle him with the canvas: not a perfect murder but a perfect murder of an esthete. It wouldn't be easy, either, to send a healthy specimen like that into the next world, Sommerwild is tall and slim, of "dignified" appearance, white-haired and "kindly," a mountain-climber and proud of having participated in two world wars and winning a medal for athletics. A tough opponent, in tiptop condition. There was nothing for it but to dig up a valuable metal objet d'art, made of bronze or gold, perhaps marble would do, but I couldn't very well go to Rome first and make off with something from the Vatican Museum.

While the bathwater was running, I happened to think of Blothert, an important member of the group whom I had only seen twice. He was a kind of "Rightist counterpart" to Kinkel, also a politican but with a different background and from a different "milieu"; Züpfner was to him what Fredebeul was to Kinkel: a kind of disciple, a "spiritual heir," but to call up Blothert would have been even more senseless than to ask the walls of my apartment for help. The only thing which aroused a halfway recognizable sign of life in him was Kinkel's baroque madonnas. The way he compared them with his own showed me how abysmally they hated each other. He was president of something or other which Kinkel would like to have been president of, they still called each other by first names as they had gone to school together. On each of the two occasions I saw Blothert I got a shock. He was of medium height, very fair and looked about twenty-five, when someone looked at him he grinned, when he said anything he first ground his teeth for half a minute, and of every four words he said two were "the Cabinet" and "Catholon"—and then you suddenly saw he was over fifty, and he looked like a student aged by secret vices. A weird character. Sometimes he tied himself in knots when he said a few words, began to stammer and said "the Ca Ca Ca Ca," and I felt sorry for him till he finally spat out the rest of the word, "binet" or "tholon." Marie had told me about him, that he was "spectacularly intelligent." I have never received any proof of this claim, and on only one occasion did I hear him say more than twenty words: when the group were talking about the death penalty. He had been "unreservedly in favor," and what surprised me about this statement was the fact that he did not pretend the contrary. As he spoke his face wore an expression of triumphant bliss, he got tangled up again in his Ca Ca and it sounded as if with every Ca he was cutting off someone's head. Now and then he would look at me, and every time in surprise as if he was refraining from saying "Incredible," he didn't refrain from shaking his head. I believe someone who is not a Catholic simply doesn't exist for him. I kept thinking that if the death penalty were introduced he would plead for the execution of all non-Catholics. He also had a wife, children, and a telephone. Then I decided after all to phone my mother again instead. I remembered Blothert when I thought of Marie, for he would be constantly in and out of the house, he had something to do with the Executive Committee, and the thought of his being one of her regular visitors horrified me. I am very fond of her, and perhaps her girl guide's words, "I must take the path that I must take," were to be taken as the valediction of an early Christian martyr who is about to be thrown to the wild beasts. I also thought of Monika Silvs and knew that one day I would accept her compassion. She was so pretty and so sweet, and she had seemed to me to fit into the group even less than Marie. Whether she was busy in the kitchen—I had once helped her to make sandwiches too—whether she was smiling, dancing, or painting, it was all so natural, even though I did not care for the pictures she painted. She had listened too long to Sommerwild holding forth about annunciation and revelation and almost all she ever painted now was madonnas. I would try and talk her out of that. It simply can't be a success, even if you believe in it and can paint well. They should leave all that madonna painting to children or devout monks who don't consider themselves artists. I wondered whether I would succeed in talking Monika out of her madonna painting. She is not an amateur, she is still young, twenty-two or three, without a doubt still a virgin—and this terrified me. The horrible thought occurred to me that the Catholics had assigned me the role of being her Siegfried. She would end up by living with me for a few years, being nice to me, until the principles of order began to take effect, and then she would return to Bonn and marry Von Severn. I blushed at the thought and abandoned it. Monika was such a nice girl, and I didn't like making her the object of wicked thoughts. If we arranged a date, I would first have to talk her out of Sommerwild, that ladies' man who looked so much like my father. Except that my father makes no claim beyond that of being a halfway decent exploiter, and this claim he lives up to. With Sommerwild I always have the feeling he could just as well be a hotel or concert manager, a public relations officer in a shoe factory, a well-groomed popular singer, perhaps even the editor of a fashionable "literary" magazine. Every Sunday he preaches at St. Korbinian's. Marie took me along twice. The performance is more embarrassing than anything Sommerwild's superiors ought to permit. I would rather read Rilke, Hofmannsthal and Newman one by one than have someone mix me a kind of syrup out of all three. During the sermon I started to sweat. There are certain deviations from the norm which are more than my vegetative nervous system can bear. That that which is, is, and that that which is in suspension is suspended—I shudder when I hear expressions like that. Then I would rather listen to some inept, pudgy pastor stammering out the incomprehensible truths of this religion from his pulpit without deluding himself that he is delivering a polished sermon. Marie was sad because nothing in Sommerwild's sermons had impressed me. What was especially depressing was that after the sermon we all sat around in a café not far from St. Korbinian's, the whole café filled up with artistic people who had been to hear Sommerwild's sermon. Then he came himself, a kind of circle formed around him, and we were drawn into the circle, and this synthetic stuff that he had uttered so glibly from the pulpit was chewed over two or three or even four times. A very pretty young actress with golden long hair and the face of an angel who, so Marie whispered to me, was already "three quarters" converted, was almost ready to kiss Sommerwild's feet. I don't think he would have stopped her.

I turned off the bathwater, took off my jacket, pulled my shirt and undershirt over my head and threw them in the corner, and I was just getting into the tub when the phone rang. I know only one person who can make the phone ring with such a vigorous, virile sound: Zohnerer, my agent. He speaks so closely and intimately into the telephone that I am afraid every time of getting his spit in my face. When he wants to say something nice to me he begins the conversation with: "You were magnificent yesterday"; he just says that, without knowing whether I was really magnificent or not; when he wants to say something unpleasant, he begins with: "Now listen, Schnier, you're not Chaplin, you know"; this doesn't mean at all that I am not as good a clown as Chaplin, but merely that I am not famous enough to be able to afford to do something which has annoyed Zohnerer. Today he would not even say anything unpleasant, nor would he announce the imminent end of the world, the way he always did when I canceled a performance. He would not even accuse me of a "mania for canceling." Probably Offenbach, Bamberg, and Nuremberg had canceled too, and he would add up over the phone all the expenses accumulating on my account. The phone went on ringing, manly, vigorous, virile, I was just about to throw a sofa cushion over it—but I pulled on my bathrobe, went into the living room, and stopped in front of the ringing telephone. Managers have strong nerves, persistence, words like "sensitiveness of the artistic soul" are to them words like "Lager Beer," and any attempt to talk seriously to them about art and artists would be just waste of breath. They also know perfectly well that even an unscrupulous artist has a thousand times more conscience than a scrupulous manager, and they possess one all-conquering weapon: the sheer knowledge of the fact that an artist simply cannot help doing what he does: painting pictures, traveling up and down the country as a clown, singing songs, carving something "enduring" out of stone or granite. An artist is like a woman who can do nothing but love, and who succumbs to every stray male jackass. The easiest people to exploit are artists and women, and every manager is from one to ninety-nine per cent a pimp. The ringing of the phone was absolutely a pimp's ringing. He had found out from Kostert, of course, when I left Bochum, and knew for certain that I was at home. I tied the belt to my bathrobe and lifted the receiver. Immediately his beery breath hit me in the face. "Damn it all, Schnier," he said, "what's the big idea, letting me wait so long."

"I was just making the modest attempt of taking a bath," I said, "is that against my contract?"

"Your sense of humor can only be of the gallows variety," he said.

"Where is the rope," I said, "is it dangling already?"

"Cut out the symbolism," he said, "let's talk business."

"It wasn't me who started talking about symbols," I said.

"Never mind who started talking about what," he said, "so you seem to have made up your mind to commit artistic suicide."

"My dear Mr. Zohnerer," I said gently, "would you mind very much turning your face away a little from the receiver—I get your beery breath right in my face."

He swore under his breath in dialect, and then laughed: "Your impudence evidently hasn't suffered. What were we talking about?"

"Art," I said, "but if you don't mind I'd rather we talked business."

"In that case we wouldn't have much to talk about," he said, "now listen, I'm not giving you up. Understand?" I was too surprised to answer.

"We'll take you out of circulation for six months and then I'll build you up again. I hope that slimy bastard in Bochum didn't upset you seriously?"

"He did as a matter of fact," I said, "he cheated me— out of a bottle of cognac and the difference between a first and second-class ticket to Bonn."

"You were crazy to let them beat you down over the fee. A contract is a contract—and your quitting was justified because of your accident."

"Zohnerer," I said quietly, "are you really so human or. . . ."

"Rubbish," he said, "I like you. If you haven't noticed that, you are stupider than I thought, and besides, there is still a financial asset left in you. Why don't you give up this childish drinking."

He was right. Childish was the right word for it. I said: "But it has helped."

"In what way?" he asked.

"In my soul," I said.

"Rubbish," he said, "forget about your soul. We could, of course, sue Mainz for breach of contract and we would probably win—but I wouldn't advise it. Six months' break—and I'll build you up again."

"And what am I supposed to live on?" I asked.

"Well," he said, "surely your father will fork out something."

"And if he doesn't?"

"Then try and find a nice girl friend who'll help you out."

"I'd rather do the rounds of the villages and small towns," I said, "on a bike."

"You're wrong," he said, "in villages and small towns they read newspapers too, and at the moment I couldn't find a job for you at twenty marks a night in a youth club."

"Have you tried?" I asked.

"Yes," he said, "I've been on the phone all day on your account. Not a hope. There's nothing more depressing for people than a clown they feel sorry for. It's like a waiter coming up in a wheelchair to bring you your beer. Don't kid yourself."

"What about yourself?" I asked. He was silent, and I said: "I mean, thinking I could have another try in six months' time."

"Maybe," he said, "but it's your only chance. It would be even better to wait a full year."

"A year," I said, "do you know how long a year is?"

"Three hundred and sixty-five days," he said, inconsiderately turning his face toward me again. His beery breath nauseated me.

"Supposing I tried under another name," I said, "with a new nose and different turns. Songs to the guitar and a bit of juggling."

"Nothing doing," he said, "your singing is terrible and your juggling downright amateurish. Forget it. You have the makings of quite a good clown, possibly even a good one, and don't show up again until you have practiced eight hours a day for at least three months. Then I'll come and have a look at your new turns—or old ones, but practice, give up this stupid drinking."

I said nothing. I could hear him breathing heavily, drawing on his cigarette. "Try and find another faithful soul," he said, "like the girl who traveled around with you."

"Faithful soul," I said.

"Yes," he said, "forget about the rest. And don't imagine you can get along without me and clown around in lousy clubs. That's all right for three weeks, Schnier, you can do a bit of nonsense at fire brigade anniversary dinners and go round with a hat. As soon as I find out about it I'll cut it right off."

"You bastard," I said.

"Yes," he said, "I'm the best bastard you can find, and if you start going round on your own you'll be completely washed up in two months at the outside. I know this business. Do you hear?"

I was silent. "I said, Do you hear?" he asked quietly.

"Yes," I said.

"I like you. Schnier," he said, "I've liked working with you—or I wouldn't be spending all this money on a phone call."

"It's after six," I said, "and I'd say it's costing you about two marks fifty."

"Yes," he said, "maybe three marks, but at the moment no agent would invest that much in you. So: I'll see you in three months' time and with at least six first-class turns. Squeeze as much as you can out of your old man. Goodbye now."

He actually hung up. I went on holding the receiver, heard the buzzing tone, waited, finally replaced it after a long pause. He had cheated me on a few occasions but

103

he had never lied to me. At a time when I had probably been worth two hundred and fifty marks a night he had got hundred and eighty mark contracts for me—and probably made quite a nice profit out of me. It was only after I had put back the receiver that I realized he was the first person I would have liked to go on talking to on the phone. He ought to give me some other chance —than to wait six months. Perhaps that was a group of artistes who needed someone like me, I was not heavy, I never got dizzy and after some training I could join in a bit of acrobatics quite nicely, or work out some skits with another clown. Marie had always said I need an "opposite number," then I wouldn't get so bored with the turns. I was sure Zohnerer hadn't considered all the angles. I decided to call him up later, went back to the bathroom, took off my bathrobe and threw the rest of my clothes onto the floor, and got into the tub. A hot bath is almost as good as sleep. When we were on the road I had always taken a room with bath, even when we were still short of money. Marie always said my background was responsible for this extravagance, but that's not so. At home they had been stingy with hot water as they were with everything else. A cold shower, that was something we could have any time, but a hot bath was considered an extravagance at home too, and even Anna, who otherwise often closed one eye, was not to be budged over this. At her I.R. 9 a hot bath had evidently been considered a kind of deadly sin.

Even in the bathtub I missed Marie. She had sometimes read aloud to me as I lay in the tub, from the bed, once from the Old Testament the whole story of Solomon and the Queen of Sheba, another time the war of the Maccabees, and now and again from Thomas Wolfe's *Look Homeward, Angel*. Here I was, lying completely deserted in this stupid terra cotta bathtub, the bathroom was done in black tiles, but the tub, soapdish, shower handle and toilet seat were terra cotta. I missed Marie's voice. Come to think of it, she couldn't even read the Bible with Züpfner without feeling like a traitor or a whore. She would be bound to think of the hotel in Düsseldorf where she had read aloud to me about Solomon and the Queen of Sheba till I fell asleep in the tub from exhaustion. The green carpeting in the hotel room, Marie's dark hair, her voice, then she brought me a lighted cigarette, and I kissed her.

I lay in foam up to my neck and thought about her. She couldn't do a thing with him or near him without thinking of me. She couldn't even screw the top on the toothpaste when he was around. How many times we had had breakfast together, skimpy or luxurious, hurried or leisurely, very early in the morning or almost at noon, with plenty of jam or none at all. The idea of her having breakfast with Züpfner every morning at the same time, before he got into his car and drove off to his Catholic office, almost made me religious. I prayed it might never happen: breakfast with Züpfner. I tried to picture Züpfner: his brown hair, fair skin, straight build, a kind of Alcibiades of German Catholicism, only not so mercurial. According to Kinkel his position was "in the center but still somewhat more Right than Left." This Left-and-Right business was one of their chief topics of conversation. To be honest, I had to add Züpfner to the four people who seemed to me to be authentic Catholics: Pope John, Alec Guinness, Marie, Gregory—and Züpfner. No doubt he too, however much he might be in love, was influenced by the fact that he had saved Marie from a sinful situation and placed her in a sinless one. Obviously his holding hands with Marie hadn't meant anything serious. I had spoken to Marie about it afterwards, she had blushed, but nicely, and told me, "there were many things involved" in this friendship: that their fathers had both been persecuted by the Nazis, and Catholicism, and "his manner, you know. I am still fond of him."

I let out some of the bathwater, lukewarm by this time, ran in some hot, and shook some more of the bath stuff into the water. I thought of my father, who has an interest in this bath stuff factory too. Whether I buy cigarettes, soap, writing paper, popsicles or wieners: my father has an interest. I imagine he even has an interest in the inch of toothpaste I use now and again. But at home no one was allowed to talk about money. When Anna wanted to do the accounts with my mother and show her the books, my mother always said "Money—what a disagreeable topic." We got very little pocket money. Luckily we had a great many relatives, when the whole bunch got together there were fifty or sixty uncles and aunts, and some of them were nice and gave us a little money from time to time, my mother's stinginess being proverbial. To cap it all, my mother's mother was an aristocrat, a Von Hohenbrode, and to this day my father feels like a graciously accepted son-in-law, although his father-in-law was called Tuhler, only his mother-in-law had been a Von Hohenbrode. Germans today are even more infatuated with titles than in 1910. Even people who are considered intelligent will do anything to get to know an aristocrat. One day I ought to draw the attention of Mother's Executive Committee to this fact. It is a racial matter. Even a sensible man like my grandfather can't get over the fact that in the summer of 1918 the Schniers were supposed to be raised to the nobility, that the papers were "so to speak" all ready, but then at the critical moment the Kaiser, who was supposed to sign the document, hopped it—he probably had other things on his mind—if he ever had anything on his mind at all. This story of the "near aristocracy" of the Schniers is still told today on every possible occasion, after almost fifty years. "They found the papers on His Majesty's desk," my father always says. I am surprised no one went to Doorn and had the thing signed. I would have sent off a messenger on horseback, then at least the matter would have been settled in proper style.

I thought of how Marie used to unpack the suitcases while I was already in the bath. How she would stand in front of the mirror, take off her gloves, smooth her hair; how she would take the hangers out of the wardrobe, hang up her dresses on them and put the hangers back in the wardrobe; they would squeak on the brass rod. Then the shoes, the faint click of the heels, the shuffling sound of the soles, and the way she set out her tubes, bottles and jars on the glass top of the dressing table; the big jar of cold cream, or the slim bottle of nail polish, the box of powder and the hard metallic sound of the lipstick being stood on end.

I suddenly realized I had begun to cry in the bathtub, and I made a surprising physical discovery: my tears felt cold. At other times they had always felt hot, and during the past few months I had wept hot tears several times when I was drunk. I also thought of Henrietta, of my father, of Leo who had converted, and was surprised I hadn't heard from him yet.

12

It was in Osnabrück that she told me for the first time that she was afraid of me, when I refused to go to Bonn, and she was determined to go there to breathe "Catholic air." I didn't like the expression, I said there were plenty of Catholics in Osnabrück too, but she said I just didn't understand her and didn't want to understand her. We had already been in Osnabrück two days, between two bookings, and still had three days ahead of us. It had been raining since early morning, there wasn't a single film showing that I might have wanted to see, and I hadn't even bothered to suggest we play parchesi. The day before when we had played, Marie had worn an expression like that of a particularly long-suffering nursemaid.

Marie was lying on the bed reading, I was standing at the window smoking and looking down on the Hamburgerstrasse, sometimes onto the station square, where people were running in the rain from the station to the waiting streetcar. We couldn't do "the thing" either. Marie was sick. She had not actually had a miscarriage but something of the sort. I had never found out exactly what it was, and no one had told me. Anyhow she had thought she was pregnant, now she wasn't any more, she had only spent a few hours in the morning at the hospital. She was pale, tired, and edgy, and I had said it certainly wouldn't be good for her to make the long train journey now. I would like to have known more about it, whether she had been in pain, but she told me nothing, just cried sometimes, but in a strange irritable way.

I watched the little boy coming along the street from the left, toward the station square, he was wet through and held his school satchel open in front of him in the pouring rain. He had turned back the cover of the satchel and carried it in front of him with an expression of his face like I've seen in pictures of the Three Kings offering the infant Jesus frankincense, gold and myrrh. I could make out the wet book covers, almost coming apart. The boy's expression reminded me of Henrietta. Dedicated, oblivious, exalted. Marie asked me from the bed: "What are you thinking about?" And I said: "Nothing." I watched the boy go across the square, slowly, then disappear into the station and I was afraid for him; for this exalted quarter of an hour he would have to do five minutes' bitter penance: a scolding mother, a worried father, no money in the house for new books. "What are you thinking about," Marie asked again. I wanted to say "nothing" again, then I thought of the boy and I told her what I was thinking about: how the boy arrived home, in some village close by, and how he would probably lie, because no one could believe what he had actually done. He would say he had slipped and fallen, his satchel had fallen into a puddle, or he had put it down for a few minutes, right under a drainpipe from a roof, and suddenly water had come pouring down, right into the satchel. I told Marie all this in a quiet monotonous voice, and she said, from the bed: "What are you trying to do? Why are you telling me all this nonsense?" "Because that's what I was thinking about when you asked me." She didn't believe any of my story about the boy, and I lost my temper. We had never lied to each other or accused each other of lying. I got so mad I forced her to get up, put on her shoes, and run over to the station with me. I was in such a hurry I forgot the umbrella, we got wet and didn't see the boy at the station. We went through the waiting room, even to the Traveler's Aid, and I finally asked the ticket collector at the barrier whether a train had just left. He said, yes, for Bohmte, two minutes ago. I asked him whether a boy had come through the barrier, wet through, with fair hair, about so tall, he became suspicious and asked "What's the matter? Has he been up to something?" "No," I said, "I only want to know whether he got on the train." We were both wet, Marie and I, and he looked at us suspiciously from head to foot. "Are you from the Rhineland?" he asked. It sounded as if he was asking me if I had a police record. "Yes," I said. "I can only give out information of this kind with the permission of my superiors," he said. I expect he had had trouble with someone from the Rhineland, probably in the army. I knew a stagehand who had once been swindled by a Berliner in the army, and ever since then treated everybody from Berlin as a personal enemy. During the performance of a female acrobat from Berlin he suddenly switched off the light, she lost her footing and broke her leg. The thing was never proved, they said it was a "short circuit," but I am sure that stagehand only switched off the light because the girl was from Berlin and he had once been swindled in the army by a Berliner. The ticket collector at the barrier in Osnabrück looked at me with an expression that quite scared me. "I have a bet with this lady," I said, "it's a bet." That was a mistake, because it was a lie and anyone can tell at once when I'm lying. "I see," he said, "a bet. When Rhinelanders start betting." It was hopeless. For an instant I considered taking a taxi and driving to Bohmte, waiting at the station for the train and seeing the boy get out. But of course he might get out at any little place before or after Bohmte. We were wet through and very cold when we got back to the hotel. I pushed Marie into the bar downstairs, stood at the counter, put my arm around her and ordered cognac. The bartender, who was also the hotel owner, looked at us as if he would like to call the police. The day before we had played parchesi for hours and had ordered ham sandwiches and tea sent up to us, that morning Marie had gone to the hospital, and come back looking pale. He put down the cognac in front of us so that half of it slopped over, and looked pointedly past us. "Don't you believe me?" I asked Marie, "I mean about the boy." "I do," she said, "I do believe you." She was only saying so out of pity, not because she really believed me, and I was furious because I didn't have the nerve to tell the bartender off about the spilled cognac.

Next to us stood a burly fellow who smacked his lips as he drank his beer. After each gulp he licked the foam from his lips, looked at me as if at any moment he was going to speak to me. I am afraid of being spoken to by half-drunk Germans of a certain age, they always talk about the war, think it was wonderful, and when they are quite drunk it turns out they are murderers and think it wasn't really "all that bad." Marie was shivering with cold, looked at me and shook her head when I pushed our cognac glasses across the stainless steel counter to the bartender. I was relieved because this time he pushed them toward us carefully, without spilling a drop. It removed the feeling I had had of being a coward. The chap next to us was noisily sipping a schnapps and began to talk to himself. "In forty-four," he said, "we drank schnapps and cognac by the bucket —in forty-four by the bucket—we poured the rest onto the street and set fire to it—not a drop for the bastards." He laughed. "Not a drop." When I pushed our glasses across the counter toward the bartender again, he only filled one glass, looked at me doubtfully before filling the second, and it was only then that I realized Marie had left. I nodded, and he filled the second glass. I drained both, and I still feel relieved that I managed to leave then. Marie was lying upstairs on the bed in tears, when I put my hand on her forehead she pushed it away, quietly, gently, but she pushed it away. I sat down beside her, took her hand, and she did not pull it away. I was glad. Outside it was already getting dark, I sat beside her on the bed for an hour and held her hand before I began to speak. I spoke softly, told her the story of the boy again, and she pressed my hand, as if to say: Yes, I do believe you. I also asked her to tell me just what they had done to her at the hospital, she said it had been "something gynecological—nothing serious, but horrible." The word gynecological scares me stiff. To me it sounds sinister, because I am completely ignorant in these things. I had been with Marie for three years when I first heard about the "gynecological" business. I knew, of course, how women have children, but I knew nothing about the details. I was twenty-four years old and lived with Marie for three years when I found out about it for the first time. Marie had laughed when she realized how ignorant I was. She drew my head to her breast and kept saying: "You're sweet, you really are." The second person to tell me about it was Karl Emonds, my school friend, who was always fussing over his horrible conception charts.

Later on I went to the pharmacy for Marie, got her some sleeping pills and sat by her bed till she fell asleep. I still don't know what was the matter with her and what complications the gynecological business had involved. Next morning I went to the public library, read everything I could find on the subject in the encyclopedia, and felt relieved. Then toward midday Marie left for Bonn alone, taking only an overnight bag. She never even mentioned my coming along. She said: "We'll meet the day after tomorrow then, in Frankfurt." In the afternoon, when the vice squad arrived, I was glad Marie had left, although the fact that she had left caused me a lot of embarrassment. I assume the manager had reported us. Naturally I always said Marie was my wife, and only two or three times did we have any trouble. In Osnabrück it became awkward. Two police officers, a woman and a man, arrived, in plain clothes, very polite, punctilious in a way which had probably been drilled into them as producing "agreeable" results. There are certain forms of politeness on the part of the police which I particularly dislike. The policewoman was pretty, nicely made up, did not sit down until I asked her to, even accepted a cigarette, while her companion was "unobtrusively" sizing up the room. "Miss Derkum is no longer with you?" "No," I said, "she has gone on ahead, I am meeting her in Frankfurt, the day after tomorrow." "You are an artiste?" I said yes, although it was not true, but I thought it would be simpler to say yes. "Please understand," said the policewoman, "we have to do a certain amount of spot-checking when people traveling through are taken ill"—she cleared her throat—"abortively." "I quite understand," I said—I hadn't read anything about abortive in the encyclopedia. The police officer declined to sit down, politely, but continued to look around unobtrusively. "May I have your home address?" asked the policewoman. I gave her our address in Bonn. She stood up. Her colleague glanced at the open wardrobe. "Are those Miss Derkum's clothes?" he asked. "Yes,"

112

I said. He gave his colleague a "speaking" look, she shrugged her shoulders, so did he, looked once more attentively at the carpet, bent down over a spot, looked at me, as if he expected I would now confess to the murder. Then they left. They remained extremely polite to the very end of the performance. As soon as they had gone I hurriedly packed all the suitcases, sent for the bill, and a porter from the station, and left by the next train. I even paid the hotel for the full day. I checked the luggage through to Frankfurt and got onto the next southbound train. I was afraid and wanted to get away. While I was packing I had seen spots of blood on Marie's towel. Even on the station platform, before I was sitting in the Frankfurt train at last, I was afraid I would suddenly feel a hand on my shoulder and a courteous voice would ask me from behind: "Do you confess?" I would have confessed anything. It was already past midnight when the train went through Bonn. It didn't occur to me to get out.

I traveled all the way to Frankfurt, arrived there toward four in the morning, went to a much too expensive hotel and telephoned Marie in Bonn. I was afraid she might not be home, but she came to the phone at once and said: "Hans, thank heaven you called, I was so terribly worried." "Worried," I said. "Yes," she said, "I phoned Osnabrück and found you had left. I'll come right away to Frankfurt, right away." I had a bath, ordered breakfast in my room, fell asleep and was woken about eleven by Marie. She was like a different woman, very affectionate and almost gay, and when I asked: "Have you breathed enough Catholic air?" she laughed and kissed me. I didn't tell her anything about the police.

13

I wondered whether I should let in some more hot water, but it was all used up, I felt I had to get out. The bath hadn't done my knee much good, it was swollen again and almost stiff. As I got out of the tub I slipped and nearly fell onto the splendid tiles. I wanted to phone Zohnerer then and there and suggest he get me into an acrobatic troupe. I dried, lit a cigarette, and looked at myself in the mirror: I had lost weight. At the sound of the telephone I hoped for one moment it might be Marie. But it was not her ring. It might have been Leo. I hobbled into the living room, lifted the receiver and said: "Hullo."

"Oh," said Sommerwild's voice, "I hope I didn't disturb you in the midst of a double sommersault."

"I am not an acrobat," I said, furious, "I am a clown —there is a difference, at least as much difference as between Jesuits and Dominicans—and the only double thing which could happen here would be a double murder."

He laughed. "Schnier, Schnier," he said, "I'm really worried about you. I suppose you've come to Bonn to declare war on us all over the phone?"

"Look, did I call you," I said, "or did you call me?"

"Oh for heaven's sake," he said, "does that really matter?" I did not reply. "I am well aware," he said, "that you don't like me, it will surprise you, I like you, and you must admit I have the right to straighten out the things which I believe in and which I stand for."

"By force if necessary," I said.

"No," he said, his voice sounded quite clear, "no, not by force, but firmly, as the person concerned has a right to expect."

"Why do you say person and not Marie?"

"Because I am anxious to keep the matter as objective as I possibly can."

"That is your great mistake, Prelate," I said, "the matter is as subjective as it could possibly be."

I felt cold in my bathrobe, my cigarette had got damp and wasn't burning properly. "I shall not only kill you, I shall also kill Züpfner if Marie doesn't come back."

"For God's sake," he said impatiently, "leave Heribert out of this."

"Very funny," I said, "some fellow takes my wife away from me, and he is the very person I am supposed to leave out of it."

"He is not some fellow, Miss Derkum was not your wife—and he didn't take her away from you, she left."

"Entirely of her own free will, I suppose?"

"Yes," he said, "entirely of her own free will, although conceivably in a conflict between the natural and the supernatural."

"And where does the supernatural come in?" I said.

"Schnier," he said impatiently, "in spite of everything I believe you are a good clown—but you know nothing about theology."

"I know this much," I said, "that you Catholics are as hard on an unbeliever like me as the Jews are on the Christians, and the Christians on the heathen. All I ever hear is: law, theology—and when you come right down to it, this is all on account of a stupid bit of paper which the state—the state, mind you—has to issue."

"You are confusing motive and cause," he said, "I understand what you mean, Schnier," he said, "I understand."

"You don't understand anything," I said, "and the result will be double adultery. The one Marie commits when she marries your Heribert, and the second one she commits when one day she goes off with me again. I suppose I am not sufficiently sensitive and not enough of an artist, above all not enough of a Christian, for a

115

prelate to say to me: Schnier, if only you had just kept her on as a concubine."

"You misunderstand the theological essence of the difference between your case and the one we were arguing about that evening."

"What difference?" I asked, "I suppose you mean that Besewitz is more sensitive—and a kind of faith dynamo for your lot?"

"No," he actually laughed. "No. The difference is one of ecclesiastical law. B. lived with a divorced woman whom he couldn't possibly have married in church, while you—well, Miss Derkum was not divorced and there was nothing to stop your getting married."

"I was prepared to sign," I said, "even to convert."

"Prepared in a contemptible way."

"Am I supposed to pretend to feelings, to a faith, that I don't have? If you insist on justice and law—purely formal things—why do you accuse me of lacking certain feelings?"

"I'm not accusing you of anything."

I was silent. He was right, I realized, and it hurt. Marie had left, and of course they had welcomed her with open arms, but if she had wanted to stay with me, no one could have forced her to leave.

"Hullo, Schnier," said Sommerwild. "Are you still there?"

"Yes," I said, "I'm still here." I had pictured my phone conversation with him quite differently. Waking him at two thirty in the morning, insulting and threatening him.

"What can I do for you?" he asked gently.

"Nothing," I said, "if you will tell me that those secret conferences in the hotel in Hanover were aimed simply and solely at encouraging Marie to be faithful to me—then I'll believe you."

"You evidently fail to realize, Schnier," he said, "that Miss Derkum's relationship to you had reached a crisis."

"And you people have to get into the act right away," I said, "and show her a legal and ecclesiastical loophole allowing her to leave me. I always thought the Catholic church was against divorce."

"For God's sake, Schnier," he shouted, "you can't expect me as a Catholic priest to encourage a woman to persist in concubinage."

116

"Why not?" I said. "You are driving her into fornication and adultery—if as a priest you can be a party to that, go ahead."

"Your anti-clerical outlook surprises me. I have only come across that in Catholics."

"I am not in the least anticlerical, don't kid yourself, I am merely anti-Sommerwild, because you have been unjust and you're two-faced."

"Good God," he said, "in what way?"

"To listen to your sermons, anyone would imagine your heart is as big as a barn, but then you go around whispering and conniving in hotel lobbies. While I am earning my daily bread by the sweat of my brow, you are having consultations with my wife without listening to my side. Unjust and two-faced, but what else can you expect from an esthete?"

"Carry on," he said, "abuse me, malign me, I can understand you so well."

"You don't understand a thing, you have made Marie swallow some damned synthetic stuff. I happen to prefer pure drinks: I'd rather have pure applejack than synthetic cognac." "Please," he said, "do go on—you really sound as if you were emotionally involved."

"I am involved, Prelate, emotionally and physically, because it concerns Marie."

"The day will come when you realize you have done me an injustice, Schnier. Over this as in everything—" his voice became almost tearful, "and as for my synthetic stuff, maybe you forget that many people are thirsty, just plain thirsty, and that they might prefer something synthetic to drink rather than nothing at all."

"But in your Holy Scriptures there is this business about pure, clear water—why don't you pour out some of that?"

"Possibly," he said, his voice shaking, "because—to keep to your metaphor—I am at the end of a long chain of people who are drawing water from a well, I may be the hundredth or thousandth in line and the water is not quite so fresh any more—and besides, Schnier, are you listening?"

"I'm listening," I said.

"You can love a woman without living with her."

117

"Is that so?" I said, "I suppose now you're going to talk about the Virgin Mary."

"Don't mock, Schnier," he said, "it doesn't suit you."

"I am not mocking," I said, "I am quite capable of respecting something I don't understand. I simply regard it as a fatal mistake to offer the Virgin Mary as a model to a young girl who does not intend entering a convent. I even gave a lecture about it once."

"Did you?" he said, "where?"

"Right here in Bonn," I said, "to some girls. To Marie's group. I came over from Cologne on one of their club evenings, I did a bit of clowning for the girls and talked to them about the Virgin Mary. Ask Monika Silvs. Naturally I couldn't talk to the girls about what you call desires of the flesh! Are you still listening?"

"I am listening," he said, "and I am amazed. You are becoming very drastic, Schnier."

"Damn it all," I said, "the procedure which leads to the conception of a child is a fairly drastic affair—if you prefer we can talk about the stork. Everything which is said, preached and taught about this drastic business is pretense. In your heart of hearts you people regard it as something obscene which is permissible in marriage as a form of self-defense against nature—or you kid yourselves and separate the physical from that other part of it—but it is precisely that other part of it which complicates matters. Not even the wife who merely tolerates her lord and master is merely a body—and not even the filthiest drunk who goes to a whore is merely a body, neither is the whore. You all treat this thing like a Christmas cracker—and it's dynamite."

"Schnier," he said in a subdued voice, "I am astonished at how much thought you have given the matter."

"Astonished," I shouted, "you ought to be astonished at the thoughtless bastards who regard their wives simply as legal property. Ask Monika Silvs what I told the girls about it. Ever since I found out that I am a member of the male sex I have given more thought to this than almost anything else—and that astonishes you?"

"You have simply no idea whatever of *justice* and *law*. These things—however complicated they may be—have somehow to be governed by regulations."

"Yes," I said, "and I've had a dose of your regulations.

118

You shove nature onto a track which you call adultery —and when nature intervenes in marriage, you get scared. Confessed, forgiven, sinned—etc. All governed by regulations."

He laughed. His laugh sounded unpleasant. "Schnier," he said, "I see now what's the matter with you. You are obviously as monogamous as a donkey."

"You don't even know anything about zoology," I said, "let alone *homo sapiens*. Donkeys are not in the least monogamous, although they look pious. Donkeys are completely promiscuous. Crows are monogamous, sticklebacks, jackdaws and sometimes rhinoceroses."

"But not Marie, evidently," he said. He must have realized how this brief sentence wounded me, for he went on softly: "Sorry, Schnier, I would have gladly spared you that, do you believe me?"

I was silent. I spat out the burning cigarette butt onto the carpet, watched the glow spread, burning small black holes. "Schnier," he called imploringly, "at least believe me when I say I don't like telling you."

"Does it matter," I said, "what I believe? but all right —I believe you."

"You were just talking so much about nature," he said, "you ought to have followed your nature, gone after Marie and fought for her."

"Fought," I said, "where does that word come in your damned marriage laws."

"What you had with Miss Derkum was not a marriage."

"All right," I said, "so it wasn't. Not a marriage. I tried to telephone her almost every day, and I wrote to her every day."

"I know," he said, "I know. Now it's too late."

"So now the only thing left is open adultery," I said.

"You're incapable of that," he said, "I know you better than you think, and you can rant and threaten me as much as you like, I tell you, the terrible thing about you is that you are an innocent, I might almost say, a pure person. Can I help you . . . I mean . . ." He was silent. "You mean with money," I asked.

"That too," he said, "but I meant in your job."

"I might take you up on that," I said, "on both things, money and the job. Where is she?"

I heard him breathing, and in the silence I smelled

something for the first time: a mild shaving lotion, a little red wine, a cigar too, but faint. "They have gone to Rome," he said.

"Honeymoon, eh?" I asked hoarsely.

"That's what it's called," he said.

"To make the whoring complete," I said. I hung up, without thanking him or saying goodbye. I looked down at the little black spots the cigarette had burned in the carpet, but I was too tired to tread on them and put them out properly. I felt cold, and my knee hurt. I had stayed in the bath too long. Marie had not wanted to go to Rome with me. She had blushed when I suggested it, she said Italy yes, but not Rome, and when I asked her, why not, she said: Don't you really know. No, I said, and she did not tell me. I would like to have gone with her to Rome to see the Pope. I believe I would have even stood for hours in St. Peter's Square, clapped and shouted Evviva when he appeared at the window. When I told Marie this she got quite furious. She said she found it "somehow perverse," that an agnostic like me would want to cheer the Holy Father. She was really jealous. I have often noticed that with Catholics: they guard their treasures . . . the sacraments, the Pope—like misers. Besides, they are the most conceited lot of people I know. They give themselves airs about everything: about what is strong in their church, about what is weak in it, and they expect everyone whom they regard as halfway intelligent to convert soon. Perhaps the reason Marie didn't want to go to Rome with me was because there she would have to be especially ashamed of living in sin with me. In many respects she was naive, and she really wasn't very intelligent. It was mean of her to go there now with Züpfner. They would be sure to have an audience, and the poor Pope, who would address her as My daughter and Züpfner as My good son, would have no idea that an unchaste and adulterous couple were kneeling in front of him. Perhaps she had gone to Rome with Züpfner because there was nothing there to remind her of me. We had been together in Naples, Venice and Florence, in Paris and in London, and in a lot of German cities. In Rome she could be safe from memories, and she certainly had plenty of "Catholic air" there. I decided to phone Sommerwild again and tell him I thought it particularly despicable of him to make fun of my monogamous disposition. But nearly all educated Catholics have this mean streak, either they huddle behind their protective wall of dogmas, tossing off principles knocked together out of dogmas, but when one seriously confronts them with their "unshakable truths" they smile and refer to "human nature." If necessary they assume a sarcastic smile, as if they had just come from the Pope and he had presented them with a little bit of his infallibility. In any case, when you start to seriously discuss the monstrous truths they so calmly proclaim, you are either a "Protestant" or have no sense of humor. If you talk seriously to them about marriage they bring up their Henry VIII, they have been firing with this cannon for the last three hundred years, they want to show how severe their church is, but when they want to show how softhearted it is, what a big heart it has, they trot out their Besewitz anecdotes, tell jokes about bishops, but only when they are with "the initiated," by which they mean—whether they are Left or Right wing is of no consequence any more—"educated and intelligent people." That time when I challenged Sommerwild to tell the bishop's story about Besewitz from the pulpit, he became very angry. When it is a case of man and wife they only fire from the pulpit with their main cannon: Henry VIII. A kingdom for a marriage! Justice! Law! Dogma!

I was feeling sick, for a number of reasons, physically because I had had nothing but cognac and cigarettes since that wretched breakfast in Bochum—spiritually, because I was imagining Züpfner in a hotel in Rome watching Marie get dressed. He would probably also poke around in her underwear. These neatly parted, intelligent, righteous and educated Catholics need compassionate women. Marie was not the right one for Züpfner. A man like that, always impeccably dressed, fashionably enough not to be old-fashioned, but not so fashionably as to seem dandified; and a man who washes thoroughly in cold water every morning and cleans his teeth as vigorously as if he was out to break a record—for a man like that Marie is not intelligent enough, and she is also much too energetic getting up in the morning. He is the type who, before he is conducted into the audience chamber to the Pope, would give his shoes one more quick wipe with his handkerchief. I felt sorry for the Pope too, before whom the two would kneel. He would smile benignly, and sincerely rejoice over this handsome, pleasant-looking Catholic German couple—and once again he would be deceived. He couldn't dream he was dispensing his blessing over two adulterers.

I went into the bathroom, dried myself off, dressed again, went into the kitchen and put on the kettle. Monika had thought of everything. There were matches on the gas stove, ground coffee in an air-tight jar, filter papers next to it, ham, eggs, canned vegetables in the refrigerator. I only like working in the kitchen when there is no other way of escaping from certain forms of adult chatter. When Sommerwild starts talking about "Eros," Blothert spits out his Ca . . Ca . . Cabinet, or Fredebeul gives a cleverly involved lecture on Cocteau—then I must say I prefer to go out to the kitchen, squeeze mayonnaise out of tubes, slice olives in half, and spread liver sausage on bread. When I want to get something for myself alone in the kitchen I feel lost. My hands become clumsy from loneliness, and the necessity of opening a can, breaking eggs into the pan, depresses me deeply. I am not a bachelor. When Marie was ill or went to work— she worked for a time at a stationer's in Cologne—I didn't mind so much doing things in the kitchen, and when she had the first miscarriage I even washed the sheets before our landlady got home from the movies.

I managed to open a can of beans without gashing my hand, I poured boiling water onto the filter, while I thought about the house Züpfner had built for himself. I had been there once, two years ago.

14

I imagined her coming home in the dark. The sharply swept lawn looked almost blue in the moonlight. Next to the garage, cut twigs, stacked up by the gardener. Between the forsythia and the hawthorn, the garbage can, ready to be carried away. Friday evening. By now she would know what the kitchen was smelling of, fish, she would also know what messages she would find, one from Züpfner on the T.V. set: "Urgent call to go to F. Love. Heribert," the other from the maid on the icebox— "Gone to movies, back at ten. Greta (Luise, Birgit)."

Open garage door, switch on light: on the whitewashed wall the shadow of a scooter and a discarded sewing machine. The Mercedes in Züpfner's stall was a sign that Züpfner had walked. "Get some fresh air, get a bit of fresh air, air." Mud on the tires and fenders indicated drives into the Eifel Mountains, afternoon speeches to the Youth Union ("keep together, stand together, suffer together").

A glance upward: everything dark in the nursery too. The houses next door separated by double driveways and wide borders. Sickly reflection of the television sets. There the homecoming husband and father is considered a nuisance, the return of the prodigal son would also have been considered a nuisance; no calf would have been slaughtered, not even a chicken would have been broiled —he would have been told to go to the refrigerator for the remains of some liver sausage.

Saturday afternoons there was fraternization, when

123

shuttlecocks flew over hedges, kittens or puppies ran away, shuttlecocks were thrown back, kittens—"oh, how sweet"—or puppies—"oh, how sweet"—handed back at garden gates or through hedge gaps. The irritation in voices was subdued, never personal; only sometimes it strayed from the smooth curve and scratched notches in the neighbors' sky, always from trivial causes, never from the true ones: when a saucer shattered, a rolling ball broke off flowers, gravel from a child's hand was tossed onto car paint, newly washed, newly ironed laundry wetted by garden hoses—then voices become shrill which are not permitted to become shrill when it's a matter of betrayal, adultery, abortion. "Oh, your ears are just too sensitive, you'd better take something for it."

Don't take anything, Marie.

Open the front door: quiet and pleasantly warm. Little Marie asleep upstairs. It doesn't take long: wedding in Bonn, honeymoon in Rome, pregnancy, confinement—brown curls on snow-white baby pillow. Do you remember how he showed us the house and virilely announced: There's room for twelve children here—and how he sizes you up now in the morning at breakfast, the unspoken Well? on his lips, and how simple-minded church and party friends shout after the third glass of brandy: "From one to twelve, leaves eleven to go!"

They are whispering in town. You were at the movies again, on this beautiful sunny afternoon at the movies. And again at the movies—and again.

All evening alone in the group, at Blothert's, hearing nothing but Ca Ca Ca, and this time it wasn't even finished off with—binet but with—tholon. The word rolls around in your ear like a foreign body. It sounds as if it might be a clicker, also sounds a bit like a carbuncle. Blothert has the Geiger counter which can track down the catholon. "He's got it—he hasn't—she's got it—she hasn't." It's like picking off petals: she loves me, she loves me not. She loves me. Football clubs and party friends, government and opposition, are tested for catholon. Like a racial feature he looks for it and doesn't find it; Nordic nose, Mediterranean mouth. One of them has it for sure, he's swallowed it, the longed for, the ardently looked for. Blothert himself, watch out for his eyes, Marie. Belated lust, a seminarist's idea of the sixth commandment, and when he speaks of certain sins, then only in Latin. *In sexto, de sexto.* Of course, it sounds like sex. And the darling children. The oldest ones, Hubert, eighteen, Margret, seventeen, are allowed to stay up a little longer, to reap the benefits of the adult conversation. About catholon, corporative state, capital punishment, which produces such a strange flicker in Mrs. Blothert's eyes, sends her voice up to a stimulated pitch where laughter and tears erotically unite. You have tried to console yourself with Fredebeul's stale Left-wing cynicism: in vain. In vain will you have tried to get angry at Blothert's stale Right-wing cynicism. There is a lovely word: nothing. Think of nothing. Not of cabinet and catholon, think of the clown who weeps in the bath, and whose coffee drips onto his slippers.

15

I could place the sound but didn't know the proper response, I had heard it many times but had never had to react to it. At home the maids reacted to the sound of the front door bell, the shop bell at Derkums' I had heard often but I had never got up. In Cologne we had lived in a boarding house, in hotels the only thing that ever rings is the phone. I heard the ringing but didn't register it. It was unfamiliar, I had only heard it twice in this apartment, once when a boy delivered some milk and once when Züpfner sent Marie some roses. When the roses arrived I was in bed, Marie came into the room, showed them to me, thrust her nose ecstatically into the bouquet, and an awkward scene followed because I thought the flowers were for me. Women admirers had sometimes sent me flowers to the hotel. I said to Marie: "What lovely roses, you keep them," and she looked at me and said: "But they are for me." I flushed. I was embarrassed, and it occurred to me that I had never ordered any flowers for Marie. Of course I brought back for her all the flowers given me on stage, but I had never bought her any, usually it was I who had to pay for the flowers presented to me on stage. "Who are they from?" I said. "Züpfner," she said. "Damn it all," I said, "what's the idea?" I remembered how they had held hands. Marie colored and said: "Why shouldn't he send me flowers?" "The question should be the other way round," I said: "Why should he send you flowers?" "We've known each other a long time," she said, "and perhaps

126

he admires me." "All right," I said, "let him admire you, but all those expensive flowers, it's overdoing it. To my mind it's in poor taste." She was offended and left the room.

When the boy came with the milk we were sitting in the living room, and Marie went out, opened the door to him and gave him the money. The only visitor we ever had in our apartment was Leo, before he converted, but he had not rung the bell, he had come up with Marie.

In an odd sort of way the ringing sounded both diffident and stubborn. I had a terrible fear it might be Monika, perhaps even sent by Sommerwild on some pretext or other. I immediately got my Nibelung complex again. I ran out into the hall in my soaking wet slippers, couldn't find the button I had to press. While I was looking for it, I remembered that of course Monika had the front door key. I finally found the button, pressed it and heard a sound like a bee buzzing against a windowpane. I went out on the landing and stood by the elevator. The In Use signal went red, the figure One lit up, then the Two, I stared anxiously at the numbers, till I suddenly noticed someone was standing beside me. I jumped, and turned: a pretty woman, very fair, not too slim, with charming light gray eyes. Her hat was a little too red for my taste. I smiled, she smiled too and said: "You must be Mr. Schnier—I am Mrs. Grebsel, your neighbor. I am so pleased to meet you in the flesh"—"I am pleased too," I said—I really was pleased. In spite of her hat being too red, Mrs. Grebsel was a sight for sore eyes. I saw she was carrying a newspaper, "The Voice of Bonn," she saw my glance, blushed and said: "Don't let it bother you." "I'll give that dirty dog a punch in the nose," I said, "if you only knew what a miserable, hypocritical creature he is—and he cheated me too, did me out of a whole bottle of schnapps." She laughed. "My husband and I would be delighted," she said, "if we could really become neighbors. Will you be here for some time?" "Yes," I said, "I'll drop in one day, if I may—is everything in your flat terra cotta too?" "Of course," she said, "terra cotta is the trademark of the fifth floor." The elevator had paused for a minute at the third floor, now the Four showed red, the Five, I flung open the door and took a step back in my astonishment. My father

127

came out of the elevator, held the door open for Mrs. Grebsel as she went in, and turned toward me. "Good God," I said, "Father." I had never said Father to him before, just Dad. He said "Hans," made an awkward attempt to embrace me. I went ahead of him into the apartment, took his hat and coat, opened the door to the living room and pointed to the sofa. He seated himself ponderously.

We were both very embarrassed. Embarrassment seems to be the sole means of communication between parents and children. Probably my greeting him as "Father" had sounded rather dramatic, and that enhanced the embarrassment, which was inevitable in any case. My father sat down in one of the terra cotta armchairs, and shook his head as he looked at me: with my soaking wet slippers, wet socks, in the bathrobe which was not only much too long but unfortunately also flaming red. My father is not tall, he is slight and so expertly yet casually well-groomed that the television people will do anything to get hold of him when there are economic matters to be discussed. He also radiates kindness, good sense, and is now more famous as a television star than he could ever have been as one of the brown-coal Schniers. He loathes every kind of brutality. You would expect him, when you see him like that, to smoke cigars, not fat ones but light, slim cigars, but for him to smoke cigarettes seems surprisingly dashing and progressive for a capitalist of nearly seventy. I can understand why they send him along to all the discussions which have to do with money. You can see that he not only radiates kindness but is kind too. I offered him cigarettes, gave him a light, and as I bent forward he said: "I must admit I don't know much about clowns, but I do know a few things. I had no idea they bathed in coffee." He can be very witty. "I don't bathe in coffee, Father," I said, "I just wanted to make some coffee and didn't quite succeed." It was here at the latest that I should have said Dad again, but it was too late. "Would you like a drink?" He smiled, looked at me suspiciously, and asked: "What have you got?" I went to the kitchen: in the refrigerator there was the cognac, there were also a few bottles of mineral water, lemonade and a bottle of red wine. I took one bottle of each, carried them into the living room, and lined them

128

up on the table in front of my father. He took his glasses out of his pocket and studied the labels. Shaking his head he pushed the cognac aside first. I knew he liked cognac and said, somewhat hurt: "But it seems like a good brand." "The brand is excellent," he said, "but the best cognac is no good when it is ice-cold."

"Good God," I said, "shouldn't you keep cognac in the refrigerator?" He looked at me over the top of his glasses, as if I had just been convicted of sodomy. In his own way he is an esthete too, he is quite capable of sending the toast back to the kitchen three or four times till Anna produces exactly the right shade of brown, a silent battle renewed each morning, for anyway Anna regards toast as "Anglo-Saxon nonsense." "Cognac in the refrigerator," said my father contemptuously, "did you really not know—or are you just pretending? One never knows where one is with you!"

"I didn't know," I said. He gave me a searching look, smiled, and seemed convinced.

"And to think of all the money I spent on your education," he said. It was meant to sound ironical, the way a father of nearly seventy talks to his grown-up son, but the irony misfired, it froze on the word money. With a shake of his head he rejected the lemonade too, and the red wine, and said: "In the circumstances it seems to me that soda water is the safest drink." I fetched two glasses from the sideboard, opened a bottle of soda water. That at least I seemed able to do properly. He nodded benevolently as he watched me.

"Do you mind," I said, "if I stay in my bathrobe?"

"Yes," he said, "I do mind. Please get properly dressed. Your attire and your—your odor of coffee lend a certain comical aspect to the situation which is not in keeping. I wish to have a serious talk with you. And besides —forgive me for being so frank—I detest, as you no doubt recall, any evidence of sloppiness."

"It isn't sloppiness," I said, "it's just a sign of relaxation."

"I don't know," he said, "how often during your lifetime you have really obeyed me, now you are no longer obliged to do so. I am merely asking you to do me a favor."

I was amazed. My father used to be rather shy, almost taciturn. Television had taught him how to discuss and argue, with a "compelling charm." I was too tired to dodge this charm.

I went into the bathroom, took off the coffee-soaked socks, dried my feet, put on my shirt, trousers, jacket, went into the kitchen in my bare feet, heaped the warmed-up white beans onto a plate and simply broke the soft-boiled eggs over the beans, scraped the remains of egg out of the shells with a spoon, took a slice of bread, the spoon, and went into the living room. My father looked at my plate with an expression which accurately conveyed a blend of surprise and disgust.

"Excuse me," I said, "I haven't had anything to eat since nine this morning, and I don't imagine you particularly want me to faint at your feet." He forced a laugh, shook his head, sighed, and said: "Well, all right—but you know, protein alone is simply not good for you."

"I'll have an apple afterwards," I said. I stirred the beans and eggs together, bit into the bread, and took a spoonful of my mush, which tasted very good.

"You ought at least to put some of that tomato stuff on it," he said.

"There isn't any," I said.

I ate much too fast, and the inevitable noises I made while eating appeared to annoy my father. He suppressed his disgust, but not very successfully, and I finally stood up, went to the kitchen, finished my plate standing by the refrigerator, and looked at myself in the mirror hanging over it while I ate. I had not even stuck to the most important part of my training during the last few weeks: facial exercises. A clown, whose main effect is his immobile face, must keep his face very mobile. I used to always stick out my tongue at myself before I began my exercises, so as to get quite close to myself before I could withdraw from myself again. Later on I stopped doing that, and without any tricks whatever just stared at myself, every day for half an hour, until finally I wasn't there at all: as I have no narcissistic tendencies, I often came close to going mad. I simply forgot it was me whose face I was looking at in the mirror, turned the mirror around when I had finished my exercises, and if I happened to glance in a mirror later on in the day I got a shock: that was some strange fellow in my bathroom, on the toilet, I didn't know whether he was serious or comic, a long-nosed, pale ghost—and I would run as fast as I could to Marie to see myself in her face. Since she has left I can't do my facial exercises any more: I am afraid of going mad. I always went up, after my exercises, quite close to Marie, till I saw myself in her eyes: tiny, a bit distorted, yet recognizable: that was me, and yet it was the same person I had been afraid of in the mirror. How was I to explain to Zohnerer that without Marie I just couldn't go on practicing in front of the mirror? To watch myself eating was merely sad, not frightening. I could hang on to the spoon, could recognize the beans, traces of egg white and egg yolk in them, the slice of bread, getting smaller all the time. The mirror confirmed for me things of such touching reality as an empty plate, a dwindling slice of bread, a slightly smeared mouth, which I wiped with my sleeve. I was not practicing. There was no one there to bring me back out of the mirror. I slowly returned to the living room.

"Much too fast," said my father, "you eat too quickly. Do sit down. Aren't you going to drink anything?"

"No," I said, "I wanted to make some coffee, but it was a flop."

"Shall I make some for you?" he asked.

"Do you know how to?" I asked.

"I have the reputation of making very good coffee," he said.

"Oh, never mind," I said, "I'll have some soda water, it's not that important."

"But I'd be glad to do it," he said.

"No," I said, "thanks. The kitchen is in an appalling mess. A huge puddle of coffee, open cans, eggshells on the floor."

"Very well then," he said, "as you wish." He appeared disproportionately hurt. He poured me out some soda water, held out his cigarette case to me, I took one, he lit it for me, we smoked. I felt sorry for him. Probably I had completely thrown him with my plate of beans. No doubt he had counted on finding me in what he imagined to be Bohemian surroundings: a sophisticated confusion and all sorts of modern stuff on the ceiling and walls, but the apartment happens to be completely lacking in style, almost suburban, and I saw that this depressed him. We had chosen the sideboard from a catalogue, the pictures on the walls were all just reproductions, only two abstracts among them, the only attractive ones were two water-colors by Monika Silvs, hanging over the chest of drawers: Rhine Landscape III and Rhine Landscape IV, in shades of dark gray with barely visible traces of white. The few attractive things we do have, chairs, a few vases and the tea wagon in the corner, were bought by Marie. My father is a person who needs atmosphere, and the atmosphere in our apartment made him irritable and tongue-tied. "Did Mother tell you I was here?" I asked finally, when we lit the second cigarette without having said a single word.

"Yes," he said, "why can't you spare her that sort of thing."

"If she hadn't answered the phone in her committee voice, everything would have been different," I said.

"What's wrong with this committee?" he asked quietly.

"Nothing," I said, "it's a very good thing that racial differences should be reconciled, but my idea of race is different from the committee's. Negroes, for instance, have become the latest thing—I wanted to offer mother a negro I know well as a Nativity figure, and when you think that there are several hundred negro races. The committee will never be out of a job. Or gypsies," I said, "Mother should invite some to tea some day. Right off the street. There's still a lot to be done."

"That's not what I wanted to talk to you about," he said.

I said nothing. He looked at me and said in a low voice: "I wanted to talk to you about money." I remained silent. "I assume you are financially embarrassed. Please say something."

"Embarrassed is a nice way of putting it. I shall probably not be able to perform for a year. Look at this." I pulled up my trouser leg and showed him my swollen knee, I let my trouser down again and pointed with the forefinger of my right hand to my left breast. "And this," I said.

"Good God," he said, "heart?"

"Yes," I said, "heart."

"I'll give Drohmert a call and ask him to see you. He's the best heart specialist there is."

"You don't understand," I said, "I don't need to consult Drohmert."

"But didn't you say: heart?"

"Maybe I should have said soul, feelings, emotions—heart seemed to me the right word."

"Oh I see," he said drily, "that business." No doubt Sommerwild had told him about that "business" over a game of skat at the Union Club, between jugged hare, beer and a no trump game.

He got up, began to walk up and down, then stood behind the chair, leaned on the back and looked down at me.

"It probably sounds foolish," he said, "if I make a solemn pronouncement, but do you know what's the matter with you? You lack the very thing that makes a man a man: the ability to accept a situation."

"I heard that once before today," I said.

"Then hear it a third time: accept the situation."

"Please," I said, wearily.

"How do you imagine I felt when Leo came to me and said he was going to become a Catholic. It was as painful for me as Henrietta's death—it would have hurt me less if he had said he was going to become a Communist. That's something I can understand, when a young person dreams a false dream of social justice and so on. But that." He clung to the back of the armchair and shook his head vigorously. "That. No. No." Apparently he was serious. He had gone quite pale and looked much older than his age.

"Sit down, Father," I said, "and have a cognac." He sat down, nodded toward the cognac bottle, I got a glass from the sideboard, poured him a drink, and he took the cognac and drank it without thanking me or raising his glass to me. "I don't suppose you understand that," he said. "No," I said.

"I am afraid for every young person who believes in this thing," he said, "that's why it shocked me so terribly, but even that I have accepted—accepted. Why are you looking at me like that?"

"I owe you an apology," I said, "when I saw you on television I thought you were a magnificent actor. Even a bit of a clown."

He looked at me suspiciously, almost hurt, and I said

quickly: "No really, Dad, magnificent." I was glad to have found the Dad again.

"They simply forced me into this role," he said.

"It suits you," I said, "and whatever part you act in it you act well."

"I don't act any of it," he said seriously, "none of it, I don't need to act anything."

"That's bad," I said, "for your opponent."

"I have no opponents," he said indignantly.

"Even worse for your opponents," I said.

He gave me another suspicious look, then laughed and said: "But I really don't see them as opponents."

"Even worse than I thought," I said, "don't those fellows you are always talking to about money know that you people always keep quiet about the most important thing —or have you come to an agreement before you are conjured onto the screen?" He poured himself some cognac, looked at me questioningly: "I wanted to talk to you about your future."

"Wait a moment," I said, "I just want to know how it's done. You people always talk about percentages, ten, twenty, five, fifty per cent—but you never say what per cent of what?" He looked almost stupid as he raised the cognac glass, drank and looked at me. "What I mean is," I said, "I didn't learn much arithmetic, but I know that a hundred per cent of half a pfennig is half a pfennig, while five per cent of a billion is fifty million . . . see what I mean?"

"For God's sake," he said, "do you have so much time to watch TV?"

"Yes," I said, "since this business, as you call it, I watch TV a lot—it makes me feel so beautifully empty. Utterly empty, and when you only see your father once every three years you enjoy seeing him on television. In some bar or other, over a glass of beer, in the semi-darkness. Sometimes I am really proud of you, the skillful way you prevent anyone from asking about the percentage figure."

"You are mistaken," he said coolly, "I don't prevent anything at all."

"Isn't it a bit of a bore not to have any opponents?" He got up and looked at me angrily. I got up too. We both stood behind our armchairs, leaning our arms on

134

the backs. I laughed and said: "As a clown I'm naturally interested in the modern forms of pantomime. Once when I was sitting alone in the back room of a bar I switched off the sound. It was wonderful. L'art pour l'art turning up in wage policy, in the economic system. It's a pity you have never seen the turn I do called Board of Directors' Meeting."

"It may interest you to know," he said, "that I have spoken to Genneholm about you. I asked him to have a look at some of your performances and let me have a—a kind of expert opinion."

I suddenly had to yawn. It was rude, but I couldn't help it, and I was fully aware of the discourtesy. I had slept badly during the night and had had a trying day. When someone sees his father for the first time in three years, and has a serious conversation with him for what was really the first time in his life—it is quite true that nothing could be less appropriate than a yawn. I was all worked up, but dead tired, and I was sorry I had to yawn at that particular moment. The name Genneholm acted on me like a sedative. People like my father must always have *the best:* Drohmert, the best heart specialist in the world, Genneholm, the best theater critic in the Federal Republic, the best tailor, the best champagne, the best hotel, the best author. It's a bore. My yawning became almost a cramp, my jaw muscles cracked. The fact that Genneholm is a pansy doesn't prevent his name filling me with boredom. Pansies can be very amusing, but it is the amusing people I find boring, especially eccentrics, and Genneholm was not only a pansy but eccentric too. He usually came to Mother's parties and moved right up close to you so that every time you had to smell his breath and share in his last meal, which I could have done without. The last time I met him, four years ago, he had smelled of potato salad, and in view of this smell his scarlet waistcoat and honey-colored Mephistophelean moustache no longer seemed in the least bizarre to me. He was very witty, everyone knew he was witty, and so he had to be witty all the time. A tiring existence.

"I beg your pardon," I said, when I could be sure my yawning fit was over for the time being. "What did Genneholm say?"

My father was offended. He is always offended when you let yourself go, and my yawning pained him objectively, not subjectively. He shook his head as he had over my bean mush. "Genneholm is watching your development with great interest, he is very favorably inclined toward you."

"A pansy never gives up hope," I said, "they're a persistent bunch."

"That's enough," said my father sharply, "be glad that you have such an influential and expert well-wisher behind you."

"I am quite glad," I said.

"But he has a number of objections to what you have been doing so far. He feels you ought to avoid all the Pierrot side of it, that you certainly have a gift for Harlequin, but that you're too good for that—and that as a clown you are impossible. He believes your opportunity lies in devoting yourself entirely to pantomime . . . are you listening at all?" His voice got sharper and sharper.

"Of course," I said, "I am listening to every word, every single one of these clever, apt words, don't let it bother you if I keep my eyes closed." While he was quoting Genneholm I had shut my eyes. It felt so good and released me from the sight of the dark brown chest of drawers against the wall behind Father. A revolting piece of furniture that somehow reminded me of school: the dark brown color, the black knobs, the pale yellow inlay along the top edge. The chest of drawers had come from Marie's parents' house.

"Please," I said softly, "do go on." I was dead tired, my stomach hurt, my head ached, and I was standing there so stiffly behind the chair that my knee began to swell still more. Behind my closed lids I saw my face as I knew it from the mirror from a thousand hours of practice, completely immobile, painted snow white, not even my eyelashes moved, or my eyebrows, only my eyes, slowly they moved from side to side like a frightened rabbit, to achieve the effect that critics like Genneholm had called "that extraordinary ability to portray animal melancholy." I was dead and locked in with my face for a thousand hours—with no chance of rescuing myself in Marie's eyes.

"Go on," I said.

"He advised me to send you to one of the best teachers. For one year, for two, for six months. Genneholm believes you should concentrate, study, become so fully conscious of yourself that you can become simple again. And practice, practice, practice—and, are you still listening?" His voice sounded less severe, thank God.

"Yes," I said.

"And I am prepared to finance that for you."

My knee felt as fat and round as a gasometer. Without opening my eyes I groped my way around the chair, sat down, groped for the cigarettes on the table like a blind man. My father cried out in alarm. I can pretend to be a blind man so well that people believe I am blind. I felt blind too, maybe I would stay blind. What I was acting was not a sightless man but a man who has just lost his sight, and when I had finally got the cigarette into my mouth I felt flame from Father's lighter, felt, too, how violently it trembled.

"Son," he said anxiously, "are you ill?"

"Yes," I said softly, drew on the cigarette, inhaled deeply, "I am terribly ill, but not blind. Pains in my stomach, my head, my knee, a rapidly proliferating depression—but the worst thing is, I know perfectly well Genneholm is right, about ninety-five per cent, and I even know what he went on to say. Did he mention Kleist?"

"Yes," said my father.

"Did he say I must first lose my soul—be totally empty, then I could afford to have one again. Did he say that?"

"Yes," said my father, "how do you know?"

"Hell," I said, "after all I know his theories, and where he gets them from. But I don't want to lose my soul, I want to get it back."

"You've lost it?"

"Yes."

"Where is it?"

"In Rome," I said, opened my eyes and laughed.

My father had really gone quite pale and haggard with fear. His laugh sounded relieved and yet annoyed.

"You rascal," he said, "was the whole thing put on?"

"Unfortunately," I said, "not entirely and not well. Genneholm would say: still far too naturalistic—and he is right. Pansies are usually right, they have a tremendous sense of empathy—but nothing else. However."

"You rascal," said my father, "you really took me in."

"No," I said, "no, I didn't take you in any more than a genuinely blind person takes you in. Believe me, all that groping and feeling around for support is not absolutely necessary in every case. Many a blind man acts the blind man though he really is blind. Right now, before your very eyes, I could hobble from here to the door in such a way that you would cry out with pain and pity and call a doctor immediately, the best surgeon in the world, Fretzer. Shall I?" I had already got up.

"Don't, please," he said, distressed, and I sat down again.

"Please, do sit down yourself," I said, "I wish you would, it gets on my nerves when you stand around like that."

He sat down, poured himself some soda water and gave me a puzzled look. "I can't make you out," he said, "will you give me a straight answer. I will pay the fees for your tuition, you can go where you like. London, Paris, Brussels. Only the best will do."

"No," I said wearily, "that's just it, it won't. Studying is no good to me any more, all I need now is work. I studied when I was thirteen, fourteen, till I was twenty-one. Only you never noticed. And if Genneholm believes I could go on studying now—then he's stupider than I thought."

"He is an expert," said my father, "the best I know." "The best there is, even," I said, "but he's only an expert, he knows something about theater, about tragedy, commedia dell'arte, pantomime. But just look what happens to his own attempts at comedy when he suddenly turns up with mauve shirts and black silk ties. Any amateur would be ashamed of himself. It isn't critics being critical that is so bad—the worst thing about them is that they are so uncritical and lacking in humor toward themselves. It's a shame. Of course, he really is an expert—but if he thinks I ought to begin studying again after six years on the stage—that's nonsense!"

"You don't need the money then?" asked my father. A slight trace of relief in his voice made me suspicious. "Oh yes I do," I said, "I need the money." "Then what do you want to do? Go on performing, under these circumstances?"

"What circumstances?" I asked.

"Well," he said, embarrassed, "you know what your press is like."

"My press?" I said, "for the last three months I've only been appearing in the provinces."

"I managed to get hold of the reviews," he said, "I have been through them with Genneholm."

"Damn it all," I said, "how much did you pay him?" He flushed. "Never you mind," he said, "now, what are your plans?"

"To practice," I said, "to work, for six months, a year, I don't know yet."

"Where?"

"Here," I said, "where else?" He hardly managed to hide his dismay.

"I won't bother the family and I won't compromise you, I won't even come to your At Home days," I said. He flushed. I had gone a few times to their At Homes, like any other guest, without going to see them privately, as it were. I had had cocktails and olives, a cup of tea, and as I left I had put cigarettes in my pocket, so blatantly that the servants saw and turned aside in embarrassment.

"Oh," was all my father said. He turned in his chair. What he really wanted to do was get up and stand by the window. Now he just looked down and said: "I would prefer you to choose the sensible way which Genneholm suggests. I don't care for financing something uncertain. Haven't you saved any money? Surely you must have made quite a nice bit these last few years."

"I haven't saved a single pfennig," I said, "I possess one solitary mark." I took the mark out of my pocket and showed it to him. He actually leaned over and looked at it as if it were a strange insect.

"I find it hard to believe you," he said, "I certainly didn't bring you up to be a spendthrift. About how much would you need a month, what had you in mind?"

My heart was hammering. I hadn't thought he would want to give me such direct help. I considered. Not too little and not too much, and still I had to have enough, but I had no idea, not the faintest, how much I would

139

need. Electricity, phone, and of course somehow or other I had to live. I was sweating with anxiety. "First of all," I said, "I need a thick rubber mat, as big as this room, twenty by fifteen, you could get that cheaper for me from your Rhenish Rubber Company."

"Fine," he said with a smile, "I'll even make you a present of it. Twenty by fifteen—but Genneholm feels you shouldn't fritter yourself away on acrobatics."

"I won't, Dad," I said, "aside from the mat I suppose I would need a thousand marks a month."

"A thousand marks," he said. He got up, his dismay was genuine, his lips quivered.

"All right then," I said, "how much did you think?" I had no idea how much money he really had. A thousand marks for a year—I could calculate that much—was twelve thousand marks, and a sum like that wouldn't kill him. He really was a millionaire, Marie's father had carefully explained it to me and worked it all out once when I was there. I didn't remember exactly. He had shares and "a finger in the pie" all over the place. Even in this bath stuff factory.

He paced up and down behind his chair, silently, moving his lips as if he were counting. Maybe he really was but it took a very long time.

I remembered again how shabbily they had behaved when I left Bonn with Marie. Father had written me that for moral reasons he refused me all support and that he expected me to "go to work" to support myself "and that unfortunate, respectable girl whom you have seduced," and that, as I knew, he had always thought highly of old Mr. Derkum, both as a political opponent and a man, and it was a scandal.

We lived in a boarding house in Cologne-Ehrenfeld. The seven hundred marks which Marie's mother had left her were gone in a month, and I thought we had managed very economically and sensibly.

We lived close to the Ehrenfeld station, the window of our room looked out on the red-brick wall of the station embankment, brown-coal trains rumbled into the city full, came out empty, a comforting sight, a stirring sound, it always reminded me of the stable financial situation at home. The view from the bathroom out onto galvanized tubs and washing lines, sometimes when it was dark the sound of a falling can or a bagful of garbage which someone had furtively thrown from a window into the yard. I often lay in the bath and sang liturgical songs, till the landlady first forbade me to sing— "People think I have a renegade pastor for a lodger"— and then cut off my bath credit. In her opinion I took too many baths, she found them unnecessary. Sometimes she raked around with a poker in the parcels of garbage that had been thrown into the yard, to determine the despatcher from the contents: onion skin, coffee grounds, chop bones, gave her material for involved combinations, which she supplemented by means of information casually obtained in the butcher shops and grocery stores, never with any success. The garbage never admitted of conclusive deductions as to individuality. Threats which she sent up into the laundry-hung sky were formulated in such a way that everyone took them personally: "No one can put anything over on me, I know what's what." In the morning we always lay by the window and watched for the postman, who sometimes brought us parcels from Marie's friends, Leo, Anna, at very irregular intervals checks from Grandfather, but from my parents only demands that I "take my fate in hand and overcome my misfortune by my own efforts."

Later on my mother wrote that she had "cast me out." She is capable of such vile taste that at times it borders on idiocy, for she took the expression from a novel by Schnitzler called *The Divided Heart*. In this novel a girl is "cast out" by her parents because she refuses to bear a child which has been fathered by a "noble but weak artist," an actor, I think. Mother quoted a sentence word for word from Chapter 8 of the novel "My conscience compels me to cast you out." She considered this a suitable quotation. In any case, she "cast me out." I am sure she only did it because it was a way of avoiding conflict in her conscience as well as her bank account. At home they expected me to start a heroic career: go into a factory or take a construction job in order to support my mistress, and they were all disappointed when I didn't.

Even Leo and Anna made no bones about their disappointment. In their mind's eye they already saw me setting off at daybreak with sandwiches and Thermos, blowing a kiss up to Marie's window, saw me coming home in the evening "tired but contented," reading the paper and watching Marie knitting. But I made no effort whatever to turn this vision into living reality. I stayed with Marie, and Marie much preferred it when I stayed with her. I felt I was an "artist" (much more than I ever did later), and we made our childish ideas of Bohemian life come true: with Chianti bottles and unbleached cotton curtains and gaily colored raffia. The memory of that year still moves me to tears. When Marie went to our landlady at the end of the week to ask for a postponement of the rent, the landlady always began to argue and ask why I didn't go out to work. And Marie would say with her wonderful pathos: "My husband is an artist, you see, an artist." Once I heard her call out from the dirty staircase into the landlady's open room: "Yes, an artist," and the landlady called back in her hoarse voice: "What, an artist? And he's your husband too? The Marriage License Bureau must have been pleased about that." What annoyed her most was that we nearly always stayed in bed till ten or eleven. She hadn't enough imagination to realize that this was the easiest way for us to save a meal and current for the little electric radiator, and she didn't know that I usually couldn't go and practice in the little parish hall till close to noon, because in the mornings there was always something going on there: Child Care, Communion instruction, cooking lessons, or a Catholic building co-op's counseling service.

We lived near the church where Heinrich Behlen was chaplain, and he had got me this little hall with a stage as a place to practice, also the room in the boarding house. In those days a lot of Catholics were very kind to us. The woman who gave the cooking lessons in the church house always let us have the leftovers, usually just soup and pudding, sometimes meat as well, and when Marie helped her tidy up she would occasionally stuff a package of butter or a bag of sugar into Marie's pocket. Sometimes she stayed behind when I started my practicing, laughing herself sick, and made some coffee in the afternoon. Even when she found out we were not married she was still nice. I had the feeling she never expected artists to be "properly married." Some days, when it was cold, we went over there earlier. Marie joined in the cooking lessons, and I sat in the cloakroom beside an electric radiator and read. Through the thin wall I heard the giggling in the hall, then serious talks on calories, vitamins, weights and measures, yet on the whole it all sounded very cheerful. On the days when there was Child Care, we were not allowed to turn up till it was all over. The young woman doctor in charge was very firm, in a friendly way, and was terribly scared of the dust I stirred up when I hopped around on the stage. Later she maintained that the dust was still hanging in the air next day and was dangerous for the babies, and she saw to it that I was not allowed to use the stage for twenty-four hours before she had her consulting hours. Heinrich Behlen even got into trouble over it with his pastor, who had no idea I practiced there every day and who told Heinrich "not to carry brotherly love too far." Sometimes I also went to church with Marie. It was so nice and warm there, I always sat over the heating duct; it was absolutely quiet too, the street noises outside seemed infinitely far away, and in a comforting way the church was empty: only seven or eight people, and at times I had the sensation of being one of this quiet sad gathering of survivors of something which in all its impotence had a majestic quality. Apart from Marie and me, nothing but old women. And the undramatic way in which Heinrich Behlen conducted the service suited the dark, ugly church so well. Once I even helped him out when his altar boy didn't turn up, at the end of the Mass when the book is carried from right to left. I simply noticed that Heinrich suddenly faltered, lost the rhythm, and I quickly ran over, brought the book from the right, genuflected when I reached the center of the altar, and carried it to the left. I would have felt I was being discourteous had I not helped Heinrich in his dilemma. Marie went scarlet, Heinrich smiled. We had known each other a long time, he had been captain of the football team at school, older than I was. Generally we waited for Heinrich outside by the sacristy after Mass, he would invite us for breakfast, buy eggs, ham, coffee and cigarettes at the grocer's on credit, and he was always as happy as a kid when his housekeeper was sick.

I thought of all the people who had helped us, while at

home they sat huddled over their stinking millions, had cast me out and gloated over their moral reasons.

My father was still pacing up and down behind his chair and moving his lips as he counted. I was on the point of telling him I didn't want his money, but somehow, so it seemed to me, I had a right to get something from him, and with one solitary mark in my pocket I didn't want to indulge in heroics which I would be sorry for later. I really did need some money, urgently, and he hadn't given me a pfennig since I had left home. Leo had given us his entire pocket money, Anna sometimes sent us a loaf of home-made white bread, and later on even Grandfather sent us money now and again, "crossed" non-negotiable checks for fifteen, twenty marks, and once, for some reason which I never discovered, twenty-two marks. We always had a terrible time with these checks: our landlady had no bank account, nor did Heinrich, he knew no more about non-negotiable checks than we did. The first check he simply paid into the welfare account of his parish, had the bank explain to him the purpose and nature of a crossed check, then he went to his priest and asked him for a cash check for fifteen marks—but the priest nearly exploded with anger. He told Heinrich he couldn't give him a cash check because he would have to state what it was for, and a welfare account was a ticklish thing, it was always inspected, and if he wrote: "check to accommodate Chaplain Behlen, equal in value to private check," he would get into trouble, for after all a parish welfare was not a place for exchanging crossed checks "of dubious origin." He would only be able to declare the crossed check as a donation for a definite purpose, as direct support from Schnier for Schnier, and pay me the corresponding amount in cash as an allowance from the welfare. That could be done, although it was not really quite proper. It took altogether ten days for us to actually get the fifteen marks, for of course Heinrich had a thousand other things to do, he couldn't devote himself exclusively to the cashing of my crossed check. I got a shock every time after that when I received a crossed check from Grandfather. It was maddening, it was money and yet it was not money, and it was never what we really needed: ready money. Finally Heinrich opened a bank account himself so he could give us cash checks for the non-negotiable checks, but he was often away for three or four days, once he was away on vacation for three weeks when the check for twenty-two marks arrived, and I finally got hold of the only person in Cologne I had known as a boy, Edgar Wieneken, who held some kind of official position—cultural adviser with the Socialist Party, I think. I found his address in the phone book, but didn't have a nickel to call him up, and walked from Cologne-Ehrenfeld to Cologne-Kalk, found he wasn't home, waited till eleven at night at the front door because his landlady refused to let me into his room. He lived near a very large and very dark church in the Engels-strasse (I still don't know whether he felt obliged to live in the Engels-strasse because he belonged to the Socialist Party). I was completely worn out, dead tired, hungry, was out of cigarettes, and knew Marie was sitting at home worrying. And Cologne-Kalk, the Engels-strasse, the chemical factory close by—the surroundings were not salutary for victims of melancholia. I finally went into a bakery and asked the woman behind the counter if I could have a roll. She was young, but nothing to look at. I waited till the shop was empty for a moment, went in quickly and said without wishing her good evening: "Could you spare me a roll?" I was afraid someone might come in—she looked at me, her thin, sullen mouth first got even thinner, then became rounder and fuller, then without a word she put three rolls and a piece of cake into a bag and gave it to me. I don't believe I even said thank you as I took the bag and quickly went out of the shop. I sat down on the doorstep of the house where Edgar lived, ate the rolls and the cake and from time to time felt for the crossed check for twenty-two marks in my pocket. Twenty-two marks was an odd figure, I racked my brains as to how it could have been arrived at, maybe it was the remains of some account, maybe it was even supposed to be a joke, probably it was simply accidental, but the strange thing was that the figure 22 as well as the words twenty-two were on the check, and Grandfather must surely have had something in mind when he wrote them. I never discovered what it was. Later I found out I had only waited an hour and a half for Edgar in Kalk in the Engels-strasse: it seemed like an eternity of gloom: the dark house fronts, the vapors from the chemical factory. Edgar was glad to see me again. He beamed, patted me on the shoulder, took me up to his room where a large photo of Brecht was hanging on the wall, beneath it a guitar and a lot of pocket books on a home-made shelf. I heard him scolding his landlady outside because she had not let me in, then he came back with some schnapps, told me gleefully he had just won a battle in the theater committee against the "scruffy bastards of the CDU" and asked me to tell him everything that had happened to me since we had last met. As boys we had been friends for years. His father was in charge of a swimming pool, later grounds supervisor at the stadium near our house. I asked him to forego the story of my life, brought him up to date briefly on my situation, and asked if he wouldn't cash the check for me. He was terribly nice, understood completely, at once gave me thirty marks in cash, didn't want to accept the check at all, but I implored him to take it. I believe I almost wept as I begged him please to take the check. He took it, a bit offended, and I invited him to come and see us and watch me practicing. He came with me as far as the streetcar stop by the Kalk post office, but when I saw a free taxi on the other side of the square I ran across, got in, and just caught sight of Edgar's large face, startled, hurt, pale. It was the first time I had indulged in a taxi, and if ever a man deserved a taxi it was me that evening. I couldn't have borne to go trundling right across Cologne by streetcar and having to wait another hour before I saw Marie again. The taxi cost nearly eight marks. I gave the driver a fifty pfennig tip and ran upstairs in our boarding house. Marie fell on my neck in tears, and I was crying too. We had both been so frightened, had been separated for ages, we were too desperate to kiss, we just whispered over and over again that we would never, never be separated again, "until death do us part," whispered Marie. Then Marie "got ready," as she called it, made up her face, put on some lipstick, and we went to one of the booths on the Venlo-strasse, we each had two portions of goulash, bought ourselves a bottle of red wine and went home.

Edgar never quite forgave me for taking that taxi. Afterwards we saw him quite often, and he even helped

146

us out again with money when Marie had the miscarriage. Nor did he ever mention the taxi, but a feeling of suspicion remained with him which has never been erased.

"For God's sake," said my father loudly and at a new pitch which I had never heard him use before, "speak up clearly and open your eyes. You're not going to fool me with that trick again."

I opened my eyes and looked at him. He was angry.

"Have I been talking?" I asked.

"Yes," he said, "you've been mumbling to yourself, but the only word I understood was now and again stinking millions."

"That's all you can understand and all you're meant to understand."

"And crossed check I understood," he said.

"Yes, yes," I said, "come on, sit down again and tell me what you have had in mind—as monthly support for a year."

I went over to him, took him gently by the shoulder and pressed him down into his chair. He got up at once and we stood face to face.

"I have been thinking the matter over very carefully," he said quietly, "if you will not agree to my terms of a sound, supervised training but want to work here. . . . I would say—well, I thought two hundred marks a month would do." I was certain he had meant to say two hundred and fifty or three hundred but at the last moment had said two hundred. He seemed shocked at the look on my face, he said more rapidly than was appropriate to his well-groomed exterior: "Genneholm was saying that asceticism was the basis of pantomime." I still said nothing. I just looked at him, with "empty eyes," like one of Kleist's marionettes. I was not even furious, only amazed, in a way which made what I had taken such pains to learn, to have empty eyes, my natural expression. He was upset, there were tiny beads of sweat on his upper lip. My first reaction was still neither rage nor bitterness nor even hatred; my empty eyes slowly filled with pity.

"Dad," I said gently, "two hundred marks is not nearly as little as you seem to believe. It's quite a nice sum, I won't argue with you about that, but I wonder if you know that asceticism is a luxury, anyway the asceticism

Genneholm has in mind; what he means is diet and not asceticism, plenty of lean meat and salad—the cheapest form of asceticism is starvation, but a starving clown— oh well, it's better than a drunk one." I stepped back, it embarrassed me to stand so close to him that I could watch the beads of sweat on his lips getting bigger.

"Listen," I said, "let's stop discussing money and talk about something else, as befits gentlemen."

"But I really want to help you," he said desperately, "I'll be glad to let you have three hundred."

"I don't want to hear any more about money now," I said, "I just wanted to tell you what was the most extraordinary experience of our childhood."

"What was it then?" he asked and looked at me as if he were expecting a death sentence. He was probably thinking I would bring up the subject of his mistress, for whom he had built a villa in Godesberg.

"Don't get excited," I said, "you'll be surprised; the most extraordinary experience of our childhood was when we realized we never got enough grub at home."

He winced at the word grub, swallowed, then, with a bitter little laugh, asked: "You mean you never really had enough to eat?" "Exactly," I said quietly, "we never really had enough to eat, not at home anyway. To this day I don't know whether it was a matter of stinginess or principle, I would prefer to believe it was stinginess— but I wonder if you know what a child feels when he has spent the whole afternoon riding a bike, playing football, swimming in the Rhine?"

"I imagine he has an appetite," he said coolly.

"No," I said, "he is hungry. Damn it, all we knew as children was that we were rich, very rich—but of all this money we had nothing—not even enough to eat."

"Did you children ever lack for anything?"

"Yes," I said, "that's what I'm telling you: food—and pocket money too. Do you know what I was always hungry for as a child?"

"For heaven's sake," he said uneasily, "what?"

"Potatoes," I said. "But in those days Mother was already crazy about keeping slim—you know how she was always ahead of the times—and our place was always crawling with silly fools who all had different diet theories, unfortunately the potato didn't feature in a single one of

148

those diet theories. Sometimes the maids in the kitchen would cook themselves some, when you and Mother were out: potatoes in their jackets with butter, salt and onions, and sometimes they would wake us up and let us come down in our pajamas and eat as many potatoes as we liked on condition we never said a single word about it. Generally we went to Wienekens on Fridays, they always had potato salad then, and Mrs. Wieneken piled our plates up extra high. And then at home there was always too little bread in the bread basket, a measly piddling affair our bread was, that damned crisp-bread, or a few slices which "for health reasons" were stale—when I went to Wienekens and Edgar had just been to get some bread, his mother would hold the loaf firmly against her chest with her left hand and with her right hand cut off fresh slices which we caught in our hands and spread with jam."

My father nodded wearily, I held out the cigarettes to him, he took one, I lit it for him. I felt sorry for him. It must be terrible for a father to have his first real talk with a son who is almost twenty-eight. "There were hundreds of other things too," I said, "liquorice, for instance, and balloons, Mother regarded balloons as pure extravagance. She was right. They are pure extravagance—but we couldn't possibly have been extravagant enough to blow all your stinking millions sky-high in the form of balloons. And those cheap candies Mother had such clever and intimidating theories about, proving that they were absolute poison. But then, instead of giving us non-poisonous ones, she didn't give us any at all. At school they all wondered," I said softly, "why I was the only one who never grumbled about the food, ate it all up and found the meals wonderful."

"Well, then," he said feebly, "it had its good side after all." It did not sound very convincing and certainly not very happy, his remark.

"Oh," I said, "I have no doubts whatever as to the theoretical and educational value of an upbringing like that—but that's the point, it was all theory, education, psychology, chemistry—and a deadly grimness. At Wienekens I always knew when they had money, on Fridays, at Schniewinds and Holleraths, too, you could tell when there was money on the first or fifteenth of the month—

149

there was always something extra, everyone got an extra-thick slice of sausage, or some cake, and on Friday mornings Mrs. Wieneken always went to the hairdresser because in the late afternoon—well, you might say a sacrifice was offered up to Venus."

"What," exclaimed my father, "you don't mean. . . ." His color rose and he shook his head as he looked at me.

"Yes," I said, "I do mean that. Every Friday afternoon the kids were sent to the movies. Before that they were allowed to go and eat ice creams so that they would be out of the house for at least three and a half hours, when their mother got back from the hairdresser and their father came home with the pay envelope. You know, working class homes aren't all that big." "You mean to say," said my father, "you mean to tell me that you all knew why the children were sent to the cinema?"

"Of course we didn't know exactly," I said, "and most of it occurred to me later on when I thought about it—and it wasn't till much later that it dawned on me why Mrs. Wieneken always blushed so touchingly when we got back from the movies and had potato salad. Later on, when he took over the job at the stadium, it all changed —I suppose he was home more often. As a boy I merely noticed she was somehow embarrassed—and it wasn't till afterwards that I understood why. But in a flat consisting of one big room and a kitchen, and with three children—I don't suppose they had any alternative."

My father was so shocked that I was afraid he would think it in poor taste to bring up the subject of money again. For him our meeting had an element of high tragedy, but he was beginning to rather enjoy this tragedy, to find it attractive in a way, on a level of noble suffering, and then it would be hard to get him back to the three hundred marks a month he had offered me. With money it was like with "desires of the flesh." Nobody really talked about it, really thought about it, it was either—as Marie had said about the carnal desires of priests— "sublimated" or considered vulgar, never as the thing it was at the moment: food or a taxi, a packet of cigarettes or a room with bath.

My father was suffering, it was painful to watch. He turned toward the window, pulled out his handkerchief and dried a few tears. I had never seen that before: my

150

father crying and actually using his handkerchief. Every morning two clean handkerchiefs were laid out for him, and every evening he would throw them into the laundry hamper in the bathroom, slightly crumpled but not noticeably soiled. There had been times when my mother, trying to be economical because soap was scarce, had long arguments with him as to whether he couldn't carry around the handkerchiefs for at least two or three days. "All you do is carry them around with you anyway, and they are never really dirty—and there is such a thing as an obligation toward the nation." This was an allusion to the "war on waste." But Father—the only occasion I can recall—had put his foot down and insisted on getting his two clean handkerchiefs every morning. I had never seen a droplet or a speck of dust, anything, on him which would require him to wipe his nose. Now he was standing at the window and not only drying his tears but even wiping something as vulgar as sweat from his upper lip. I went out into the kitchen because he was still crying, and I even heard a sob or two. There are not many people you want to have around when you are crying, and it seemed to me that your own son, who you hardly know, would be the last person you would choose for company. As for me, I only knew one person who I could be with when I cried, Marie, and I didn't know whether Father's mistress was the kind of person he could have around when he was crying. I had only seen her once, she seemed sweet and pretty, and stupid in a nice way, but I had heard a lot about her. Our relatives had described her to us as grasping, but in our family everyone was considered grasping who was shameless enough to point out that now and again you have to eat, drink, and buy shoes. Anyone who maintains that cigarettes, hot baths, flowers, and schnapps are necessities has every chance of going down in history as being "recklessly extravagant." I imagine a mistress is quite expensive: she has to buy stockings, dresses, pay the rent and be constantly cheerful, which is only possible in a "stable financial situation," as Father would have put it. After all, when he went to her after those deathly boring board meetings, she had to be cheerful, smell nice, have been to the hairdresser. I couldn't imagine that she was grasping. Probably she was just expensive, and in our family that was the same as grasping. When Henkels the gardener, who sometimes helped out old Fuhrmann, suddenly pointed out with remarkable modesty that the minimum rate for casual labor had, "for the last three years, as a matter of fact," been higher than the wages he was getting from us, my mother gave a two-hour lecture in her shrill voice on the "grasping attitude of certain people." Once she gave our postman a thirty-five cent tip at New Year's and was indignant when next morning she found the thirty-five cents in the letterbox in an envelope on which the postman had written: "Madam, I haven't the heart to rob you." Of course she knew the right man in the Postmaster General's office and she complained to him at once about that "grasping, impertinent man."

In the kitchen I walked quickly around the coffee puddle, across the hall into the bathroom, pulled the stopper out of the bathtub, and it struck me that for the first time in years I had had a bath without singing at least the Litany of Loreto. I began quietly humming the Tantum Ergo while I rinsed off the remains of soapsuds from the sides of the emptying bathtub. I also tried it with the Litany of Loreto, I have always been fond of that Jewish girl Miriam and sometimes almost believed in her. But the Litany of Loreto was no help either, I suppose it really was too Catholic, and I was furious with Catholicism and the Catholics. I made up my mind to call up Heinrich Behlen and Karl Emonds. Since the terrible row Karl Emonds and I had had two years before, I hadn't spoken to him at all—and we had never written. He had treated me very badly for a stupid reason: when I had had to look after his youngest son, Gregor, who was a year old, while Karl and Sabina went to the movies and Marie was spending the evening with the "group," I had beaten up a raw egg in Gregor's milk. Sabina had told me I was to warm up the milk at ten, put it in the bottle and give it to Gregor, and because the child seemed so pale and fretful (he didn't even cry, he just whimpered pitifully), I thought a raw egg beaten up in the milk would do him good. While the milk was warming I carried him in my arms up and down in the kitchen and talked to him "There now! What's our little man going to have now, what are we going to give him then—a nice little egg" and so on, then broke the egg, beat it up in the mixer and poured it into Gregor's milk. Karl's other children were sound asleep, I was all alone in the kitchen with Gregor, and when I gave him the bottle it seemed to me he was thoroughly enjoying the egg in the milk. He smiled and fell asleep at once afterwards, without whimpering. When Karl came home from the movies he saw the egg shell in the kitchen, came into the living room where I was sitting with Sabina and said: "What a good idea, to make yourself an egg." I said I hadn't eaten the egg myself but had given it to Gregor—and a storm of abuse immediately broke loose. Sabina got positively hysterical and called me a "murderer," Karl shouted at me: "You tramp—you lecher," and that infuriated me so much that I called him a "frustrated pedagogue," picked up my coat and left in a rage. He called out after me onto the landing: "You irresponsible bum," and I shouted up to the landing: "You hysterical philistine, you miserable ass-whacker." I am really fond of children, I can handle them quite well too, especially babies, I can't imagine that an egg can be bad for a one-year-old child, but Karl calling me a "lecher" hurt me more than Sabina's "murderer." After all, one can make allowances and excuses for an overwrought mother, but Karl knew perfectly well I was not a lecher. Our relationship was strained in an idiotic kind of way because in his heart of hearts my "free mode of life" seemed "marvelous" to him, and in my heart of hearts I found his bourgeois existence attractive. I could never make him understand the almost deadly monotony of my life, the pedantic regularity of train journey, hotel, practice, performance, parchesi, and beer-drinking—and how the life he led, just because it was so bourgeois, appealed to me. And of course he, like everyone else, thought we had no children on purpose, Marie's miscarriages looked "suspicious" to him; he didn't know how badly we wanted children. In spite of all this I had sent him a telegram asking him to call me, but I wasn't going to ask him for a loan. By this time he had four children and had a hard time making ends meet.

I gave the bathtub one more rinse, went quietly out into the hall and glanced through the open living-room door. My father was standing by the table again and had stopped crying. With his red nose, his moist, fur-

rowed cheeks, he looked like any old man, shivering, surprisingly vacant and almost stupid. I poured him a small
cognac, took the glass over to him. He took it and drank.
The surprisingly stupid expression on his face was still
there, the way he emptied his glass, held it out to me
mutely, with a helpless imploring look in his eyes, had
something almost inane about it that I had never seen
in him before. He looked like someone who has lost interest in everything, everything, except thrillers, one particular wine, and stupid jokes. The crumpled damp handkerchief he had simply laid on the table, and this faux pas
—for him a terrible one—seemed deliberately disobedient
—like a naughty child who has been told a thousand
times one doesn't put handkerchiefs on the table. I
poured a little more cognac, he drank it and made a
gesture which I could only interpret as "Please get me
my coat." I did not respond. Somehow or other I had to
get him back on the subject of money. All I could think
of was to take my mark out of my pocket and juggle a
bit with the coin: I let it roll down my outstretched
right arm—then back the same way. His amusement at
this trick appeared somewhat forced. I threw the mark
into the air, almost up to the ceiling, caught it again
—but he merely repeated his gesture: "My coat, please."
I tossed the mark up again, caught it on the big toe of
my right foot and held it high up, almost under his
nose, but he only made a slight gesture of annoyance and
emitted a growling "That's enough now." With a shrug
I went into the hall, got his coat and hat from the
closet. He was already standing beside me, I helped him,
picked up his gloves, which had fallen out of his hat, and
handed them to him. He was close to tears again, made
some funny little movements with his nose and lips and
whispered: "Have you nothing nice to say to me?"

"Yes," I said quietly, "it was nice of you to put your
hand on my shoulder when those fools passed sentence
on me—and it was especially nice of you to save Mrs.
Wieneken's life when that imbecile of a major wanted
to have her shot."

"Well, well," he said, "I'd almost forgotten about all
that."

"The fact that you have forgotten it," I said, "is
especially nice—I haven't."

154

He looked at me and implored me dumbly not to say Henrietta's name, although I had meant to ask him why he had not been nice enough to forbid her to go on the school anti-aircraft outing. I nodded, and he understood: I would not mention Henrietta. No doubt he sat there during the board meetings, doodling little men on a sheet of paper and sometimes an H, and another H, maybe sometimes even her whole name: Henrietta. He was not to blame, only stupid in a way which excluded tragedy or perhaps was the basis for it. I didn't know. He was so distinguished and frail and silver-haired, he looked so kind and he hadn't even sent me a pittance when I was in Cologne with Marie. What was it that made this kind man, my father, so hard and so strong, why did he talk on the TV screen about social obligations, about national consciousness, about Germany, about Christianity even, which he admitted he didn't believe in, and, what was more, in such a way that you were forced to believe him? It could only be money, not the concrete kind you use to buy milk and take a taxi, keep a mistress and go to the movies—but money in the abstract. I was afraid of him, and he was afraid of me: we both knew we were not realists, and we both despised those who talked about "Realpolitik." There was much more to it than those idiots would ever understand. I read it in his eyes: he couldn't give his money to a clown who would do only one thing with it: spend it, the very opposite of what you were supposed to do with money. And I knew, even if he had given me a million, I would have spent it, and to spend money was in his eyes synonymous with wasting it.

While I was waiting in the kitchen and bathroom to let him cry by himself, I had been hoping he would be so deeply moved that he would give me a large lump sum, without the ridiculous conditions, but now I read it in his eyes, he couldn't. He was not a realist, and I wasn't either, and we both knew that the others in all their triteness were realists, stupid as puppets which touch their collars a thousand times without ever discovering the string they are dangling on.

I nodded again, to reassure him completely: I would mention neither money nor Henrietta, but I thought about her in a way which didn't seem right, I pictured her as she would be now: thirty-three, probably divorced from an industrialist. I couldn't imagine her being involved in all that nonsense, flirting and parties and "holding fast to Christianity," sitting around in committees and "being especially nice to the Socialists, otherwise they get even more complexes." I could only picture her as being desperate, doing something the realists would find outrageous because they have no imagination. Pouring a cocktail down the collar of one of the innumerable presidents, or ploughing her car into the Mercedes of one of the head hypocrites. What else could she have done if she hadn't been able to paint or make ashtrays on a potter's wheel? She would be bound to feel it, as I felt it, wherever there was life, this invisible wall where money ceased to be there to be spent, where it became inviolate and dwelled in tabernacles in the form of figures and columns.

I stepped aside for my father. He began to sweat again and I felt sorry for him. I hurried back into the living room and picked up the dirty handkerchief from the table and put it in his coat pocket. My mother could become very unpleasant if she found something missing when she checked the laundry once a month, she would accuse the maids of theft or carelessness.

"Shall I call a cab for you?" I asked.

"No," he said, "I'll walk a bit. Fuhrmann is waiting for me near the station." He walked past me, I opened the door, went with him to the elevator and pressed the button. I took my mark out of my pocket once more, laid it on my outstretched left hand and looked at it. My father looked away in disgust and shook his head. I thought he might at least get out his wallet and give me fifty or a hundred marks, but pain, noble sentiment and the realization of his tragic position had driven him up onto such a high level of sublimation that any thought of money was abhorrent to him, my attempts to remind him of it were sacrilege. I held open the elevator door for him, he embraced me, suddenly began to sniff, tittered and said: "You really do smell of coffee—what a pity, I would have so much liked to make you some decent coffee—I really can, you know." He released me, got into the elevator, and I saw him press the button inside and give a crafty little smile before the elevator began to move. I stood there for a minute and watched the figures light up: four, three, two, one—then the red light went out.

16

I felt like a fool as I went back into the apartment and shut the door. I should have accepted his offer to make me some coffee and kept him there for a bit. At the critical moment when he was serving the coffee, pouring it out, happy over his achievement, I ought to have said "Let's have the money" or "Hand over the money." At the critical moment one always has to be primitive, barbaric. Then one says: "You get half of Poland, we get half of Rumania—and how about it, would you like two thirds of Silesia or only half. You get four ministerial seats, we get the Piggyback Company." I had been a fool to give way to my mood and his instead of just grabbing his wallet. I should simply have brought up the subject of money and talked to him about it, about dead, abstract, tied-up money, which for a lot of people was a matter of life and death. "Money, money, money"—my mother was forever uttering this cry of dismay even when we asked her for thirty pfennigs to buy a copybook. Money, money, money. Love, love, love.

I went into the kitchen, cut myself some bread, spread butter on it, went into the living room and dialed Bella Brosen's number. I only hoped that in his present state—shivering with emotion—my father, rather than go home, would go to his mistress. She looked as if she would put him to bed, fix him a hot-water bottle, and feed him honey and milk. Mother had a damnable way, when one was feeling lousy, of carrying on about pulling oneself together and will power, and for some time now she has regarded cold water as "the only remedy."

"Mrs. Brosen speaking," she said, and I was glad to note she did not emit any odor. She had a wonderful voice, contralto, warm and affectionate.

I said: "This is Schnier—Hans—remember?"

"Remember," she said warmly, "and how—and how I feel for you." I didn't know what she was talking about, not until she went on. "You must bear in mind," she said, "that all critics are silly, vain, and egotistical."

I sighed. "If only I could believe that," I said, "I would feel a lot better."

"Then just believe it," she said, "just believe. You can't imagine how iron determination to believe something helps."

"And if someone says I'm good, what do I do then?"

"Oh," she laughed and turned the Oh into a charming coloratura, "then you simply believe that he happens to have had an attack of honesty and has forgotten his egotism."

I laughed. I didn't know whether I should address her as Bella or Mrs. Brosen. We didn't know one another at all, and there is no book where you can look up to see how you address your father's mistress. I finally said "Madame Bella," although this artistic form seemed in the highest degree inane. "Madame Bella," I said, "I am in a fix. Father was here, we talked about all sorts of things, and I never got around to the subject of money—and yet," I could tell she was blushing, I felt she was very conscientious, I believed that her relationship with Father really had something to do with "true love," and that "money matters" embarrassed her. "Please listen," I said, "forget everything that's going through your mind now, don't feel embarrassed, all I ask is, if Father should talk to you about me—I mean, perhaps you could bring him round to the idea that I'm desperate for money. Cash. Right away, I'm flat broke. Are you listening?"

"Yes," she said, so softly that I was scared. Then I could hear her sniffling.

"You must think I'm a bad woman, Hans," she said, she was crying openly now, "a mercenary creature, like so many others. You *must* think that's what I'm like. Oh."

159

"Not in the least," I said raising my voice, "I never thought that of you—really I didn't." I was afraid she might start talking about her soul and my father's soul, to judge by her violent sobbing she was pretty sentimental, and it was even possible she might bring up Marie. "Honestly," I said, not quite convinced, for the fact that she tried to make the mercenary creatures so contemptible made me a bit suspicious, "honestly," I said, "I have always been convinced of your fine feelings and I have never thought badly of you." That was true. "And besides," I would have liked to say her name again, but couldn't bring myself to utter that ghastly Bella, "besides I am almost thirty. Are you still there?"

"Yes," she sighed, and sobbed away there in Godesberg as if she were in the confessional.

"Just try and get it across to him that I need money."

"I think," she said feebly, "it would be wrong to talk to him directly about it. Anything to do with his family, you understand, is taboo for us—but there is another way." I was silent. Her sobs had subsided to modest sniffs. "Now and again he gives me money for needy colleagues," she said, "he lets me do as I like with it, and—don't you think it would be a good idea if I gave you the benefit of these small sums as a temporarily needy colleague?" "I really am a needy colleague, not just temporarily but for the next six months at least. But would you mind telling me what you mean by small sums?"

She cleared her throat, emitted another Oh, but without coloratura this time, and said: "They are usually donations in actual emergency cases, when someone dies or gets sick, or a woman has a baby—what I mean is, they're not permanent support but kind of special allowances."

"How much?" I asked. She hesitated, and I tried to picture her. I had seen her once five years ago, when Marie managed to drag me to an opera. Madame Brosen had sung the role of a peasant girl who had been seduced by a count, and I had been surprised at Father's taste. She was quite a sturdy person, of medium height, obviously blonde and with the required heaving bosom, who, leaning against a cottage or a farm wagon, finally on a hay fork, sang of simple emotions in a fine powerful voice.

"Hullo?" I called, "hullo?"

"Oh," she said, and she managed another coloratura, though a weak one this time. "Your question is so direct."

"It's in keeping with my situation." I said. I was getting panicky. The longer she remained silent, the smaller would be the amount she named.

"Well," she said at last, "the amounts vary between ten and, say, thirty marks."

"And suppose you were to invent a colleague who has got into an exceptionally difficult situation: let's say, has had a serious accident and can do with an allowance of a hundred marks or so for a few months?"

"My dear Hans," she said lowering her voice, "you don't expect me to cheat, do you?"

"No," I said, "I really have had an accident—and anyway aren't we colleagues? Artistes?"

"I'll try," she said, "but I don't know whether he'll bite."

"What?" I exclaimed.

"I don't know whether I'll succeed in putting it to him in such a way that he's convinced. I haven't got much imagination."

She didn't have to tell me that, I was beginning to believe she was the silliest female I had ever come across.

"How would it be then," I said, "if you tried to get me a booking, at the theater here—small roles, of course, I am good at bit parts."

"No, no, my dear boy," she said, "I don't feel comfortable as it is, being mixed up in this conspiracy."

"All right then," I said, "I just want you to know that small sums are welcome too. Goodbye and thanks." I hung up before she could say any more. I had a feeling that this source would yield nothing. She was too stupid. The way she had said bite had made me suspicious. It was not impossible that she simply pocketed these "donations for needy colleagues." I felt sorry for my father, I would have liked him to have a pretty and intelligent mistress. I still regretted not having given him the chance to make me some coffee. That stupid hussy would probably smile, secretly shake her head like a frustrated schoolteacher, if he went into the kitchen to make coffee, and then she would be all false smiles and

161

praise the coffee, as if he were a dog fetching a stone. I was furious when I left the phone and went to the window, opened it and looked out onto the street. I was afraid that one day I might have to take up Sommerwild's offer. All of a sudden I took my mark out of my pocket, threw it down into the street and regretted it the same instant, I looked, didn't see it, but thought I heard it fall onto the roof of a passing streetcar. I picked up the slice of bread and butter from the table, ate it, while I looked out onto the street. It was nearly eight o'clock, I had been in Bonn for nearly two hours, had talked on the phone with six so-called friends, spoken to my mother and father, and instead of having one mark more than when I arrived I had one less. I would have liked to go down to pick up the coin from the street, but it was getting on for half-past eight, Leo might call up or arrive any minute.

Marie was doing all right, she was in Rome now, in the bosom of her church, and was wondering what to wear for an audience with the Pope. Züpfner would get hold of a photo of Jacqueline Kennedy for her, would have to buy her a Spanish mantilla and a veil, for strictly speaking Marie was now almost a kind of "first lady" of German Catholicism. I made up my mind to go to Rome and request an audience with the Pope. There was something of a wise old clown about him too, and after all the figure of Harlequin had originated in Bergamo; I would find out for sure from Genneholm, who knew everything. I would explain to the Pope that my marriage with Marie had actually broken up over the question of the civil ceremony, and I would ask him to regard me as a kind of opposite number to Henry the Eighth: he had been polygamous and a believer, I was monogamous and an unbeliever. I would tell him how conceited and mean "leading" German Catholics are, and that he shouldn't let himself be duped. I would do a few turns for him, nice light little things like Going to School and Returning from School, but not the one called Cardinal; that would hurt his feelings, because he had once been a cardinal after all—and he was the last person I wanted to hurt.

Time and again I become the prey of my imagination: I pictured my audience with the Pope so minutely, saw myself kneel down and as an unbeliever ask his blessing, I saw the Swiss Guards at the door and some benevolent, only slightly disgusted smiling Monsignore in attendance—that I almost believed I had already been to see the Pope. I would be tempted to tell Leo that I had been to see the Pope and had been granted an audience. During those minutes I *was* with the Pope, saw his smile and heard his wonderful peasant's voice, told him how the local buffoon of Bergamo had become Harlequin. Leo is very strict in such things, he is always calling me a liar. It always infuriated Leo when I saw him and asked: "Do you remember how we sawed through that wood together?" He exclaims: "But we *didn't* saw through any wood together." In a very unimportant, ridiculous way, he is right. Leo was six or seven, I was eight or nine, when he came across a chunk of wood in the stables, the remains of a fence post, he also found a rusty saw in the stables and asked me to saw through the fence post with him. I asked him why on earth he wanted to saw through such a silly chunk of wood; he couldn't give any reason, he just wanted to saw; it seemed utterly senseless to me, and Leo cried for half an hour—and much later, not till ten years later, when we were discussing Lessing in our German literature class with Father Wunibald, suddenly in the middle of the class and à propos of nothing at all I realized what Leo had wanted: he just wanted to saw, at that particular moment when he felt the urge, to saw with me. I suddenly understood him, after ten years, and experienced his joy, his anticipation, his excitement, everything that had moved him, so intensely that in the middle of the lesson I began making sawing movements. I saw Leo's face opposite me, flushed with pleasure, I pushed the rusty saw toward him, he pushed it back—till Father Wunibald suddenly caught me by the hair and "brought me to my senses." Since then I have really sawed that wood with Leo—he can't understand it. He is a realist. Today he no longer understands that something which seems stupid must be done immediately. Even Mother sometimes has fleeting impulses; to play cards by the fire, to make apple-blossom tea in the kitchen with her own hands. All of a sudden she must long to sit at the well-polished mahogany table and play cards, be a happy family. But whenever she feels this urge, none of us has the urge; there used to be scenes, Misunderstood-Mother stuff, then she would insist on our duty to be obedient, the Fourth Commandment, but then she would realize it would be a strange kind of pleasure to play cards with children who join in *only* from a sense of duty—and she would retire weeping to her room. Sometimes she would try it with bribes, promise to produce something "specially good" to drink or eat—and it would become one of those tearful evenings again of which Mother supplied us with so many. She didn't know the reason we all so firmly refused was because the seven of hearts was still in the pack and reminded us of Henrietta every time we played cards, but no one told her, and later on, when I remembered her vain efforts to play the happy family at the fireside I played cards with her alone in my mind's eye, although card games which two can play are dull. I really *did* play with her, "Sixty-six" and "Gin Rummy," I drank apple-blossom tea, with honey in it even, Mother—an admonitory forefinger coyly raised—even gave me a cigarette, and somewhere in the background Leo was playing his Études, while we all knew, even the maid, that Father was with "that woman." Somehow or other Marie must have found out about these "lies," for she always looked at me doubtfully when I told her anything, and yet I really *did* see that boy in Osnabrück. Sometimes it happens to me the other way round: that something I really *did* experience seems to me untrue and not real. Like the fact that I went from Cologne to Bonn to talk to Marie's youth group about the Virgin Mary. Those things which other people call non-fiction seem very fictitious to me.

17

I stepped back from the window, gave up hope for my mark down there in the dirt, went into the kitchen to fix myself another slice of bread and butter. There was not much left to eat: a can of beans, a can of plums (I don't like plums, but Monika couldn't know that), half a loaf, half a bottle of milk, about a quarter of a pound of coffee, five eggs, three slices of bacon, and a tube of mustard. In the box on the living-room table there were four cigarettes left. I felt so miserable that I gave up hope of ever being able to practice again. My knee was so swollen that my trouser leg was beginning to feel tight, my headache was so bad that it was almost unearthly: a steady piercing pain, in my soul it was blacker than ever, then the "desires of the flesh"—and Marie was in Rome. I needed her, her skin, her hands on my chest. I have, as Sommerwild once put it, "a lively and genuine relationship to physical beauty," and I like having pretty women around, like my neighbor, Mrs. Grebsel, but I don't feel any "desires of the flesh" toward these women, and most women are hurt by this, although, if I did feel any and attempted to satsify it, they would call for the police. It is a complicated and grim business, this carnal desire, for men who are not monogamous it is probably a never-ending torture, for the monogamous ones like me it means a constant compulsion to latent discourtesy, most women are somehow hurt if they do not sense what they know as Eros. Even Mrs. Blothert, respectable, devout, was always slightly offended. Sometimes I can even understand the sex-fiends the newspapers talk about so much, and the thought that there is something called "marital duty" makes me break out in a cold sweat. There must be something monstrous about these marriages if a woman is contractually obligated by state and church to do this thing. One can't dictate compassion, after all. I wanted to try and talk to the Pope about this too. I am sure he is misinformed. I buttered another slice of bread, went into the hall and from my coat pocket took the evening paper I had bought on the platform in Cologne. Sometimes the evening paper is a help: it makes me feel as empty as television. I turned over the pages, glanced at the headlines, till I discovered an item which made me laugh. Federal Cross of Merit for Dr. Herbert Kalick. Kalick was the boy who had denounced me for being a defeatist and who during the trial had insisted on being ruthless, ruthless. In those days he had had the brilliant idea of mobilizing the orphanage for the final battle. I knew he had meanwhile become a big shot. It said in the paper that he had been awarded the Federal Cross of Merit for "his services in spreading democratic ideas among the young." Two years ago he had invited me over for a reconciliation. Was I supposed to forgive him for the fact that Georg, the orphan, had been killed while practicing with a bazooka—or that he had denounced me, age ten, for being a defeatist, and had insisted on being ruthless, ruthless? Marie felt you couldn't turn down an invitation to bury the hatchet, and we bought some flowers and went. He had an attractive house, amost in the Eifel Mountains, an attractive wife and one child whom they both proudly called their "offspring." His wife has that kind of attractiveness that makes you wonder whether she is alive or merely wound up. The whole time I sat next to her I was tempted to grasp her by her arms or by her shoulders, or by her legs, to make sure she wasn't a doll. Her entire contribution to the conversation consisted of two expressions: "Oh, how sweet" and "Oh, how awful." I found her boring at first, but then became fascinated and told her all sorts of things, the way one throws coins into an automat—just to see how she would react. When I told her my grandmother had just died—which wasn't true because my grandmother had died twelve years ago—she said: "Oh, how awful," and I feel that, when someone dies, you can say a lot of silly things, but "Oh, how awful" is not one of them. Then I told her someone called Humeloh (who didn't exist, whom I quickly invented so as to throw something positive into the automat) had just been awarded an honorary degree, she said: "Oh, how sweet." When I then told her that my brother Leo had converted, she hesitated a moment— and this hesitation seemed almost like a sign of life; she looked at me with her great big vacant doll's eyes to see which category this event belonged to as far as I was concerned, then said: "Awful, isn't it?"; I had at least succeeded in squeezing a variation out of her. I suggested she might as well just leave off the two Ohs, and simply say sweet and awful; she giggled, helped me to some more asparagus and then said: "Oh, how sweet." Finally during that evening we met the "offspring," a boy of five, who could have appeared on a TV commercial just as he was. This silly toothbrushing business, goodnight Daddy, goodnight Mummy, one handshake for Marie, one for me. I was surprised that commercial television had not discovered him yet. Later, when we were having coffee and cognac by the fire, Herbert spoke of the great times we were living in. Then he brought out some champagne and became emotional. He asked my forgiveness, even knelt down to ask me for what he called a "secularized absolution"—and I was on the point of kicking his behind, but instead I took a cheese knife from the table and solemnly dubbed him a democrat. His wife exclaimed: "Oh, how sweet," and when Herbert, much touched, had sat down again, I gave a lecture on the Jewish Yankees. I said that at one time it had been believed that the name Schnier, my name, had something to do with the snitch, but that it had been proved it was derived from Schneider, Schnieder, not from snitch, and that I was neither a Jew nor a Yankee, although—and then suddenly I punched Herbert in the nose, because I remembered that he had forced one of our classmates, Götz Buchel, to produce proof of his Aryan descent, and Götz had got into trouble because his mother was Italian, from a village in southern Italy— and to find out anything about *her* mother down there which would have any resemblance whatever to a proof of Aryan descent turned out to be impossible, especially as the village where Götz's mother was born had by then already been occupied by the Jewish Yankees. Those were trying, dangerous weeks for Mrs. Buchel and Götz, till Götz's teacher had the idea of getting an opinion from one of those ridiculous race experts at Bonn University. He established that Götz was "pure, hundred per cent pure Mediterranean," but then Herbert Kalick started some nonsense about all Italians being traitors, and till the end of the war Götz never knew a moment's peace. This all came back to me while I was trying to give the lecture about the Jewish Yankees—and I simply hit Herbert Kalick right in the face, threw my champagne glass into the fire, and the cheese knife after it, and pulled Marie after me by the arm, out. We couldn't get a taxi out there and had to walk, quite a way, till we got to the bus station. Marie was crying and kept saying it had been un-Christian and inhuman of me, but I said I wasn't a Christian and my confessional wasn't open yet. She also asked me if I had doubts about his, Herbert's, turning into a democrat, and I said, "No, no, no doubts at all—on the contrary—but I just don't like him and never will."

I opened the phone book and looked up Kalick's number. I was in the right mood to talk to him over the phone. I recalled having met him once afterwards at one of my parents' At Homes, he had looked at me beseechingly and shaken his head, while he was talking to a rabbi about "Jewish spirituality." I felt sorry for the rabbi. He was a very old man, with a white beard and very kind, and innocent in a way that worried me. Of course Herbert told everyone he met that he had been a Nazi and an anti-Semite, but that "history had opened his eyes." And yet the very day before the Americans marched into Bonn he had been practicing with the boys in our grounds and had told them: "The first Jewish swine you see, let him have it." What upset me about these At Homes of my mother's was the innocence of the returned emigrants. They were so moved by all the remorse and loud protestations of democracy that they were forever embracing and radiating good fellowship. They failed to grasp that the secret of the terror lay in the little things. To regret

168

big things is child's play: political errors, adultery, murder, anti-Semitism—but who forgives, who understands, the little things? The way Brühl and Herbert Kalick had looked at my father when he put his hand on my shoulder, and the way Herbert Kalick, beside himself with rage, banged with his fist on our table, looked at me with his stony eyes and said: "We've got to be ruthless, ruthless," or the way he grabbed Götz Buchel by the collar, stood him in front of the class, although the teacher protested mildly, and said: "Look at him—if that isn't a Jew!" I remember too many moments, too many details, tiny little things—and Herbert's eyes haven't changed. I was afraid, when I saw him standing there with the old, rather foolish rabbi, who was so full of the spirit of reconciliation, allowed Herbert to bring him a cocktail and listened to his drivel about Jewish spirituality. Another thing the emigrants don't know is that not many Nazis were sent to the front, most of those who fell were the others, Hubert Knieps, who lived next door to the Wienekens, and Günther Cremer, the baker's son, although they were Hitler Youth leaders they were sent to the front because they "didn't toe the line" and would have nothing to do with all that disgusting snooping. Kalick would never have been sent to the front, he toed the line then the way he toes the line today, a born conformist. The whole thing was quite different from the way the emigrants see it. Of course they can only think in terms of guilty, not guilty—Nazis, non-Nazis. The district leader Kierenhahn sometimes came to the shop of Marie's father, simply took a packet of cigarettes from the shelf without putting down either coupons or money, lit a cigarette, sat down on the counter opposite Marie's father and said: "Well, Martin, how about our putting you in a nice little concentration camp, one that's not too grim?" Then Marie's father would say: "Once a swine always a swine, and you always were one." They had known each other since they were six years old. Kierenhahn would get mad and say: "Don't go too far, Martin, don't overdo it." Marie's father would say: "I'll go even further: get out of here." Kierenhahn would say: "I'll see to it that you're sent to one of the bad concentration camps, not one of the nice ones." That's how it went, back and forth, and Marie's father would have been taken away if the Gauleiter had not held his "protecting hand" over him, for some reason we never discovered. Needless to say he didn't hold his protecting hand over everyone, not over Marx the leather merchant and Krupe the Communist. They were murdered. And the Gauleiter is doing all right today, he has his construction business. When Marie ran into him one day he said he "couldn't complain." Marie's father used to say to me: "The only way you can gauge how terrible that Nazi business was is by realizing that I actually owe my life to a swine like that Gauleiter, and not only that, I have to confirm in writing that I owe it to him."

By now I had found Kalick's number, but hesitated to dial it. I remembered that tomorrow was Mother's At Home day. I could go over there and, at my parents' expense, at least fill my pockets with cigarettes and salted almonds, take along a bag for olives, another for cheese biscuits, then go round with a hat and collect for "a needy member of the family." I had done that once when I was fifteen, collected "for a special purpose" and got nearly a hundred marks. My conscience didn't bother me when I used the money for myself, and if I collected tomorrow "for a needy member of the family" I wouldn't even be lying: I was a needy member of the family—and afterwards I could also go out into the kitchen, weep on Anna's bosom and pick up a few ends of sausage. All those idiots gathered together at my mother's would say my performance was a glorious joke, my mother herself would have to let it pass as a joke with a sour smile —and no one would know it was in deadly earnest. These people understand nothing. They all know, of course, that a clown has to be melancholy in order to be a good clown, but the fact that melancholy is for him a deadly serious business, that they don't grasp. At Mother's At Home I would meet them all: Sommerwild and Kalick, liberals and social democrats, six different varieties of president, even ban-the-bomb people (my mother had once been a ban-the-bomb campaigner for three days, but then when a president of something or other explained to her that a consistent ban-the-bomb policy would lead to a drastic fall in the stock market, she dashed at once—literally that minute—to the phone, called up the committee, and "dissociated" herself.) I would—but not till the end, when
170

I had already gone round with my hat, publicly punch Kalick in the nose, call Sommerwild a popish hypocrite and accuse the other members of the executive committee of German Catholicism of inciting to lechery and adultery. I took my finger off the dial and did not call Kalick. I had only wanted to ask him whether he had lived down his past by now, whether his relationship to power was still all right, and whether he could enlighten me about Jewish spirituality. Kalick had once given a talk at a Hitler Youth meeting entitled "Machiavelli, or the Attempt to Achieve a Relationship to Power." It didn't make much sense to me, all I understood was Kalick's "frank affirmation of power, which we see clearly expressed here," but from the faces of the other Hitler Youth leaders present I could tell that even for them this speech went too far. As it was, Kalick hardly spoke about Machiavelli, only about Kalick, and the expression of the other leaders showed that they regarded this talk as a public scandal. There are fellows like that, you read a lot about them in the papers: scandalizers. Kalick was nothing but a political scandalizer, and wherever he appeared he left scandalized people behind him.

I was looking forward to the At Home. At last I would benefit from my parents' money: olives and salted almonds, cigarettes—I would pocket cigars by the bundle and sell them at a discount, I would rip the decoration off Kalick's chest and hit him in the face. Compared with him, even my mother seemed human. The last time I ran across him, in the cloakroom at my parents' house, he had looked at me sadly and said: "For every man there is a chance, Christians call it grace." I didn't answer. After all, I wasn't a Christian. I recalled that during that lecture he had spoken of the "Eros of cruelty" and of the Machiavellian aspect of sex. When I thought of his sexual Machiavellianism I felt sorry for the whores he went to, the way I felt sorry for the wives who were contractually obligated to some fiend. I thought of the countless pretty girls whose fate it was to do the thing without wanting to, either for money with types like Kalick or with a husband without getting paid for it.

18

Instead of Kalick's number I dialed the number of the place where Leo lives. It was about time they finished dinner and their sex-tranquillizing salads. I was glad when the same voice came to the phone again. He was smoking a cigar now, and the smell of cabbage was less pronounced. "Schnier speaking," I said, "remember?"

He laughed. "Of course," he said, "I hope you didn't take me literally and really burn your St. Augustine."

"Certainly I did," I said. "Tore the thing up and fed the pages into the stove."

He was silent a moment. "You're joking," he said hoarsely.

"No," I said, "in matters like that I am consistent."

"For heaven's sake," he said, "didn't you grasp the dialectic in what I said?"

"No," I said, "I'm just a straightforward, honest, simple guy. How about my brother," I said, "when will they be good enough to have finished dinner?"

"The dessert has just been brought in," he said, "it won't be long now."

"What is there?" I asked.

"For dessert?"

"Yes."

"Actually I'm not supposed to say, but I'll tell you. Stewed plums with a dollop of cream. Looks quite nice. Do you like plums?"

"No," I said, "my dislike of plums is as inexplicable as it is insurmountable."

"You ought to read Hoberer's treatise on idiosyncrasy. All tied up with very, very early experiences—mostly pre-natal ones. Interesting. Hoberer has made a detailed study of eight hundred cases. Do you suffer from melancholia?"

"How did you know?"

"I can tell by your voice. You should pray and take a bath."

"I've just had a bath, and I can't pray," I said.

"I'm sorry about that," he said, "I'll make you a present of a new St. Augustine. Or Kierkegaard."

"I've got him," I said, "tell me, could you give my brother another message?"

"Certainly," he said.

"Tell him to bring me some money. As much as he can lay hands on."

He muttered something, then said out loud: "I'm just writing it down. Bring as much money as possible. By the way, you really ought to read Bonaventura. Magnificent—and don't be so contemptuous of my nineteenth century. Your voice sounds as if you don't think much of the nineteenth century."

"Right," I said, "I detest it."

"You're wrong," he said, "nonsense. Even the architecture wasn't as bad as it's made out to be." He laughed. "Wait till the end of the twentieth century before you detest the nineteenth. Do you mind if I have my dessert while I'm talking."

"Plums?" I asked.

"No," he said, he laughed thinly: "I am in disgrace and don't get the masters' food, only the servants'; today it's caramel pudding. By the way," he evidently already had a spoonful of pudding in his mouth, he swallowed, then went on with a titter, "by the way, I'm having my revenge. I phone long distance for hours with one of the brothers in Munich who used to be here. He used to be a pupil of Scheler's too. Sometimes I call Hamburg, the movie information service, or Berlin, the weather bureau, for revenge. You can't tell, you see, with direct dialing." He took another mouthful, tittered, then whispered: "The church is rich, stinking rich. It really does stink of money—like the corpse of a rich man. Poor corpses smell all right—did you know that?"

"No," I said. I felt my headache getting better and drew a red circle round the number of the place.

"You are an unbeliever, aren't you? Don't say no: I can tell from your voice that you are an unbeliever. Am I right?"

"Yes," I said.

"That makes no difference, no difference at all," he said, "there is a place in Isaiah which St. Paul even quotes in the Epistle to the Romans. Listen carefully: To whom he was not spoken of, they shall see: and they that have not heard shall understand." He gave a wicked little laugh. "Did you get it?"

"Yes," I said, with a sigh.

He raised his voice: "Good evening, sir, good evening," and hung up. His last words had sounded horribly servile.

I went over to the window and looked out at the clock on the corner. It was nearly half-past eight. It seemed to me they ate pretty copiously. I would have liked to talk to Leo, but almost the only thing I was concerned with by this time was the money he would lend me. The seriousness of my position gradually dawned on me. At times I don't know whether what I have experienced tangibly and realistically is true, or whether my real experience is the true one. I get it all mixed up. I could not have sworn I had seen the boy in Osnabrück, but I would have sworn I had sawed wood with Leo. I also couldn't have sworn whether or not I walked to Edgar Wieneken's place in Kalk to turn Grandfather's check for twenty-two marks into cash. The fact that I remember the details so vividly is no guarantee—the green blouse the woman at the bakery had on, the one who gave me the rolls, or the holes in the sock of the young workman who passed me while I was sitting on the doorstep waiting for Edgar. I was absolutely positive I had seen beads of sweat on Leo's upper lip when we sawed through the wood. I also recalled every detail of the night Marie had her first miscarriage in Cologne. Heinrich Behlen had managed to get me a few little performances to young audiences for twenty marks an evening. Marie usually went along, but that evening she stayed home as she wasn't feeling well, and when I got back later with the nineteen marks net profit in my pocket I found the room empty, saw the blood-stained sheet in the turned-back

174

bed and found the message on the chest of drawers: "Am in hospital. Nothing serious. Heinrich knows about it." I dashed off at once, was told by Heinrich's surly housekeeper what hospital Marie was in, hurried over there, but they wouldn't let me in, I first had to locate Heinrich in the hospital, have him called to the phone, before the nun at the gate would let me in. By this time it was half-past eleven at night, and when at last I got to Marie's room it was all over, she was lying there in bed, very pale, crying, beside her a nun reciting the Rosary. The nun calmly went on praying while I held Marie's hand, and in a quiet voice Heinrich tried to explain to her what would happen to the soul of the creature she had not been able to give birth to. Marie seemed firmly convinced that the child—that's what she called it—would never be able to go to Heaven because it had not been baptized. She kept saying it would remain in Purgatory, and that night I learned for the first time the terrible things Catholics are taught in their religious instruction. Heinrich was quite helpless in the face of Marie's fears, and the very fact that he was so helpless struck me as comforting. He spoke of God's mercy, which "must be greater than the more legalist thinking of the theologians." All this time the nun went on telling her beads. Marie—in religious matters she can be very obstinate —asked over and over again where the diagonal runs between law and mercy. I remember the word diagonal. Finally I went outside, I felt like an outcast, completely superfluous. I stood by a window in the corridor, smoked, looked beyond the opposite wall into an automobile graveyard. The wall was covered with election posters. Put Your Trust in the Socialist Party. Vote Christian Democratic Union. Evidently the idea was to depress any patients who might see the wall from their rooms with their indescribable stupidity. Put Your Trust in the SPD was positively inspired, almost literary compared to the fatuousness of simply having VOTE CDU printed on a poster. It was now almost two in the morning, and afterwards I quarrelled with Marie as to whether what I saw then really did happen or not. A stray dog appeared from the left, he sniffed at a lamppost, then at the SPD poster, at the CDU poster, and peed against the CDU poster and trotted on, along the street which over to

175

the right was completely dark. When we discussed that dreary night later on, Marie always denied that I had seen the dog, and if she allowed the dog to be "true," she denied that he had peed against the CDU poster. She said I had been so much under her father's influence that, without being aware of lying or distorting the truth, I would claim the dog had done his "mess" against the CDU poster even if it had been the SPD poster. And yet her father had had a much greater contempt for the SPD than for the CDU—and what I saw, I saw.

It was nearly five when I took Heinrich home and as we walked through Ehrenfeld he kept murmuring to me, pointing to the house doors: "These are my flock, these are my flock." His nagging housekeeper with the yellowy legs, her angry "what's the meaning of this?" I went home, secretly washed out the sheet in cold water in the bathroom.

Ehrenfeld, brown-coal trains, clothes lines, ban on baths, and sometimes at night the bags of garbage whizzing past our window, like dud bombs whose potential danger evaporated as they smacked the ground, or was barely sustained by the sound of an eggshell rolling away.

Heinrich got into trouble again with his priest on our account because he wanted some money from the Catholic welfare fund. I then went once more to Edgar Wieneken, and Leo sent us his watch to pawn, Edgar managed to scrape up something for us out of a workmen's welfare fund, and we were able at least to pay for the medicines, the taxi and half the doctor's fee.

I thought of Marie, the nun and her Rosary, the word diagonal, the dog, the election posters, the automobile graveyard—and of my cold hands after I had washed out the sheet—, and I really couldn't have sworn to all that. I wouldn't have liked to swear, either, that the man in Leo's hostel had told me he called up the weather bureau in Berlin so as to harm the church financially, and yet I had heard it, just as I had heard him smacking his lips and swallowing as he ate the caramel pudding.

19

Without giving it much thought or knowing what I wanted to say to her, I dialed Monika Silvs' number. The first ring was hardly over when she lifted the receiver and said: "Hullo."

Just the sound of her voice was enough to give me a lift. It is intelligent and firm. I said: "Hans speaking, I wanted . . ." but she interrupted me and said: "Oh, it's you . . ." It sounded neither unkind nor unpleasant, only it was obvious she had been expecting someone else's call, not mine. Maybe she was waiting for a call from a friend, from her mother—still, my feelings were hurt.

"I just wanted to thank you," I said, "for being so kind." I could distinctly smell her perfume, Cuir de Russie, or whatever it was, much too sophisticated for her.

"I am so sorry about everything," she said, "it must be terrible for you." I didn't know what she meant it: the Kostert review, which all Bonn had read apparently, or Marie's marriage, or both.

"Is there anything I can do?" she asked in a low voice.

"Yes," I said, "you could come over here and take pity on my soul, on my knee too, it's pretty badly swollen."

She was silent. I had expected her to say Yes at once, I dreaded the thought she might really come. But she only said: "Not today, I'm expecting a visitor." She should have told me who she was expecting, she might at least have said: man or woman. The word "visitor" depressed me. I said: "Oh well, perhaps tomorrow, I shall probably have to stay in bed for at least a week."

"Isn't there anything else I can do for you, I mean something I can do by phone." She said this in a voice which made me hope her visitor might be a woman after all.

"Yes," I said, "you could play me Chopin's Mazurka in B Flat, Opus 7."

She laughed and said: "What an idea!" At the sound of her voice I wavered for the first time in my monogamy. "I don't care much for Chopin," she said, "and I play him badly."

"Never mind," I said, "that doesn't matter. Have you got the music there?"

"It must be around somewhere," she said. "Just a moment." She put down the receiver on the table, and I could hear her walking across the room. It was a few minutes before she came back, and I remembered what Marie had once told me, that sometimes even saints had had girl friends. Only spiritually, of course, but still: whatever the thing had of a spiritual nature, these women had given them. I didn't even have that.

Monika picked up the receiver. "Yes," she said with a sigh, "I have the mazurkas here."

"Then please," I said, "play the B Flat Opus 7 Number 1."

"I haven't played Chopin for years, I would have to practice a bit."

"Maybe you don't want your visitor to hear you playing Chopin?"

"Oh," she said with a laugh, "I don't mind him listening."

"Sommerwild?" I asked, almost in a whisper, I heard her exclaim in surprise and I went on: "If it really is him, slam the piano lid down on his head."

"He hasn't deserved that," she said, "he's very fond of you."

"I know," I said, "I believe it too, but I wish I had the guts to kill him."

"I'll practice a bit and play you the mazurka," she said quickly. "I'll ring you."

"Yes," I said, but neither of us hung up. I could hear her breathing, for how long I don't know, but I could

178

hear it, then she hung up. I would have gone on holding the receiver for a long time just to hear her breathe. My God, at least a woman's breathing.

Although the beans I had eaten still lay heavily on my stomach and I was getting more and more depressed, I went into the kitchen, opened the second can of beans, tipped the contents into the saucepan in which I had heated the first lot, and lit the gas. I threw the filter paper with the coffee grounds into the garbage pail, took a clean filter, put four spoons of coffee into it, put the kettle on, and tried to tidy up the kitchen. I threw the floorcloth over the coffee puddle, the empty cans and eggshells into the pail. I hate untidy rooms, but I am incapable of tidying them up myself. I went into the living room, took the dirty glasses, put them into the sink in the kitchen. Now there was nothing untidy any more in the apartment, yet it didn't look tidy. Marie had such a clever, swift way of making a room look tidy, without doing anything to it which you could put your finger on. It must be something to do with her hands. The thought of Marie's hands—just the idea that she might put her hands on Züpfner's shoulders—heightened my depression to the point of despair. A woman can express or pretend so much with her hands that men's hands always seem to me like glued-on hunks of wood. Men's hands are handshaking hands, hitting hands, and of course shooting hands and signing hands. Shake, hit, shoot, sign non-negotiable checks—that's all men's hands can do, and, of course, work. Women's hands have almost ceased to be hands: whether they spread butter on bread or smooth hair away from the forehead. No theologian has ever thought of preaching about women's hands in the Gospels: Veronica, Mary Magdalene, Mary and Martha —all those women's hands in the Gospels which treated Christ tenderly. Instead they preach about laws, principles of order, art, state. In his private life, so to speak, Christ dealt almost entirely with women. Of course he needed men, because, like Kalick, they have a relationship to power, a sense of organization and all that crap. He needed men, the way you need packers to move house, for the heavy work, and Peter and John were so kind they could hardly be called men, while Paul was as virile as befitted a Roman. At home we had the Bible

179

read to us on every possible occasion, because our family swarms with pastors, but not one of them ever talked about the women in the Gospels, or about something as intangible as unjust Mammon. It was the same with the Catholics in the "group," they never wanted to talk about unjust Mammon, Kinkel and Sommerwild always smiled self-consciously when I mentioned it to them—as if they had caught Christ out in an embarrassing lapse, and Fredebeul spoke of the abuse this expression had suffered at the hands of history. What worried him about it was its "irrational aspect," as he put it. As if money were something rational. In Marie's hands even money lost its dubious quality, she had a wonderful way of handling it carelessly and yet at the same time very carefully. Since on principle I refused checks and other "means of payment," I always got my fee in cash, so we never needed to plan ahead for more than two or at most three days. She gave money to almost everyone who asked her for it, sometimes even to people who hadn't asked her for it at all but who, as it turned out during the conversation, were in need of money. Once she gave some money to a waiter in Göttingen to buy a winter coat for his son who was just starting school, and she was always paying the surcharge for helpless grandmothers who had strayed into first-class compartments on trains on their way to funerals. There is no end to the number of grandmothers who travel by train to the funerals of children, grandchildren, daughters-in-law and sons-in-law, and who—at times, of course, with a certain coy grandmotherly helplessness—stumble laboriously into a first-class compartment, weighed down with heavy suitcases and parcels stuffed with smoked sausage, bacon and cakes. Marie would then make me stash away the heavy suitcases and parcels in the luggage rack, although everyone in the compartment knew that Granma only had a second-class ticket in her purse. She would then go out into the corridor and "arrange" things with the conductor, before Granma's attention was drawn to her mistake. Marie always began by asking how far she was going and who had died—so she could pay the right surcharge. The grandmothers' comments usually consisted of some such gracious remark as: "Young people are not nearly as bad as they're made out to be," the fee took the form of hefty ham sandwiches. Especially between Dortmund and Hanover—so it always seemed—there are a great many grandmothers traveling every day to funerals. Marie was always ashamed of our traveling first class, and would have thought it intolerable if someone had been thrown out of our compartment because he only had a second-class ticket. She had unlimited patience when it came to listening to long-winded descriptions of family relationships and looking at photos of complete strangers. Once we spent two hours sitting next to an old peasant woman from Bückeburg who had twenty-three grandchildren and a photo of each one of them in her purse, and we listened to twenty-three life stories, looked at twenty-three photos of young men and young women who had all done well: municipal inspector in Münster, or married to a railway official, manager of a sawmill, and another one had "an important job in this party we always vote for—you know the one I mean," and of another one, who was in the army, she maintained he had "always played safe." Marie was always completely absorbed by these stories, she found them tremendously thrilling and talked about "real life," I found the element of repetition tiring. There were so many grandmothers between Dortmund and Hanover whose grandsons were railway officials and whose daughters-in-law died young because they "don't give birth to all their children, the women nowadays—that's what it is." Marie could be very kind and nice to old people who needed help; she was also constantly helping them to telephone. I once told her she ought to have worked at the Catholic Travelers' Aid, and she said, somewhat nettled: "And why not?" I hadn't meant it at all unkindly or disapprovingly. Now she really had landed in a kind of Catholic Travelers' Aid, I believe Züpfner married her to "save" her, and she married him to "save" him, and I was not sure if he would allow her to use his money to pay for express and first-class surcharges for grandmothers. He was certainly not stingy, but in a maddening way, like Leo, his needs were small. Not like St. Francis of Assisi, who could picture the needs of others though his own needs were small too. I found the idea of Marie now having Züpfner's money in her purse unbearable, like the word honeymoon and the idea that I might fight for Marie. Fight could only be meant in the physical sense. Even a clown out of training like me was better than either Züpfner or Sommerwild. Before they had even got into position I would have already done three somersaults, come at them from behind, got them down on their backs, and clamped a half-nelson on them. Or were they perhaps thinking of real brawls? I wouldn't put even such perverse variations of the Nibelung saga past them. Or did they mean it in a spiritual sense? I was not afraid of them, and why was Marie not allowed to answer my letters, which were after all a kind of spiritual challenge? They used words like wedding trip and honeymoon and dared call me obscene, those hypocrites. They should listen to what waiters and chambermaids tell each other about honeymoon couples. Every scruffy bastard in the train, in the hotel, wherever they show themselves, whispers "honeymoon" as they go by, and everyone knows they do the thing constantly. Who takes the sheets off the bed and washes them? When she puts her hands on Züpfner's shoulders, surely she must remember how I warmed her icy hands in my armpits.

Her hands, which she uses to open the front door, to straighten the covers on little Marie's bed upstairs, plug in the toaster downstairs in the kitchen, put the kettle on, take a cigarette out of the pack. This time she finds the maid's message on the refrigerator instead of the kitchen table. "Gone to movies. Back at ten." in the living room on the TV set, Züpfner's message. "Urgent call from F. Love and kisses, Heribert." Refrigerator instead of kitchen table, love and kisses instead of love. In the kitchen, while you are spreading lots of butter, lots of liver sausage on slices of toast, and putting three spoons of cocoa in the cup instead of two, you are aware for the first time of what a slimming diet does to your nerves, do you remember the way Mrs. Blothert exclaimed, when you took the second piece of cake: "But that's a total of over fifteen hundred calories, can you afford it?" The way the butcher looks at your waistline, a look that silently says: "No, you can't afford it." O Holy of Holies, Ca- ca- ca-, Thou -binet and -tholon! "Oh yes, you're beginning to put on weight." They are whispering it in the city, the city of whispers. Why this restlessness, this desire to be alone in the dark, in movies and churches, now in the dark living room with cocoa and toast. How did you reply to the young chap at the dance who shot out the question: "Tell me quickly what it is you love, Madam, quickly!" You will have told him the truth: "Children, confessionals, movies, Gregorian chant and clowns." "And not men, Madam?" "Oh, yes, one" you will have said. "Not men as such, they're stupid." "May I print that?" "Oh no, for goodness' sake, don't." If she could say one, why didn't she say which one? If you love one man, surely you can only mean your own, the one you are married to.

The maid returns. Key in the lock, open the door, close the door, key in the lock. Light on in the hall, off, on in the kitchen, open the refrigerator door, close it, light off in the kitchen. In the hall a gentle knock at the door. "Good night, Madam." "Good night. Has Marie been a good girl?" "Yes, very." Light off in the hall, footsteps going upstairs. ("She was sitting there all alone in the dark listening to church music.")

With those hands that washed out the sheets, that I warmed in my armpits, you touch everything: record player, record, lever, button, cup, bread, child's hair, child's bedclothes, the tennis racket. "Why don't you play tennis any more, I wonder?" Shrug of the shoulders. Don't feel like it, just don't feel like it. Tennis is so good for wives of politicians and prominent Catholics. No, no, the two terms are not quite that identical yet. It keeps you slim, supple and attractive. "And F. loves playing tennis with you. Don't you like him?" Yes, of course. There is something so sincere about him. Indeed there is, they say he got to be Minister with sheer "B.S. and push." Everyone says he is a scoundrel, a schemer, and yet his affection for Heribert is sincere: the corrupt and the brutal sometimes take to the conscientious and the incorruptible. How touchingly scrupulous it was, the way Heribert went about building his house: no special credits, no "assistance" from party and church friends with connections in the building trade. It was only because he wanted a "hillside lot" that he had to pay a bonus, which he considered actually corrupt. But it was precisely this hillside lot that proved to be troublesome. Anyone who builds on a hillside has the choice of a garden sloping up or a garden sloping down. Heribert chose to have it slope down—this turns out to be a disadvantage when little Marie starts to play ball, the ball is forever rolling down toward the neighbor's hedge, sometimes through it and into the rock garden, snaps off twigs, flowers, rolls over delicate, costly mosses, and necessitates awkward scenes of apology. "How can you possibly be cross with such an adorable little girl?" You can't. Silvery voices gaily pretend unconcern, mouths strained by slimming diets, tired throats with tense muscles, give out gaiety, where only a good row with sharp words flying would relieve the situation. Everything swallowed, covered up with false neighborly gaiety, till some time later on quiet summer evenings behind closed doors and drawn blinds fine china is thrown at embryo ghosts. "I wanted to have it—it was you who didn't." Fine china does not sound fine when it is thrown against the kitchen wall. Ambulance sirens scream up the hill. Snapped-off crocus, damaged moss, a child's hand rolls a child's ball into the rock garden, screaming sirens announce the undeclared war. Oh if only we had chosen a garden sloping up.

The phone ringing made me jump. I lifted the receiver, flushed, I had forgotten Monika Silvs. She said, "Hullo, Hans?" I said: "Yes," still didn't know why she was calling. It was only when she said: "You will be disappointed" that I remembered the mazurka. I couldn't go back now, couldn't say "I'd rather not," we had to go through with this terrible mazurka. I heard Monika put the receiver down on the piano, begin to play, she played extremely well, the tone was superb, but while she played I began to cry from sheer wretchedness. I should not have attempted to repeat that moment: when I came home from being with Marie, and Leo was playing the mazurka in the music room. You can't repeat moments or communicate them. That autumn evening, in our garden, when Edgar Wieneken did the hundred meters in 10.1. I clocked him myself, measured the distance for him myself, and he ran it that evening in 10.1. He was in top form, in just the right mood for it—but of course nobody believed us. It was our mistake to speak of it at all and so try to perpetuate the moment. We ought to have been content to know he really ran 10.1. Afterwards, of course, he kept running his usual 10.9 and 11.0 and nobody believed us, they laughed at us. It is bad enough to talk about such moments, to try and repeat them is suicide. It was a kind of suicide I was committing when I listened on the phone now to Monika playing the mazurka. There are certain ritual moments which contain their own repetition: the way Mrs. Wieneken cut the loaf—but I had tried to repeat this moment with Marie too by once asking her to cut the loaf the way Mrs. Wieneken had. The kitchen in a workman's home is not a hotel room, Marie was not Mrs. Wieneken—the knife slipped, she cut her left arm, this experience made us ill for three weeks. This is what sentimentality can lead to. One should leave moments alone, never repeat them.

I was so miserable I couldn't even cry any more when Monika came to the end of the mazurka. She must have sensed it. When she came to the phone all she said, in a low voice, was: "There, you see." I said: "I am to blame —not you—forgive me."

I felt as if I were lying drunk and stinking in the gutter, covered with vomit, my mouth full of foul curses, and as if I had told someone to photograph me and had sent Monika the picture. "May I call you again?" I asked quietly. "In a few days perhaps. I only have one explanation for my terrible behavior, I feel so utterly miserable I can't even describe it." I heard nothing, only her breathing, for a few moments, then she said: "I'm going away, for two weeks."

"Where to?" I asked.

"Into retreat," she said, "and to do a bit of painting."

"When are you coming over here," I asked, "to make me a mushroom omelette and one of your decorative salads?"

"I can't come," she said, "not now."

"Later on?" I asked.

"I'll come," she said; I could hear her crying, then she hung up.

20

I thought I ought to have a bath, I felt so dirty, and I thought I must stink the way Lazarus stank—but I was perfectly clean and didn't smell. I crept into the kitchen, turned off the gas under the beans, under the kettle, went back to the living room, raised the cognac bottle to my lips: it didn't help. Even the phone ringing didn't arouse me from my stupor. I lifted the receiver, said: "Yes?" and Sabina Emonds said: "Hans, what on earth are you up to?" I was silent, and she said: "Sending telegrams, it seems so dramatic. Are things that bad?"

"Bad enough," I said limply.

"I had been for a walk with the children," she said, "and Karl is away for a week, at camp with his class—and I had to get someone to stay with the kids before I could phone." She sounded as if she was in a hurry, and a bit short-tempered too, the way she always sounds. I couldn't bring myself to ask her for money. Ever since his marriage Karl has been figuring out his minimum living expenses very carefully; he had three children when I had that row with him, the fourth was on the way, but I hadn't the nerve to ask Sabina if it had arrived yet. The air in the apartment was always full of this by now more or less unchecked irritability, wherever you looked you saw his damned notebooks in which he calculated how he could make ends meet, and when I was alone with him Karl always became "frank" in a revolting kind of way and embarked on one of his man-to-man talks, about conceiving a child, and he would start accusing

186

the Catholic church (to me, of all people!), and there always came a point when he looked at me like a whining dog, and usually at that moment Sabina would come in, give him a bitter look because she was pregnant again. To my mind there is hardly anything more painful than a woman looking bitterly at her husband because she is pregnant. They ended up huddling there side by side crying their eyes out because they really did care for each other. In the background the noise of the children, chamberpots blissfully overturned, sopping washcloths thrown against brand-new wallpaper, while Karl is always talking about "discipline, discipline"[2] and "complete and unconditional obedience," and I had no alternative but to go into the nursery and do a few tricks for the children to quiet them down, but it never did quiet them down, they would squeal with delight, try to imitate me, and in the end we would all be sitting around, a child on each lap, the children would be allowed to sip from our wine glasses. Karl and Sabina would start talking about the books and calendars where you can look up the times when it is impossible for a woman to conceive. And then they are forever having babies, and it never struck them that this conversation must be specially agonizing for Marie and me, seeing how we weren't able to have children. Then when Karl was drunk he would start despatching curses to Rome, heaping maledictions on cardinals' heads and popes' minds, and the fantastic thing about it was that I would start defending the Pope. Marie knew far more about it and explained to Karl and Sabina that Rome couldn't do otherwise in these matters. Finally they would exchange sly looks, as if to say: Oh you two—obviously you have some very tricky way of avoiding children, and it usually ended up by one of the overtired kids snatching the wine glass from Marie, me, Karl or Sabina and spilling the wine over the exam papers which Karl always has stacked up on his desk. Needless to say it was embarrassing for Karl, who was constantly preaching to his boys about discipline and order, to have to return their exam papers with wine stains on them. There were slaps and tears, and with an "Oh-you-men-look" in our direction Sabina would go out into the kitchen with Marie to make some coffee, and no doubt they had their woman-to-woman talk then, something which embarrasses

187

Marie as much as man-to-man talks do me. When I was alone again with Karl he would start talking about money again, in a reproachful tone of voice, as much as to say: I talk about it with you because you're a nice guy, but of course you really don't know a thing about it.

I sighed and said: "Sabina, I am utterly ruined, professionally, spiritually, physically, financially. . . . I am . . ."

"If you're really hungry," she said, "I hope you know where a bowl of soup is always waiting for you on the stove." I was silent, I was touched, it sounded so honest and simple. "Are you listening?" she said.

"I'm listening," I said, "and I'll come round tomorrow lunchtime at latest and have my bowl of soup. And if you need anyone again to look after the kids, I—I," I couldn't go on. I could hardly offer now to do something for money which I had always done in the past for them for nothing, and I remembered that stupid business with the egg I had given Gregor. Sabina laughed and said: "Come on, out with it." I said: "What I mean is, if you and Karl could recommend me to your friends, I do have a phone—and I'll do it as cheaply as anyone else."

She was silent, and I could tell she was shocked. "Hans," she said, "I can't talk much longer, but please tell me —what happened?" Apparently she was the only person in Bonn who hadn't read Kostert's review, and I realized she had no means of knowing what had gone on between Marie and me. After all, she knew none of the group.

"Sabina," I said, "Marie has left me—and married someone called Züpfner."

"Oh no," she exclaimed, "I don't believe it."

"It's true," I said.

She was silent, and I heard someone banging against the door of the phone booth. Some idiot, no doubt, who wanted to tell his skat friends how he could have won a heart trump hand without the three top trumps.

"You ought to have married her," said Sabina in a low voice, "I mean—oh, you know what I mean."

"I know," I said, "I wanted to, but then it turned out you have to have that damned certificate from the Marriage License Bureau and that I had to guarantee in writing—in writing, mind you—that I would have the children brought up as Catholics."

"But surely that wasn't the only reason, was it?" she asked. The banging on the door of the phone booth got louder.

"I don't know," I said, "that's certainly how it began —but there are probably a lot of other things too which I don't understand. You'd better hang up, Sabina dear, or that agitated German citizen at the door will murder you. The place is swarming with fiends." "You must promise me you'll come," she said, "and remember: your soup will be waiting for you on the stove all day." I heard her voice grow faint, she whispered: "How unfair, how unfair," but in her confusion she had evidently just put the receiver down on the shelf where the phone book always lies instead of on the hook. I heard the fellow say: "Well, it's about time," but Sabina seemed to have gone. I shouted into the phone: "Help, help," in a shrill, piercing voice, the fellow swallowed the bait, picked up the receiver and said: "Is there something I can do for you?" His voice sounded respectable, composed, very masculine, and I could smell that he had been eating something sour, like marinated herring. "Hullo, hullo," he said, and I said: "Are you a German, as a matter of principle I will speak only to true Germans."

"A very good principle too," he said, "what is the trouble?"

"I am concerned about the CDU," I said, "I trust you invariably vote CDU?"

"I should hope so," he said indignantly, and I said: "Then I can stop worrying," and hung up.

21

I really should have insulted the fellow, I should have asked him whether he raped his own wife, whether he had won no-trumps with two aces, and whether he had already had the mandatory two-hour chat about the war with his colleagues at the Ministry. His voice had been that of the masterful husband, the true German, and his "Well, it's about time" had sounded like "Shoulder arms!" Sabina Emonds' voice had made me feel somewhat better, she had sounded a bit short-tempered and harassed, but I knew she really did think Marie had behaved badly and that the bowl of soup would always be waiting for me on the stove. She was a very good cook, and when she was not pregnant and handing out her "Oh-you-men-looks" right and left she was a cheerful soul, and Catholic in a much nicer way than Karl, who had retained his strange seminarist's ideas on the Sextum. Sabina's reproachful glances were actually directed at the entire male sex, but they took on a specially somber tone, almost thunderous, when she looked at Karl, the originator of her condition. Usually I had tried to distract Sabina, I would do one of my turns, this made her laugh, she would laugh long and hard, till the tears came, then she generally got trapped by her tears, and there was no more laughter in them. . . . And Marie would have to take her out and comfort her, while Karl sat beside me looking glum and guilty, till in desperation he would start correcting papers. Sometimes I would give him a hand by marking the mistakes with a red ballpoint, but

190

he never trusted me, looked through everything again and was furious every time because I hadn't overlooked anything and had marked the mistakes quite correctly. He simply couldn't imagine that I would carry out a job like that fairly and the way he would do it himself. Karl's problem is only a problem of money. If Karl Emonds had a seven-room apartment, the feeling of irritation, of pressure, would probably disappear. I had once had an argument with Kinkel over his conception of "subsistence level." Kinkel was supposed to be one of the cleverest experts in this field, and I believe it was he who worked out that the subsistence level for a single person in a city, not including rent, was eighty-four marks, later increased to eighty-six. I didn't even bother to point out that he himself, to judge by the disgusting story he had told us, apparently regarded thirty-five times that sum as *his* subsistence level. Such objections are considered too personal and in poor taste, but what's really in poor taste is that a man like that should tell other people what their subsistence level is. The eighty-six marks even included an amount for cultural needs: movies probably, or newspapers, and when I asked Kinkel if they expected the person in question to see a good film for that money, a film of educational value—he lost his temper, and when I asked him what was meant by the item "Replacement of Underwear," whether the Ministry specially hired a kind old man to run all over Bonn and wear out his underpants and report to them how long he took to wear out his underpants—his wife said I was being dangerously subjective, and I told her I could see the point of Communists setting up plans, with test meals, maximum lifetime of handkerchiefs, and all that nonsense, seeing that Communists did not have the hypocritical alibi of a "spiritual nature," but that Christians like her husband should lend themselves to such presumptuous madness seemed to me fantastic—so then she said I was an out-and-out materialist and had no sense of sacrifice, suffering, fate, the nobility of poverty. With Karl Emonds I never have the impression of sacrifice, suffering, fate, the nobility of poverty. He has quite a good income, and all that was to be seen of fate and nobility was a constant irritation, because he could calculate that he would never be able to afford a big

191

enough apartment. When I realized that of all people Karl Emonds was the only one I could approach for money my situation became clear to me. I didn't have a single pfennig.

22

I also knew I would never do any of those things: go to Rome and talk to the Pope, or pinch cigarettes and cigars, stuff my pockets with peanuts, at Mother's At Home tomorrow afternoon. I no longer even had the strength to believe in it, the way I had believed in sawing through the wood with Leo. All attempts to retie the puppet strings and pull myself up by them would fail. The time would even come when I would ask Kinkel for a loan, and Sommerwild, and even that sadist Fredebeul, who would probably hold up a five-mark piece and make me jump for it. I would be glad when Monika Silvs asked me over for coffee, not because it was Monika Silvs but because of the free coffee. I would give that silly Bella Brosen another call, butter her up a bit and tell her I wasn't going to bother about the amount, that any amount, never mind how small, would be welcome, then—one day I would go to Sommerwild and prove to him "convincingly" that I was repentant, had seen the light, was ripe for conversion, and then the worst thing of all would happen: Sommerwild would stage a reconciliation with Marie and Züpfner, but if I became a Catholic my father would probably never do another thing for me. Apparently this was for him the worst of all. I had to think it out: my choice was not *rouge et noir,* but dark brown or black: brown coal or church. I would become what they had all been expecting of me for so long: a man, mature, no longer subjective but objective and ready to sit down to a brisk game of skat at the Union Club. I still had a few chances left: Leo, Heinrich, Behlen, Grandfather, Zohnerer, who might build me up into a schmaltzy guitar player, I would sing: "When the wind plays in your hair, I know that you'll be mine." I had sung it to Marie once, and she had put her hands over her ears and said it was ghastly. Finally I would do the very last thing of all: go to the Communists and perform all those turns which they could so nicely classify as anti-capitalist. I actually had gone there once and had met with some cultural Joes in Erfurt. They put on quite a welcome for me at the station, with huge bouquets of flowers, and afterwards at the hotel there was brook trout, caviar, strawberry parfait, and vast quantities of champagne. Then they asked us what we would like to see of Erfurt. I said I would like very much to see the place where Luther defended his doctor's dissertation, and Marie said she had heard there was a Catholic theological faculty in Erfurt and that she was interested in the religious life. They obviously didn't like that but couldn't do anything about it, and it all became very embarrassing: for the cultural Joes, for the theologians, and for us. The theologians must have thought we had something to do with those donkeys, and none of them spoke frankly with Marie, not even when she discussed matters of doctrine with a professor. Somehow or other he realized that Marie was not properly married to me. In the presence of the functionaries he asked her: "But you really are a Catholic, aren't you?" and she went scarlet and said: "Yes, even though I am living in sin I'm still a Catholic." It got really terrible when we realized that even the functionaries didn't like our not being married, and on our way back to the hotel for coffee one of the functionaries said there were certain manifestations of petty-bourgeois anarchy which he didn't approve of at all. Then they asked me which turns I was going to perform, in Leipzig and Rostock, whether I couldn't do the "Cardinal," "Arrival in Bonn" and "Board Meeting." How they ever found out about the Cardinal we never discovered, for I had rehearsed this number just for myself and the only person I showed it to was Marie, and she had asked me not to do it in public seeing that Cardinals wore the red of martyrs, and I told them no, I would first have to study living conditions here, for the whole point of comedy was to present people in abstract form with situations taken from their own reality, not from that of others, and in their country Bonn, Boards of Directors and Cardinals obviously didn't exist. They became uneasy, one of them turned pale and said they had thought it would be quite different, and I said so had I. It was appalling. I told them I could look around a bit if they liked and do a turn such as "Session of the Zone Committee" or "The Cultural Council Meets," or "The Party Conference Elects its Presidium"—or "Erfurt, City of Flowers"; unfortunately it so happened that around the station Erfurt looked like anything but a city of flowers—but then the boss got up and said they couldn't possibly permit any propaganda against the working class. By this time he was no longer pale, he was white in the face—a few of the others at least had the guts to grin. I replied that I didn't see that it would be propaganda against the working class if I did a quickly rehearsed number such as "The Party Conference Elects its Presidium," and I made the stupid mistake of saying Barty Gonference, that infuriated the white-faced fanatic, he banged on the table, so violently that the whipped cream slipped off my cake onto the plate, and said, "We have been mistaken in you, very much mistaken," and I said, in that case I could leave, and he said, "Yes—by all means, by the next train." I added that I could call the number "Board Meeting" simply "Session of the Zone Committee" as presumably there too the only matters they decided on would be the ones which had been decided in advance. Then they got thoroughly unpleasant, left the room, didn't even pay for our coffee. Marie was in tears, I was ready to hit someone over the head, and when we went across to the station to get the next train back there wasn't a porter in sight, and we had to carry our own bags, which I loathe. Outside the station we were lucky enough to run into one of the young theologians Marie had been talking to that morning. He flushed when he saw us, but he took the heavy suitcase from the tearful Marie, and Marie kept whispering to him that he must please not get himself into trouble.

It was dreadful. We had been a total of only six or seven hours in Erfurt, but we had got on the wrong side of everyone: the theologians as well as the functionaries.

When we got out at Bebra and went to a hotel, Marie cried all night, in the morning she wrote a long letter to the theologian, but we never found out whether he actually got it.

I had thought a reconciliation with Marie and Züpfner would be the end, but to hand myself over to the white-faced functionary and perform the Cardinal for that lot would really be the very end. I still had Leo, Heinrich Behlen, Monika Silvs, Zohnerer, Grandfather and the bowl of soup at Sabina Emonds, and presumably I could make a little money baby-sitting. I would guarantee in writing not to feed the children any eggs. Evidently that was more than a German mother could bear. What other people call the objective significance of art I couldn't care less about, but to poke fun at Boards of Directors where Boards of Directors don't exist seems pretty low.

I had once spent a lot of time rehearsing a fairly long number called "The General," and it turned out to be what is known in our circles as a success: that is, the right people laughed, and the right people were angry. When I went to my dressing room after the show, my breast swelling with pride, I found an old, tiny woman waiting for me. I am always short-tempered after a show, the only person I can bear near me is Marie, but Marie had let the old lady into my dressing room. She began talking before I had even finished closing the door, and told me her husband had also been a general, he had been killed and had written her a letter beforehand asking her not to accept a pension. "You are still very young," she said, "but you're old enough to understand" —and then she left. After that I could never do the "General" again. Whereupon the press calling itself Left Wing wrote that I had apparently been intimidated by the reactionaries, the press calling itself Right Wing wrote that I had doubtless realized I was playing into the hands of the East, and the independent press wrote that I had obviously renounced radicalism and personal involvement in any form. All utter drivel. The reason I couldn't do the number any more was because I always had to think of the little old woman, who probably had a hard time struggling along, mocked and scorned by everyone.

When I no longer enjoy something, I stop doing it—to explain that to a journalist is probably much too complicated. They must always be "sniffing around," "nosing out a story," and wherever you go you find the malicious type of journalist who can never reconcile himself to the fact that he is not an artist himself and doesn't even possess the makings of an artistic person. Those people, of course, don't even have a "nose," and they talk nonsense, preferably when there are pretty girls around who are still sufficiently naive to idolize every hack writer who happens to have a column in a paper, and "influence." There are some strange unrecognized forms of prostitution compared with which prostitution itself is an honest trade: at least you get something for your money.

Even this path—finding my salvation through the compassion of commercial love, was barred to me: I had no money. Meanwhile Marie was trying on her Spanish mantilla in her hotel in Rome in order to make the right impression as the first lady of German Catholicism. Back in Bonn she would attend countless tea parties, smile, go on committees, open exhibitions of "religious art" and "look around for a suitable dressmaker." All the women with husbands in official positions in Bonn "looked around for a suitable dressmaker."

Marie as the first lady of German Catholicism, a teacup or a cocktail glass in her hand: "Have you seen the sweet little Cardinal who is going to consecrate Krögert's Column of the Virgin? It seems that in Italy even the Cardinals are gallant. It's too sweet for words."

I couldn't even hobble properly now, I could really only creep along, I crept out onto the balcony to breathe in some of my native air: that didn't help either. I had already been in Bonn too long, nearly two hours, and by that time the Bonn climate loses its beneficial effect.

It struck me that they really had me to thank for the fact that Marie had remained a Catholic. She had some terrible religious crises, due to disillusionment over Kinkel, as well as over Sommerwild, and a fellow like Blothert would probably have turned even St. Francis into an atheist. For a time she even stopped going to church, wouldn't hear of our being married in church, she withdrew into a kind of obstinate defiance, and it wasn't till we had

197

been gone from Bonn for three years that she met the group again, although they were always inviting her. I told her at the time that disillusionment was insufficient reason. If she believed the thing as such to be true—a thousand Fredebeuls couldn't make it untrue, and after all—I said—there was Züpfner, whom I had to admit I found a bit stiff, not my type at all, but who as a Catholic was convincing. There must be a lot of convincing Catholics, I told her, I named pastors whose sermons I had listened to, I reminded her of the Pope, Gary Cooper, Alec Guinness—and it was by clinging to Pope John and Züpfner that she managed to climb up out of the pit. Strangely enough, Heinrich Behlen no longer appealed to her during this period, she said she found him smarmy, was always embarrassed when I mentioned him, so that I began to suspect he might have "made advances" to her. I never asked her about it, but I had my suspicions, and when I thought of Heinrich's housekeeepr I could understand that he "made advances" to girls. I found the idea repulsive, but I could understand it, just as I understood a lot of repulsive things that went on at boarding school.

It was only now that I realized I had been the one to offer Pope John and Züpfner as a source of comfort in her religious doubts. I had been scrupulously fair in my attitude toward Catholicism, that was just where I had gone wrong, but to me Marie was Catholic in such a natural way that I wanted to help her retain that naturalness. I woke her up when she overslept so she could get to church on time. How often had I paid for a taxi to get her there on time, I phoned around for her, when we were in Protestant areas, to try and find a Holy Mass, and she always said she found that "particularly" sweet, but then I was supposed to sign that damned paper, guarantee *in writing* that I would have the children brought up as Catholics. We had often talked about our children. I had looked forward very much to having children, had talked to my children, held them in my arms, beaten up raw eggs in milk for them, the only thing that worried me was that we would be living in hotels, and in hotels it is usually only the children of millionaires or kings who are treated well. The first thing children—at least the sons—of non-kings and non-millionaires get shouted at them is: "This isn't your home," a triple insinuation since it assumes that you behave like a pig at home, that you only enjoy yourself when you are behaving like a pig, and that in no circumstances are you supposed to enjoy yourself as a child. For girls there is always a good chance of being regarded as "sweet" and being nicely treated, but boys always start off by being shouted at if their parents aren't around. For Germans, every boy is a naughty child, the always unspoken adjective naughty is simply merged with the noun. If anyone should ever hit on the idea of testing the vocabulary most parents use when talking to their children, he would find that it makes the vocabulary of the comic strip look like a complete dictionary. It won't be long before German parents speak only in Kalick-language to their children: Oh, how sweet, and Oh, how awful; now and again they will decide to make use of such variations as "Don't argue" or "That's none of your business." I have even discussed with Marie how we would dress our children, she was all for "jaunty, light-colored raincoats," I preferred parkas, since it seemed to me that a child couldn't very well play in a puddle in a jaunty, light-colored raincoat, while a parka was ideal for playing in puddles, she —I always thought first of a girl—would be warmly dressed but with bare legs, and when she threw stones into the puddle the water need not necessarily splash her coat, it might only splash her legs, and when she scooped out the puddle with an empty can and the dirty water happened to run out of the side of the can, it wasn't bound to go on the coat, in any case the chances were that it would only dirty her legs. Marie felt she would be more careful just because she was wearing a light-colored raincoat, the question of whether our children would actually be allowed to play in puddles was never completely clarified. Marie would just smile, be evasive and say: let's wait and see.

If she was to have children with Züpfner she wouldn't be able to dress them in either parkas or jaunty, light-colored raincoats, she would have to let her children run around without coats, for we had gone thoroughly into the matter of coats of all kinds. We had also discussed long and short pants, underwear, socks, shoes—she would have to let her children run naked through the streets of Bonn if she didn't want to feel like a whore or a traitor. I also had no idea what she could give her children to eat: we had gone into all the various types of food, of feeding methods, we had agreed we didn't want stuffed children, children who are forever getting porridge or milk stuffed or poured into them. I did not want my children to be forced to eat, it had disgusted me to watch Sabina Emonds stuffing food into her two oldest children, especially the eldest, whom Karl had unaccountably named Edeltrud. I had even had an argument with Marie over the tiresome matter of eggs, she was not in favor of eggs, and when we argued about it she said they were rich people's food, then she had blushed and I had had to comfort her. I was used to being treated and regarded differently from other people merely because I am one of the brown-coal Schniers, and it only happened to Marie twice that she made a silly remark about it: the first day, when I came downstairs to her in the kitchen, and the time we talked about eggs. It's an awful thing to have wealthy parents, especially awful, of course, when one has never benefited from the wealth. At home we very seldom had eggs, my mother regarded eggs as being "distinctly harmful." In Edgar Wieneken's case it was embarrassing the other way round, he was always brought in and introduced as a child of the working class; there were even some priests who, when they introduced him, used to say: "A genuine child of the working class," it sounded as if they had said: Look, he has no horns and looks quite intelligent. It is a racial matter that Mother's executive committee ought to look into one day. The only people who behaved naturally to me over this were the Wienekens and Marie's father. They didn't hold it against me, my being one of the brown-coal Schniers, nor did they make any special fuss of me because of it.

I suddenly realized I was still standing on the balcony
looking out over Bonn. I was hanging on to the railing,
my knee was hurting like mad, but the coin I had thrown
down worried me. I would have liked to get it back, but
I couldn't go down into the street now, Leo was bound
to arrive any minute. They couldn't sit forever over their
plums, whipped cream and grace. I couldn't spot the coin
down there on the street: it was quite a long way down,
and it is only in fairy tales that coins glint clearly
enough to be found. It was the first time I ever regretted
anything to do with money: this discarded mark, twelve
cigarettes, two streetcar rides, a wiener. Without remorse,
but with a certain wistfulness, I thought of all the express and first-class surcharges we had paid for grandmothers from Lower Saxony, wistfully, the way you think
of the kisses you gave to a girl who married someone
else. There was not much to be hoped for from Leo,
he has strange ideas about money, rather like a nun's
ideas about "married life."

Nothing glinted down there on the street, through everything was well lit up, there was no fairy coin to be
seen: just cars, streetcar, bus and citizens of Bonn. I
hoped the mark had stayed on the roof of the streetcar and that someone at the depot would find it.

Of course I could throw myself on the bosom of the
Protestant church. Only: when I thought of bosom I
shivered. I could have thrown myself on Luther's breast,
but "bosom of the Protestant church"—no. If I was

going to be a hypocrite I wanted to be a successful hypocrite and get as much fun out of it as possible. I would enjoy pretending to be a Catholic, I would "keep to myself" entirely for six months, then start going to Sommerwild's evening sermons, till I began to warm with catholons like a festering wound with germs. But this would mean giving up my last chance of getting into Father's good books and of being able to sign non-negotiable checks in a brown-coal office. Perhaps my mother would find a place for me on her executive committee and give me a chance to present my race theories. I would go to America and lecture to women's clubs as a living example of the remorse of German youth. The only thing was, I had nothing to be remorseful about, nothing whatever, and so I would have to pretend remorse. I could also tell them about the time I threw ashes from the tennis court into Herbert Kalick's face, and how I was locked up in the shed and afterwards had stood before the court: before Kalick, Brühl, Lövenich. But the moment I told them that, it would be hypocrisy. I could not describe those moments and hang them around my neck like a decoration. Everyone carries the decorations of his heroic moments around his neck and on his chest. To cling to the past is hypocrisy, because no one knows those moments: how Henrietta in her blue hat had sat in the streetcar and gone off to defend the sacred German soil against the Jewish Yankees near Leverkusen.

No, the safest hypocrisy, and the one I would enjoy the most, was to "gamble on the Catholic card." There every number was a winner.

I glanced once more over the roofs of the University to the trees in the park: that was where Marie would be living, over there on the slopes between Bonn and Godesberg. Good. It was better to be near her. It would be too easy for her if she were able to think I was always on the move. She should always have to reckon with the possibility of running into me and blush with shame every time she realized how unchaste and adulterous her life was, and when I met her with her children, and they were wearing raincoats, parkas, or loden coats; her children would all of a sudden seem to her naked.

They are whispering in the city, Madam, that you let your children run around naked. That's going too far. And have you forgotten one little word, Madam, at a crucial point when you say you only love one man—you ought to have said which man. They also whisper that you are smiling at the sullen resentment harbored by everyone here against the one they call *Der Alte*. You think that in a distorted kind of way they all resemble him. After all—you think—they all regard themselves as indispensable as he does, after all, they all read mystery stories. Naturally the jackets of these books do not go with the tastefully decorated homes. The Danes have forgotten to extend their designs to the jackets of mystery stories. The Finns will be clever enough to do this and adapt their jackets to go with chairs, sofas, glasses, and pots. Even at Blothert's there are mystery stories lying around that hadn't been hidden carefully enough the evening we went over the house.

Always in the dark, Madam, in movies and churches, in dark living rooms listening to church music, avoiding the bright light of the tennis courts. Such a lot of whispering. The thirty or forty-minute confessions in the cathedral. Ill-concealed indignation on the faces of those waiting their turn. Heavens above, how on earth can she have so much to confess: she has the handsomest, nicest, most reasonable husband. A really nice man. An adorable little daughter, two cars.

The exasperated impatience in there behind the grill, the endless whispering back and forth about love, marriage, duty, love, and finally the question: "Not even religious doubts—then what is your trouble, my daughter?"

You can't put it into words, can't even think it, the thing I know. What you need is a clown—official description—comedian, no church affiliation.

I hobbled from the balcony to the bathroom to put on my make-up. It had been a mistake to face Father standing, sitting, without my make-up, but his visit was the last thing I could have expected. Leo had always been so keen to see my true opinion, my true face, my true self. Now he was going to see it. He was always afraid of my "masks," of my clowning, of what he called my "flippancy," when I wore no make-up. My make-up box hadn't arrived yet from Bochum. The moment I opened the white cabinet on the bathroom wall, I realized it was too late. I ought to have remembered the fatal sentimentality inherent in objects. Marie's tubes and jars, bottles and lipsticks: there was nothing left in the cabinet, and the fact of there being so unmistakably *nothing* left of her was as bad as if I had found one of her tubes or jars. All gone. Perhaps Monika Silvs had been merciful enough to pack it all up and put it away. I looked at myself in the mirror: my eyes were utterly empty, for the first time I didn't need to empty them by looking at myself for half an hour and doing facial exercises. It was the face of a suicide, and when I began to put on my make-up my face was the face of a corpse. I smeared Vaseline over my face and ripped open a half-dried tube of white make-up, squeezed out what was left and painted myself completely white: not a stroke of black, not a spot of red, all white, even my eyebrows painted over; my hair above it looked like a wig, my unpainted mouth dark, almost blue, my eyes, pale blue like a stony sky, as empty as a Cardinal's who will not admit to himself that he has long since lost his faith. I was not even afraid of myself. With this face I could become a success, I could even be hypocritical about the thing which in all its helplessness, in its stupidity, relatively speaking appealed most to me: the thing Edgar Wieneken believed in. This thing at least would have no taste, in its tastelessness it was the most honest of all the dishonest things, the least of the lesser evils. So in addition to the black, dark brown and blue there was another alternative, which it would be too euphemistic and too optimistic to call red, it was gray with a soft shimmer of sunrise. A sad color for a sad thing, where perhaps there was even room for a clown who was guilty of the worst of all clown sins: that of arousing pity. But the trouble was: Edgar was the last person I could betray, the last person I could pretend to. I was the only witness to the fact that he really had run the hundred meters in 10.1, and he was one of the few people who had always taken me as I was, to whom I had always appeared as I was. And the only faith he had was faith in certain people—the others believed in more than people: in God, in abstract money, in things like nation and Germany. Not Edgar. It had been bad enough for him that time I took the taxi. I was sorry now, I ought to have explained it to him, there was no one else to whom I owed any explanations. I left the mirror; I liked what I saw in it too much, I didn't think for an instant that it was me I was looking at. That was no longer a clown, it was a corpse acting a corpse.

I hobbled across to our bedroom, which I hadn't gone into yet for fear of Marie's clothes. I had bought most of them myself, even discussed the alterations with the dressmakers. She can wear almost any color except red and black, she can even wear gray without looking mousy, pink suits her very well, and green. I could probably make my living in the world of women's fashions, but for someone who is monogamous and not a pansy it would be too much of a torture. Most husbands just give their wives crossed checks and advise them to bow to the "dictates of fashion." If purple happens to be the fashion, all these women who are fed with crossed checks wear purple, and when all the women at a party who "take pride in their appearance" run around in purple, the whole thing looks like a convocation of laboriously animated female bishops. There are very few women who can wear purple. Marie looked very nice in purple. While I was still at home the sack dress suddenly became fashionable, and all the poor old hens who had been told by their husbands to dress "smartly" ran around at our At Homes in sacks. I felt so sorry for some of the women—especially the tall, stout wife of one of the innumerable presidents—that I wanted to go up to her and hang something—a tablecloth or a curtain—around her like a mantle of mercy. Her fool of a husband noticed nothing, saw nothing, heard nothing, he would have sent his wife shopping in a pink nightgown if some pansy had decreed it was the fashion. The next day he gave a lecture to a hundred and fifty Protestant clergymen on the word "know" in marriage. Probably he didn't even realize his wife has much too knobbly knees to be able to wear short dresses.

I flung open the door of the wardrobe so as to avoid the mirror: there was nothing left of Marie, nothing, not even a shoetree or a belt, the way women sometimes leave them on a hanger. Scarcely even a trace of her perfume, she ought to have been merciful and taken my

205

clothes too, given them away or burned them, but my things were still hanging there: green corduroy trousers, which I had never worn, a black tweed jacket, some ties, and three pairs of shoes on the shoerack at the bottom; in the small drawers I would find everything, everything: cufflinks and the little white collar stays, socks and handkerchiefs. I might have known it: where property is concerned, Christians are relentless, fair. I didn't even need to open the drawers: everything of mine would be there, everything of hers would be gone. How kind it would have been to take along my stuff too, but here in our wardrobe it had all been done fairly, with excruciating justice. No doubt Marie had felt sorry for me too, when she took away everything that would remind me of her, and no doubt she had wept, the tears that women in divorce films weep when they say: "I'll never forget the years I spent with you."

The tidy clean wardrobe (someone had even gone over it with a duster), was the worst thing she could have left behind for me to find, tidy, divided, her things divorced from mine. The inside of the wardrobe looked like after a successful operation. Nothing left of her, not even a button off her blouse. I left the door open, to avoid the mirror, hobbled back into the kitchen, put the bottle of cognac in my coat pocket, went into the living room and lay down on the sofa and pulled up my trouser leg. My knee was badly swollen, but the pain got less as soon as I lay down. There were four cigarettes left in the box, I lit one of them.

I thought about which would have been worse: if Marie had left her clothes here, or this way: everything tidy and clean and not even a message anywhere: "I'll never forget the years I spent with you." Maybe it was better this way, and yet she might at least have left a button or a belt on a hanger, or have taken the whole wardrobe with her and burned it.

When we got the news of Henrietta's death, the table was just being set at home, Anna had left Henrietta's napkin, which she didn't think was quite ready for the laundry, in the yellow napkin ring on the sideboard, and we all looked at the napkin, there was a bit of marmalade on it and a small brown spot of soup or gravy. For the first time I sensed how terrible are the objects

206

left behind when someone goes away or dies. Mother actually made an effort to eat, no doubt it was supposed to mean: Life goes on, or something of that sort, but I knew very well: that wasn't so, it isn't life that goes on but death. I struck the soup spoon out of her hand, ran into the garden, back again into the house where the screaming and shouting was in full swing. The hot soup had scalded my mother's face. I tore up Henrietta's room, flung open the window and threw everything I could lay hands on into the garden: boxes and dresses, dolls, hats, shoes, caps, and when I flung open the drawers I found her underwear and among it some queer little things which must have been precious to her: dried ears of wheat, stones, flowers, scraps of paper and whole bundles of letters tied up in pink ribbon. Tennis shoes, racquets, trophies, as fast as I picked them up I threw them out into the garden. Leo told me later I had looked like "a madman," and that it had all happened so fast, so terribly fast, that no one had been able to stop me. Whole drawersful I just tipped out over the windowsill, ran into the garage and carried the heavy spare can of gasoline into the garden, tipped it over the things and set fire to it: everything that lay scattered around I kicked into the tall flames, gathered together all the scraps and pieces, dried flowers, ears of wheat and the bundles of letters and threw them into the fire. I ran to the dining room, took the napkin with the ring from the sideboard, threw them into the fire! Leo said later that it was all over in less than five minutes, and before anyone realized what was happening the flames were burning skyhigh and I had thrown the whole lot in. An American officer even appeared on the scene, he thought I was burning secret documents, records of the German Werewolves, but by the time he arrived everything was scorched, black and hideous and stinking, and when he tried to grab one of the bundles of letters I struck his hand and tipped the remains of the gasoline in the can into the flames. Then even the fire trucks turned up with ridiculously big hoses, and in the background someone shouted in a ridiculously high voice the most ridiculous command I have ever heard "Water—forward march!" and they were not ashamed to play their hoses on this pathetic funeral pyre, and because a window

207

frame had caught fire a bit one of them turned his hose on it, everything inside was awash, and afterward the parquet floor warped, and Mother moaned about her ruined floor and phoned all the insurance companies to find out if it was water damage or fire damage or whether it came under the heading of general insurance.

I took a drink from the bottle, put it back in my coat pocket and gently felt my knee. When I lay down, it hurt less. If I was sensible and put my mind to it, the swelling and pain would go down. I could get myself an empty orange crate, sit in front of the station, play the guitar and sing the Litany of Loreto. I would lay my hat or my cap—as if by chance—on the step beside me, and as soon as it occurred to anyone to throw something into it, others would be encouraged to follow suit. I needed money, if only because I was almost out of cigarettes. The best thing would be to put a few nickels and pennies into the hat. Surely Leo would bring me at least that much. I pictured myself sitting there: my white face in front of the dark station façade, a blue jersey, my black tweed jacket and the green corduroy trousers, and I "lifted up my voice" against the street noises: *Rosa mystica—ora pro nobis—turris davidica—ora pro nobis —virgo, fidelis—ora pro nobis*—I would be sitting there when the trains from Rome came in and my *conjux infidelis* arrived with her Catholic husband. The wedding ceremony must have required a great deal of agonizing thought: Marie was not a widow, she was not divorced, she was no longer—this I happened to know for a fact— a virgin. Sommerwild must have been tearing his hair out, a wedding without a veil was enough to ruin the whole esthetic concept. Or did they have special liturgical regulations for fallen girls and former clowns' concubines? What had the bishop who performed the ceremony thought? They wouldn't settle for anything less than a bishop. Marie once took me along to a bishop's vestry, and all that back and forth with take off miter and put on miter, put on white band and take off white band, put the crosier there, put the crosier here, put on the red band, take off the white, had made a great impression on me, my sensitive artistic nature has a feeling for the esthetics of repetition.

I also thought about my pantomime with the keys. I

could get some Plasticine, press a key into it, pour some water in the hollow form and bake a few keys in the refrigerator; it shouldn't be too difficult to find a small portable one in which every evening before my show I would bake the keys which were to melt away during the performance. Perhaps the idea was worth something, for the moment I discarded it, it was too complicated, made me dependent on too many props and technical contingencies, and if some stagehand happened to have been swindled during the war by a Rhinelander he would open the icebox and spoil my show. The other was better: to sit on the Bonn station steps, with my true face, painted white, sing the Litany of Loreto and srike a few chords on the guitar. My hat beside me, the one I used to wear for my Chaplin imitations, all I needed was the come-on coins: a nickel would do, a nickel and a dime would be better, but best of all three coins: a nickel, a dime, and a penny. People must be able to see that I was not a religious maniac who would spurn a modest donation, and they must see that every mite, even a copper one, was welcome. Later on I would add a silver coin, it must be apparent that larger donations were not only not despised but also given. I would even put a cigarette into the hat, most people found it easier to reach for their cigarettes than for their wallets. At some point, of course, someone would turn up to put forward principles of order: streetsinger's license, or someone from the Anti-Blasphemy Executive Committee would take exception to the religious content of my offering. In case I should be asked for identification I would have a coal briquette beside me, everyone knew the inscription "Warm up with Schnier," I would underline the black Schnier with red chalk, maybe draw an H. in front of it. That would be an impractical, but unmistakable, visiting card: How do you do, my name is Schnier. And there was one thing my father really could do for me, it wouldn't even cost him anything. He could get me a streetsinger's license. All he needed to do was call up the mayor, or speak to him about it when he played skat with him at the Union Club. He must do that for me. Then I could sit on the station steps and wait for the train from Rome. If Marie could bring herself to walk past me without putting her arms

209

around me, there was always suicide. Later I hesitated to think of suicide, for a reason which may appear presumptuous: I wanted to save myself for Marie. She might leave Züpfner, then we would be in the ideal Besewitz situation, she could remain my concubine since in the eyes of the church she could never be divorced from Züpfner. All I needed then was to be discovered by television, acquire new fame, and the church would close its eyes. After all I didn't feel the need of being married to Marie in church, and they wouldn't even have to let off their worn-out Henry the Eighth cannon at me.

I was feeling better. My knee was less swollen, the pain was less, headache and depression remained, but I am as used to them as to the idea of death. An artist always carries death with him, like a good priest his breviary. I even know exactly what will happen after my death: I shall not be spared the Schnier vault. My mother will cry and maintain she was the only person who ever understood me. After my death she will tell everyone "what our Hans was really like." To this very day and probably to all eternity she is firmly convinced that I am "sensual" and "grasping." She will say: "Yes, our Hans, he was gifted, but sad to say very sensual and grasping—unfortunately completely undisciplined—but so gifted, so gifted." Sommerwild will say: "Our good friend Schnier, a remarkable man, unfortunately he was hopelessly anticlerical and had absolutely no feeling for metaphysics." Blothert will be sorry he didn't get his capital punishment through in time to have me publicly executed. For Fredebeul I shall be "a unique type, of no sociological consequence whatever." Kinkel will weep, sincerely and without restraint, he will be completely bowled over, but too late. Monika Silvs will sob as if she were my widow and be sorry she didn't come to me at once and make me that omelette. Marie will simply not believe I am dead—she will leave Züpfner, go from hotel to hotel and ask for me, in vain.

My father will make the most of the tragedy, full of regret that he did not secretly leave at least a few notes on the hall table as he left. Karl and Sabina will weep, uncontrollably, in a manner which all those at the funeral will find offensive. Sabina will grope furtively in Karl's coat pocket because she has forgotten her handkerchief again. Edgar will feel obliged to hold back his tears, and after the funeral perhaps he will pace out the hundred-meter stretch in our garden again, go back alone to the cemetery and lay a big bunch of roses at the memorial tablet for Henrietta. Apart from me no one knows that he was in love with her, no one knows that the bundles of letters I burned showed only E.W. as sender. And there is one other secret I shall take with me to the grave: that I once watched Mother go secretly into her storeroom in the basement, cut herself a thick slice of ham and eat it down there, standing, with her fingers, hurriedly, it didn't even look disgusting, only surprising, and I was touched rather than horrified. I had gone into the basement to look for old tennis balls in the luggage room, which was forbidden, and when I heard footsteps I switched off the light, I saw her take a jar of home-made applesauce off the shelf, put the jar down again, saw merely the cutting movement of her elbows, and then she stuffed the rolled-up slice of ham into her mouth. I never told anyone and I never will. My secret will rest under a marble slab in the Schnier vault. Strangely enough I like the kind to which I belong: people.

When one of my kind dies, I am sad. I would weep even at the grave of my mother. At the grave of old man Derkum I lost all self-control; I kept shoveling more and more earth onto the bare wood of the coffin and heard someone behind me whisper that it was in-decent—but I kept right on shoveling, till Marie took the shovel away from me. I never wanted to see the shop again, the house, wanted nothing to remember him by. Nothing. Marie was sensible, she sold the shop and put the money aside "for our children."

By this time I could go into the hall without hobbling and fetch my guitar. I undid the cover, shoved two armchairs together in the living room, pulled the phone toward me, lay down again and tuned the guitar. It did me good to hear the few sounds. As I began to sing I felt almost myself again: *mater amabilis—mater ad-mirabilis*—I intoned the *ora pro nobis* on the guitar. I liked the idea. With the guitar in my hand, with the open hat lying beside me, with my true face, I would wait for the train from Rome. *Mater boni consilii*. After

211

all, Marie had told me, when I came back with the money from Edgar Wieneken, we would never, never be parted again: "Till death do us part." I was not dead yet. Mrs. Wieneken used to say: "If you can sing you're still alive," and "As long as you have an appetite, there's still hope for you." I sang and I was hungry. The last thing I could imagine was Marie settling down in one place: together we had gone from town to town, from hotel to hotel, and when we stayed anywhere for a few days she would always say: "The open suitcases are staring at me like mouths wanting to be fed," and we would feed the mouths of the suitcases, and whenever I had to spend a few weeks in one place she would run through the towns as if they had just been excavated. Movies, churches, popular newspapers, parchesi. Did she really want to be present at the great ceremonial high office when Züpfner was made a Knight of Malta, surrounded by chancellors and presidents, and at home with her own hands iron out the drops of wax in his robes? A matter of taste, Marie, but not your taste. It is better to put your trust in an unbelieving clown, who wakes you early enough for you to get to Mass on time, who will even pay for a taxi for you to go to church. You'll never need to wash out my blue jersey.

24

When the phone rang I was confused for a few moments. I had been concentrating entirely on not missing the doorbell and on opening the door to Leo. I put down the guitar, stared at the ringing phone, lifted the receiver and said: "Hullo." "Hans?" said Leo.

"Yes," I said, "I'm glad you're coming." He was silent, cleared his throat, I hadn't recognized his voice right away. He said: "I have the money for you." *The* money sounded odd. Leo had odd ideas about money anyway. His requirements are almost nil, he doesn't smoke, doesn't drink, doesn't read evening papers and only goes to the movies when at least five people in whom he has complete confidence have recommended the film to him as worth seeing; that happens once very two or three years. He would rather walk than take the streetcar. When he said *the* money, my spirits fell again immediately. If he had said, *some* money, I would have known it would be two or three marks. My nervousness stuck in my throat and I asked hoarsely: "How much?" "Oh," he said, "six marks and seventy pfennig." For him that was a lot, I think that for what are called personal needs it would last him for two years: now and again a stamp, a roll of peppermints, a nickel for a beggar, he didn't even need matches, and if he ever did buy a box, to have them on hand for "superiors" who needed a light, they lasted him for a year, and even when he carried them around for a year they still looked like new. Now and again, of course, he had to have a haircut, but no doubt he took that out of the "study account" that Father had set up for him. In the past he used sometimes to spend money on concert tickets, but Mother generally gave him her complimentary tickets. Rich people have far more given to them than poor people, and what they do have to buy they generally get cheaper, Mother had a whole catalogue from the wholesalers: I wouldn't have been surprised if she had even got stamps at a reduced price. Six marks seventy —for Leo that was quite a tidy sum. For me too, at the moment—but he probably didn't know yet that I was— as we used to say at home—"temporarily without funds."

I said: "Good, Leo, thanks a lot—could you bring me a pack of cigarettes when you come?" I heard him clear his throat, no reply, and I asked: "You can hear me, can't you? Eh?" Perhaps I had offended him by asking him right away to use some of his money for cigarettes. "Yes, yes," he said, "only . . ." he stammered, stuttered: "I find it hard to tell you—I can't come."

"What?" I shouted, "you can't come?"

"It's a quarter to nine," he said, "and I have to be back in the building by nine."

"And if you're late," I said, "will you be excommunicated?"

"Don't, please," he said, hurt.

"Well, can't you ask for leave or something?"

"Not at this hour," he said, "I would have had to do that at noon."

"And what happens if you just come in late?"

"Then I get a severe exhortation!" he said in a low voice.

"That sounds like garden," I said, "if I remember my Latin correctly."

He gave a little laugh. "More like garden shears," he said, "it's pretty unpleasant."

"Oh all right then," I said, "I won't expose you to such an unpleasant inquiry, Leo—but the presence of a human being would do me good."

"It's all very complicated," he said, "you must try and understand. The exhortation wouldn't be so bad, but if I get another exhortation this week it gets into the records, and I have to account for it before a scrutinium."

"Where?" I said, "say it again, please, slowly." He

sighed, growled a bit and said very slowly: "Scrutinium."

"Damn it, Leo," I said, "it sounds as if insects were being taken apart. And 'into the records'—that's like in Anna's I.R. 9. Everything got into the records there immediately, like with criminals."

"Good God, Hans," he said, "are we going to spend these few minutes arguing about our educational system?"

"If you find it so distasteful, then by all means let's not. But there must be ways—I mean ways of getting round it, such as climbing over walls, like at I.R. 9. What I mean is, there are always loopholes in these strict systems."

"Yes," he said, "there are, like in the army, but I won't have anything to do with them. I want to keep straight."

"Can't you for my sake overcome your repugnance for once and climb over the wall?"

He sighed, and I could visualize him shaking his head. "Won't tomorrow do? I mean, I can skip the lecture and be at your place shortly before nine. Is it so urgent? Or are you leaving right away?" "No," I said, "I'm staying in Bonn for a while. At least give me Heinrich Behlen's address, I'd like to give him a call, and maybe he'll come over, from Cologne or wherever he is now. I've had an accident, to my knee, I have no money, no bookings—and no Marie. To tell the truth, tomorrow I'll still be injured, with no money, no bookings and no Marie—so it's not really urgent. But maybe Heinrich is a priest by now, has a motor scooter or something. Are you still there?"

"Yes," he said wearily.

"Please," I said, "give me his address, his phone number."

He was silent. He certainly knew how to sigh, like someone who for a hundred years has sat in the confessional and sighed over the sins and follies of mankind. "All right," he said at last, with an audible effort, "you don't know then?"

"What don't I know," I shouted, "for God's sake, Leo, speak clearly. Tell me what you mean."

"Heinrich is no longer a priest," he said quietly.

"I thought you remained one as long as you breathed."

"Of course," he said, "what I mean is, he no longer

215

holds office. He went away, disappeared months ago." He brought all this out with great difficulty. "Well," I said, "he'll turn up again," then something struck me, and I asked: "Is he by himself?"

"No," said Leo severely, "he went off with a girl." It sounded as if he had said: "He's got the plague."

I felt sorry for the girl. No doubt she was Catholic, and it must be painful for her to sit around in some dump with a former priest and put up with the details of "desires of the flesh," underwear strewn around, pants, suspenders, saucers with cigarette ends, torn movie tickets and the first signs of running out of cash, and when the girl went downstairs to get bread, cigarettes or a bottle of wine, a nagging landlady would open the door, and she couldn't even call out: "My husband is an artist, yes, an artist." I was sorry for them both, for the girl more than for Heinrich. Doubtless the church authorities were very strict in such a case, when it concerned a chaplain who not only wasn't much to look at but was also difficult. With a type like Sommerwild they would probably close their eyes. But then he didn't have a housekeeper with yellowy skin on her legs, but a pretty, blooming creature he called Maddalena, an excellent cook, always nicely dressed and cheerful.

"All right then," I said, "for the time being he's no use to me."

"My God," said Leo, you are cold-blooded, aren't you?"

"I am neither Heinrich's bishop nor seriously interested in the matter," I said, "it's only the details that worry me. Do you at least have Edgar's address or phone number?"

"Do you mean Wieneken?"

"Yes," I said. "You remember Edgar, don't you? You met at our place in Cologne, and we used to play at Wienekens' as kids and have potato salad?"

"Yes, of course," he said, "of course I remember, but Wieneken isn't in Germany at all, as far as I know. Someone told me he was on a trip with some commission or other studying conditions in India or Thailand, I don't remember exactly."

"Are you sure?" I asked.

"Pretty sure," he said, "yes, now I remember, it was Heribert who told me."

"Who?" I shouted, "who told you?"

He was silent, I couldn't even hear him sigh, and I knew now why he didn't want to come. "Who?" I shouted again, but he didn't answer. He had also acquired this little confessional cough that I had sometimes heard when I was waiting for Marie in church. "You'd better not come tomorrow either," I said in a low voice. "It would be a pity to miss your lecture. Don't tell me you've seen Marie too."

Apparently he really had learned nothing but sighing and coughing. Now he sighed again, deeply, unhappily, a long sigh. "You don't need to answer," I said, "say hullo for me to the nice man at your place I spoke to twice on the phone today."

"Strüder?" he asked softly.

"I don't know his name, but he sounded so nice on the phone."

"But nobody takes him seriously," he said, "he's—he's just being kept on out of charity." Leo actually managed a kind of laugh, "only sometimes he creeps to the phone and talks a lot of nonsense."

I got up, looked down through a gap in the curtains to the clock in the square. It was three minutes to nine. "You must go now," I said, "otherwise it will get into your record. And be sure not to miss your lecture tomorrow."

"But please try and understand," he begged.

"Damn it," I said, "I do understand. Only too well."

"What kind of a man are you?" he asked. "I am a clown," I said, "and I collect moments. Goodbye." I hung up.

25

I had forgotten to ask him about his experiences in the
army, but perhaps there would be another opportunity
some day. Doubtless he would praise the "food"—he had
never eaten so well at home—regard the hardships as
"excellent training" and the contact with ordinary folk as
"immensely instructive." I didn't have to ask him about it.
Tonight in his hostel bed he wouldn't be able to sleep, he
would toss and turn while he wrestled with his conscience
and wonder if he had done the right thing in not coming
to see me. There was so much I had wanted to tell him:
that he would do better to study in South America or
Moscow, anywhere on earth but in Bonn. Surely he must
realize there was no room here for what he called his
faith, between Sommerwild and Blothert, in Bonn, a converted Schnier, especially one who had turned priest,
would almost serve to strengthen the stock market. I
must talk to him about it all one day, the best time
would be at one of Mother's At Homes. We two apostate
sons would sit down in the kitchen with Anna over a cup
of coffee, reminisce about old times, glorious times when
there was bazooka practice in our grounds and army cars
pulled up in front of the entrance when officers were
billeted on us—a major or something, with NCO's and
soldiers, a car with a pennant, and all they ever thought
about was fried eggs, cognac, cigarettes and fooling
around with the maids in the kitchen. Sometimes they
became official, i.e., pompous: they would assemble in
front of our house, the officer would strut up and down,

rgotten to ask him about his experiences in the
t perhaps there would be another opportunity
. Doubtless he would praise the "food"—he had
ten so well at home—regard the hardships as
t training" and the contact with ordinary folk as
ely instructive." I didn't have to ask him about it.
in his hostel bed he wouldn't be able to sleep, he
ss and turn while he wrestled with his conscience
der if he had done the right thing in not coming
e. There was so much I had wanted to tell him:
would do better to study in South America or
anywhere on earth but in Bonn. Surely he must
ere was no room here for what he called his
ween Sommerwild and Blothert, in Bonn, a con-
chnier, especially one who had turned priest,
most serve to strengthen the stock market. I
k to him about it all one day, the best time
at one of Mother's At Homes. We two apostate
ld sit down in the kitchen with Anna over a cup
reminisce about old times, glorious times when
bazooka practice in our grounds and army cars
in front of the entrance when officers were
n us—a major or something, with NCO's and
a car with a pennant, and all they ever thought
as fried eggs, cognac, cigarettes and fooling
ith the maids in the kitchen. Sometimes they
official, i.e., pompous: they would assemble in
ur house, the officer would strut up and down,

sighed, growled a bit and said very slowly: "Scrutinium."

"Damn it, Leo," I said, "it sounds as if insects were being taken apart. And 'into the records'—that's like in Anna's I.R. 9. Everything got into the records there immediately, like with criminals."

"Good God, Hans," he said, "are we going to spend these few minutes arguing about our educational system?"

"If you find it so distasteful, then by all means let's not. But there must be ways—I mean ways of getting round it, such as climbing over walls, like at I.R. 9. What I mean is, there are always loopholes in these strict systems."

"Yes," he said, "there are, like in the army, but I won't have anything to do with them. I want to keep straight."

"Can't you for my sake overcome your repugnance for once and climb over the wall?"

He sighed, and I could visualize him shaking his head. "Won't tomorrow do? I mean, I can skip the lecture and be at your place shortly before nine. Is it so urgent? Or are you leaving right away?" "No," I said, "I'm staying in Bonn for a while. At least give me Heinrich Behlen's address, I'd like to give him a call, and maybe he'll come over, from Cologne or wherever he is now. I've had an accident, to my knee, I have no money, no bookings—and no Marie. To tell the truth, tomorrow I'll still be injured, with no money, no bookings and no Marie—so it's not really urgent. But maybe Heinrich is a priest by now, has a motor scooter or something. Are you still there?"

"Yes," he said wearily.

"Please," I said, "give me his address, his phone number."

He was silent. He certainly knew how to sigh, like someone who for a hundred years has sat in the confessional and sighed over the sins and follies of mankind. "All right," he said at last, with an audible effort, "you don't know then?"

"What don't I know," I shouted, "for God's sake, Leo, speak clearly. Tell me what you mean."

"Heinrich is no longer a priest," he said quietly.

"I thought you remained one as long as you breathed."

"Of course," he said, "what I mean is, he no longer

holds office. He went away, disappeared months ago." He brought all this out with great difficulty. "Well," I said, "he'll turn up again," then something struck me, and I asked: "Is he by himself?"

"No," said Leo severely, "he went off with a girl." It sounded as if he had said: "He's got the plague."

I felt sorry for the girl. No doubt she was Catholic, and it must be painful for her to sit around in some dump with a former priest and put up with the details of "desires of the flesh," underwear strewn around, pants, suspenders, saucers with cigarette ends, torn movie tickets and the first signs of running out of cash, and when the girl went downstairs to get bread, cigarettes or a bottle of wine, a nagging landlady would open the door, and she couldn't even call out: "My husband is an artist, yes, an artist." I was sorry for them both, for the girl more than for Heinrich. Doubtless the church authorities were very strict in such a case, when it concerned a chaplain who not only wasn't much to look at but was also difficult. With a type like Sommerwild they would probably close their eyes. But then he didn't have a housekeeper with yellowy skin on her legs, but a pretty, blooming creature he called Maddalena, an excellent cook, always nicely dressed and cheerful.

"All right then," I said, "for the time being he's no use to me."

"My God," said Leo, you are cold-blooded, aren't you?"

"I am neither Heinrich's bishop nor seriously interested in the matter," I said, "it's only the details that worry me. Do you at least have Edgar's address or phone number?"

"Do you mean Wieneken?"

"Yes," I said. "You remember Edgar, don't you? You met at our place in Cologne, and we used to play at Wienekens' as kids and have potato salad?"

"Yes, of course," he said, "of course I remember, but Wieneken isn't in Germany at all, as far as I know. Someone told me he was on a trip with some commission or other studying conditions in India or Thailand, I don't remember exactly."

"Are you sure?" I asked.

"Pretty sure," he said, "yes, now I remember, it was Heribert who told me."

"Who?" I shouted, "who told you?

He was silent, I couldn't even knew now why he didn't want to co again, but he didn't answer. He h little confessional cough that I had s I was waiting for Marie in churc come tomorrow either," I said in a be a pity to miss your lecture. Don Marie too."

Apparently he really had learned and coughing. Now he sighed again, long sigh. "You don't need to answe for me to the nice man at your plac the phone today."

"Strüder?" he asked softly.

"I don't know his name, but he the phone."

"But nobody takes him seriously,' just being kept on out of charity." I a kind of laugh, "only sometimes he and talks a lot of nonsense."

I got up, looked down through a to the clock in the square. It was th "You must go now," I said, "othe your record. And be sure not to n morrow."

"But please try and understand,"

"Damn it," I said, "I do understan

"What kind of a man are you?" clown," I said, "and I collect mo hung up.

I had army, some never "exce "imme Tonig would and w to see that l Mosc realize faith, verte woul must woul sons of co there pulle billet soldi abou arou beca fron sometimes even tuck his hand into his tunic like a fourth-rate actor impersonating a colonel, shout something about "final victory." Embarrassing, ridiculous, senseless. When it was discovered that Mrs. Wieneken and a few other women had secretly gone through the woods one night, through the German and American lines, to get bread from her brother's bakery over there, the pompousness became lethal. The officer wanted to have Mrs. Wieneken and two other women shot for espionage and sabotage (when she was being questioned, Mrs. Wieneken had admitted having spoken to an American soldier over there). But then my father—for the second time in his life, as far as I can remember—put his foot down, got the women out of the improvised prison, our ironing room, and hid them in the boatshed down by the river bank. He showed real spirit, shouted at the officer and the officer shouted back. The most ridiculous thing about the officer was his decorations, which trembled with indignation on his chest, while my mother said in her mild voice: "Gentlemen, gentlemen—there is a limit, you know." What embarrassed her about the whole thing was the fact that two "gentlemen" were shouting at each other. My father said: "Before anything happens to these women you will have to shoot me—go ahead" and he actually unbuttoned his jacket and stuck out his chest at the officer, but the soldiers left then because the Americans were already on the slopes of the Rhine, and the women could come out of the boatshed. The most embarrassing thing about the major, or whatever he was, was his decorations. Undecorated he might perhaps have had a chance of preserving a certain dignity. When I see those narrow-minded bastards standing around at Mother's At Homes wearing their decorations, I always think of that officer, and then even Sommerwild's decoration seems bearable: *Pro Ecclesia* something or other. At least Sommerwild does things of lasting value for his church: he keeps his "artists" in line and has enough decency to regard the decoration "as such" as embarrassing. He only wears it during processions, special church services, and TV discussions. In his case too, television destroys the last remnants of the decency which I must admit he possesses. If our era deserves a name, it would have to be called the era of prostitution. People

219

are becoming accustomed to the vocabulary of whores. I once met Sommerwild after one of those discussions ("Can Modern Art be Religious?"), and he asked me: "Was I good? Did you like me?" word for word the questions whores ask their departing suitors. I almost expected him to ask: "Please recommend me to your friends." I said to him at the time: "I don't think you are good, so I couldn't have liked you yesterday." He was completely heartbroken, although I had expressed my opinion of him very tactfully. He had been dreadful; for the sake of scoring a few cheap cultural points he had "slaughtered" or "shot down," perhaps just "cracked up," his opponent, a somewhat inept socialist. How tricky to ask: "I see, so you find early Picasso abstract?" and in the presence of ten million viewers to murder the old gray-haired man, who mumbled something about involvement, with the remark: "Oh, I suppose you mean social art—or possibly social realism?" When I saw him on the street the next day and told him I hadn't liked him, he was really crushed. That *one* among the ten million hadn't liked him was a severe blow to his vanity, however he was richly rewarded by a "real wave of acclaim" in all the Catholic newspapers. They wrote that he had scored a victory for the "good cause."

I lit my last cigarette but two, picked up the guitar and strummed a few notes. I thought about all the things I wanted to tell Leo, and all the things I wanted to ask him. Always, when I had to have a serious talk with him, he was just writing exams or afraid of a scrutinium. I also wondered if I really ought to sing the Litany of Loreto; better not: someone might get the idea I was a Catholic, they would proclaim me as "one of ours," and it might turn out to be a nice bit of propaganda for them, seeing how they use everything "to serve their own ends," and the whole thing would be confusing and misleading, the fact that I wasn't a Catholic at all but merely found the Litany of Loreto beautiful and sympathized with the Jewish girl it was dedicated to, nobody would understand that either, and by some means or other they would discover a few million catholons in me, haul me before TV cameras—and the stocks would go even higher. I would have to look for another text, too bad, I would really have preferred to sing the Litany of Loreto, but on the Bonn station steps that was bound to be misunderstood. Too bad. I had rehearsed it so well and could intone the *Ora pro nobis* so nicely on the guitar.

I stood up, to get ready for my performance. No doubt my agent Zohnerer would "drop" me too when I began singing and playing the guitar in the street. If I had really sung litanies, *Tantum ergo* and all the texts I loved to sing and had practiced for so many years in the bath, he might perhaps have "gone along" with it, it would have been a good gimmick, something like painting madonnas. I even believed him when he said he really liked me—the children of this world are more sincere than the children of light—but "businesswise" I was finished as far as he was concerned, if I sat down on the Bonn station steps.

I could walk again without noticeably limping. That meant I didn't need the orange crate, all I had to do was tuck a sofa cushion under my left arm and the guitar under my right, and go to work. I still had two cigarettes, I would smoke one, the other would look enticing enough lying there in the black hat; at least one coin next to it would have been good. I searched in my trouser pockets, turned them inside out; a couple of movie tickets, a red parchesi counter, a used Kleenex, but no money. I pulled open the drawer of the hall table: a clothesbrush, a receipt from the Bonn church paper, a coupon for a beer bottle, no money. I went through all the drawers in the kitchen, hurried into the bedroom, hunted among collar studs, collar stays, cufflinks, among socks and handkerchiefs, in the pockets of the green corduroy trousers: nothing. I pulled off my dark trousers, left them lying on the floor like a peeled-off skin, threw the white shirt down by them and pulled the pale-blue jersey over my head: grass green and pale blue, I opened the door with the mirror: excellent, I had never looked so good. I had put the make-up on too thick, during all the years it must have been lying there the grease in it had dried out, and now I saw in the mirror that the layer of paint had already cracked, showed fissures like the face of an excavated statue. My dark hair like a wig on top. I hummed a verse to myself which I had just thought up: "Catholic politics in Bonn, Are no concern of poor Pope John, Let them holler, let them go, Eeny, meeny, miny, mo." That would do to start with, and the Anti-Blasphemy Execu-

221

tive Committee couldn't object to anything in the words. I would make up a lot more verses, intone the whole thing like a ballad. I would have liked to cry: the make-up stopped me, it looked just right, with the cracks, with the places where it was beginning to flake off, tears would have ruined all that. I could cry later, if I still felt like it. A professional bearing is the best protection, only saints and amateurs are mortally vulnerable. I stepped back from the mirror, looked more deeply into myself and at the same time further away. If Marie saw me like this and was still capable of ironing the wax spots out of his Knight of Malta uniform—then she was dead, and we were divorced. Then I could start mourning at her grave. I hoped they would all have enough small change when they passed by: Leo something more than a nickel, Edgar Wieneken, when he got back from Thailand, perhaps an old gold coin, and Grandfather, when he returned from Ischia—he would at least make me out a crossed check. By this time I had discovered how to turn them into cash, my mother would probably consider two to five pfennigs appropriate, Monika Silvs might lean down and give me a kiss, while Sommerwild, Kinkel and Fredebeul, outraged at my scandalous behavior, wouldn't even throw a cigarette into my hat. Now and again, when no train was due from the south for a few hours, I would bicycle out to Sabina Emonds and have my bowl of soup. Perhaps Sommerwild would call Züpfner in Rome and advise him to leave the train at Godesberg. In that case I would ride out there on my bike, sit down in front of the villa with the sloping garden, and sing my ditty: all she had to do was come, look at me, and be dead or alive. The only person I felt sorry for was my father. It had been nice of him to save the women from being shot, and it had been nice of him to put his hand on my shoulder, and—I could see it now in the mirror—made up as I was I not only resembled him, I was amazingly like him, and I could understand now how violently he had rejected Leo's conversion. With Leo I had no sympathy, after all he had his faith.

It was not yet nine thirty when I went down in the elevator. I remembered the Christian Mr. Kostert, who still owed me the bottle of schnapps and the difference between the first and second-class ticket. I would write him an unstamped postcard and jog his conscience. Besides, he still had to send me my baggage claim check. It was a good thing my neighbor, pretty Mrs. Grebsel, didn't run into me. I would have had to explain things to her. If she saw me sitting on the steps of the station I wouldn't need to explain anything any more. All I needed now was the briquette, my visiting card.

It was chilly outside, a March evening, I turned up my collar, put on my hat, and felt for my last cigarette in my pocket. I suddenly remembered the cognac bottle, it would have looked very decorative, but it would have been a deterrent to generosity, it was an expensive brand, you could see it from the cork. The cushion tucked under my left arm, the guitar under my right, I walked back to the station. On the way I came across the first signs of what is known here as "the time of folly." A young drunk dressed as Fidel Castro tried to jostle me, I got out of his way. On the station steps a group of matadors and Spanish donnas were waiting for a taxi. I had forgotten, it was Carnival time. That suited me fine. There is no better hiding place for a professional than among amateurs. I placed my cushion on the third step from the bottom, sat down on it, took off my hat and put the cigarette in it, not quite in the middle, not at the edge, but as if it had been thrown in from above, and began to sing: "Poor Pope John," no one paid any attention to me, and it was better that way: in an hour, in two or three hours, they would begin to notice me all right. I stopped playing when I heard the announcer's voice inside. He was calling out the arrival of a train from Hamburg—and I went on playing. I gave a start when the first coin fell into my hat: it was a nickel, it hit the cigarette, and pushed it too far to the edge. I put it back where it belonged and went on singing.

SIGNET Fiction of Interest